MARQUIS OF SECRETS

Also by Marissa Doyle

The Ladies of Almack's series

The Forgery Furore
The Vanishing Volume
Lyrics and Larceny
The Cursed Canvases
Turmoil on the Thames
An Event at Epsom
The Missing Missives
Betrayal at Brighton
The Audacious Abduction

Countess of Shadows: The Ladies of Almack's Omnibus No.1

Skin Deep
By Jove

The Leland Sisters series

Bewitching Season
Betraying Season
Courtship and Curses
Charles Bewitched

Between Silk and Sand
Evergreen
What Lies Beneath

MARQUIS OF SECRETS

THE LADIES OF ALMACK'S OMNIBUS NO.2

Marissa Doyle

In association with
Book View Cafe

Published by Book View Café LLC
304 S. Jones Blvd., Suite #2906
Las Vegas, NV 89107

ISBN: 978-1-63632-099-1

https://www.bookviewcafe.com

https://www.marissadoyle.com

For Scott,
who kept asking for what happened next

TABLE OF CONTENTS

THE CURSED CANVASES

Chapter One

Late May 1810
Somerset House, London

"That cow definitely resembles Lady Hebbly," Annabel Fellbridge said, scribbling a note in the margin of her catalogue. "Don't you think so?"

Her friend Eliza Denton, who'd come down from Hampstead to visit this year's Annual Exhibition of the Royal Academy of Art, squinted judiciously at the largest cow in a canvas titled *Lowther Castle, Westmoreland: Evening* that hung in the Anteroom at Somerset House. "I don't know. I'm not acquainted with the lady in question. Don't you think that it might be the other way around, perhaps?"

Annabel looked quickly about them, but the display rooms at Somerset House were particularly sparsely attended this morning, thank goodness. It didn't do to say something like that out loud about the wife of the head of the Royal Academy's Hanging

Committee, Sir Henry Hebbly, even if it happened to be true. "Hmm. Perhaps a trifle. Antonia Hebbly's never been accused of being a beauty, but she's the dearest, kindest person I know. She's a friend of my mother's."

"What about the other cows?" Eliza pointed at a complacent-looking Belted Galloway. "That one looks very pleased with herself."

"Yes, and it also looks like Lady Hebbly." Annabel made another note. "This is bad. Very bad."

"Did they look like that the last time you were here?"

"No. The last time the monkey in *The Bath at the Harem* was the one that looked like Lady Hebbly. And Sir Henry's portrait of Lady Hebbly looked very much like a baby pig."

"But baby pigs can be quite appealing."

"Not *this* baby pig."

When Sally had told the Lady Patronesses that rumors were beginning to fly around London that there was something very odd about some of the pictures at the Annual Exhibition, the reaction had mostly been amusement. But today, on her third visit, Annabel was no longer smiling. Something *was* very wrong here—and it was being done very deliberately.

Sally had requested they take turns visiting the Exhibition multiple times and take notes on any pictures that seemed strange in any way. On her first visit, Annabel had thought that several of the portraits on display had...the only way she could think to describe it was *caricatured* features. One of them, a portrait of an elderly, august bishop, had pointed ears peeking out from beneath his wig; the portrait of his equally dignified wife had faint but definite cat whiskers. On her second visit the very next day those portraits were as they should be, sans pointed ears and whiskers—but Lady Hebbly's bore more than a passing resemblance to a not-very-appealing baby pig. Today, a few days later, it was *Lowther Castle, Westmoreland: Evening* in which all the cows somehow managed to possess uncannily human expressions.

Eliza leaned forward to examine the cows in the background more closely. "My word, they *all* resemble her!" She looked at Annabel, her eyes wide. "And you and your friends are investigating this, I presume?"

Annabel hesitated. She had not *exactly* told Eliza about Almack's other role but had intimated that there were ladies who possessed certain powers on a par with hers and who kept an eye on matters that took an out-of-the-ordinary—or yes, supernatural turn.

"Yes," she said. "We've divided up the days and assigned them so that one of us is here to take observations both morning and afternoon. We will meet shortly to compare and discuss what we've seen."

"That ought to be an interesting exercise." Eliza grimaced. "Might we sit down for a moment? Wearing new shoes today was not a good choice."

"Of course. There are benches in the Great Room." Sitting for a few minutes would allow her to catch up on her notes.

"How is he doing it?" As they moved toward the door, Eliza nodded towards a large canvas entitled *Nausicaä and Her Handmaidens,* in which the girls clustering around their princess somehow managed to look like a school of startled mackerel. "Is he sneaking in at night and—and—"

"And repainting all the pictures? I don't think so." Annabel checked her catalogue. *Nausicaä* had been painted by Sir Henry Hebbly. Hmm.

"Which is why you and your friends have found them of interest," Eliza said. The word "magic" was left unsaid but hovered between them, nevertheless.

"Yes. Whether or not we will be able to find a pattern that tells us anything about the perpetra—" Halfway through the door into the Great Room, she stopped speaking. There, standing before a picture not far from the benches that were their destination, stood her friend Lord Glenrick and another vaguely familiar-looking man, deep in conversation.

Lord Glenrick glanced up, and his serious expression melted into a broad smile. "My dear Lady Fellbridge! What an unexpected pleasure!" he said, coming to meet them.

Annabel held out her hand and smiled at him warmly. "Good morning, my lord. I beg your pardon if we've disturbed you—"

"Not in the least. Ross and I were merely chatting."

Annabel looked at the other man, who had not joined them and did not appear to share Lord Glenrick's pleasure at the interruption. It hadn't appeared to be a "chat" to her...but it was also none of her affair. "And we were just enjoying the pictures. Eliza, may I present Lord Glenrick? Lord Glenrick, my friend Mrs. Denton."

Lord Glenrick bowed and gave Eliza his usual charming smile. "Are you enjoying the Exhibition, madam?"

Eliza's lips twitched, but she restrained herself. "It's always an…er, enriching experience to have the chance to view so much art at once."

"'Enriching.'" He pulled a long face. "That's an excellent way of putting it. I shall have to remember that."

"Are you not an appreciator of art, sir?"

"I prefer literature or music to paint but will readily admit it's a failing rather than a virtue. And besides, one must be able to say yes, one has been to the Exhibition, and wasn't it a crashing bore…or a splendid show, depending on one's audience."

Annabel smiled. "My lord, you are a cynic!"

He returned her smile. "I prefer 'an honest man,' but will happily accept any name that falls from your lips." He leaned closer. "I was going to call but will take this opportunity instead to invite you to drive with me to Hampton Court on Wednesday if you are not engaged. Do say yes. It is too long since I have had the opportunity to monopolize your attention."

She laughed but was acutely aware of Eliza's presence. "Thank you. I should enjoy that very much."

"Splendid. Is eleven too early? No? Then I shall see you then. I perceive that my friend is eager to see the rest of the pictures, so I shall say *au revoir*, ladies." He bowed and turned back to his companion, who indeed had begun to look impatient. Odd that Lord Glenrick hadn't presented him or included him in the conversation, though she had finally remembered who he was when Lord Glenrick mentioned his nickname. Lord Rossing had been one of Freddy's acquaintances whom she'd met once or twice—a typical taciturn northerner, as she recalled, mostly concerned with his horses and his immense pride in his descent. Not the man she would have expected to be viewing the annual Royal Academy Summer Exhibition, but one never knew.

The two men left the room, Lord Glenrick glancing over his shoulder to smile at her once more as they did. When they had gone, Eliza hobbled to the green baize-covered bench and sank onto it with a small groan. "Oh, that's better. Annabel, isn't that the man you told me about whom Geoffrey so dislikes? Who is he, again?"

Was that the faintest edge of rebuke in her question? Instead of sitting, Annabel went to examine a nearby painting. No distortions or changes from the last time she had viewed it. She wrote a small zero next to its name in her catalogue and examined its neighbors before answering. "Yes, it is—though I still don't understand why Lord Quinceton dislikes him. He's always perfectly charming. And he's the Duke of Carrick's heir and brother to one of my fellow Lady Patronesses."

"You're going to make me stand up and follow you around if I want to talk to you, aren't you? And I thought you were kind." Eliza sighed and made to stand up again.

Annabel relented and went to sit next to her. "I still have to finish looking," she warned.

"We can finish together as soon as my feet stop throbbing. He's smitten, isn't he?"

"Who?"

"I shall now exercise vast amounts of restraint and not hit you with my catalogue," Eliza said in a long-suffering voice. "That man. Lord Glenrick. Smitten. With you."

"Oh, no—I wouldn't say that—" Goodness, was she blushing?

"I would. Are you smitten in return?"

Why was Eliza examining her so closely? "No, of course not! I—I've given up on men, I think."

Eliza snorted. "At your age? Why should you? Hmm. Maybe that's why Geoffrey can't abide him."

Annabel drew in her breath. "Eliza, that's—that's scarcely likely. Lord Quinceton doesn't care what Lord Glenrick thinks of me."

"You think so?" Eliza pursed her lips.

Annabel hesitated. Lord Quinceton had left London for a few days to confer with his bailiff at his estate in Gloucestershire after their adventure sorting out her cousin Hartley's engagement to Miss Pouli. At first, she'd been relieved to know he was elsewhere; the memory of how she'd defended him in his very presence to her Cousin Medea still made her squirm.

But that relief had been short-lived, and to her dismay she'd actually found herself *missing* the wretched man. It was an unsettling realization; just weeks ago she'd told Emily she couldn't abide the creature. But there was simply no reason to believe he cared about whether or not Lord Glenrick was smitten by her. The idea was quite nonsensical.

"I don't see why he should," she said firmly. "Why should it matter to him?"

Eliza opened her mouth to answer, but Annabel forestalled her by standing up. "Are your feet feeling better? If not, you can stay here while I look at the rest of the pictures."

Eliza seemed to understand she didn't want to pursue the conversation, bless her. She climbed to her feet with a small wince. "No, but they'll hold me up a little longer. I should like to see if there are any more pictures of cows with whom you are acquainted."

On Monday, Annabel made a tidy copy of her observations of the Exhibition's paintings to bring to the Lady Patronesses meeting. If the others had seen anything like she had, she was certain they would be undertaking a new investigation today.

She was right.

"It's a disgrace!" Frances announced when Sally asked for their reports. She tapped her catalogue, heavily penciled with notes. "Poor Lady Hebbly! Did you all see?"

All heads around the table nodded. Some of them had seen the baby pig and others the monkey, depending on what day they had visited; others had caught both Lady Hebbly's and Sir Henry's likenesses cleverly concealed in a muck-pile in a canvas entitled *A Rustic Farm, Derbyshire.*

"That wasn't the only one," Emily said. "Did anyone catch her face on all of the cows in *Lowther Castle, Westmoreland: Evening*?"

Sally held up a hand to stem the flurry of affirmations. "I think that we can agree that there is indeed something going on here. The only question is, what?"

"And who," Emily added.

"And why," Georgiana said.

"It's obvious that somebody bears a grudge against Lady Hebbly," Maria said.

"Who could dislike Lady Hebbly?" Annabel asked. "I *know* her. I can't imagine that she has an enemy in the world. And besides, it's not just her. Someone clearly has a grudge against both the Hebblys. Every single canvas of his was defaced somehow."

"What about the pictures of the Bishop of Bath and Wells and his wife? That wasn't painted by Sir Henry," Clementina put in.

"True. But pictures painted by others have also been altered—to include scurrilous images of him and Lady Hebbly. And Annabel is right: all of Sir Henry's pictures have been damaged. Every single one." Dorothea tapped the table to emphasize her words.

"Sir Henry is in charge of this year's Hanging Committee for the Exhibition," Georgiana said. "Might that have something to do with it?"

"Perhaps, but who knows? All we can say with certainty is that someone who is skilled in magic bears him a grudge," Dorothea said. "But who? This nonsense—" She gestured at the notes in front of her. "It is the malice of a child. Giving animals the features of people—a silly schoolboy prank."

"Rather a cruel schoolboy," Maria commented.

"Children are often cruel."

"Or it might be someone who has some magical ability but not enough to actually do anything harmful to the people they dislike," Clementina suggested.

"Or they're clever enough to realize that public humiliation can be the worst form of harm," Emily added.

Sally rapped on the table. "We could speculate about this for the rest of the day. I would rather we spent our time deciding how to catch the culprit. Frances, I would like you to take this investigation if you're willing. See if you can't get a feel for the magic that's being used or why. *Who* would be even better."

Annabel waited. Frances' talent was reading objects to discern who had made them or last handled them...which meant she would have to touch the paintings in order to get any impression from them. But one did not go about pawing the pictures at the Academy's Summer Exhibition, which in turn meant that she'd need to be concealed while she did so—

"Annabel, I shall need your help," Frances said, turning to her.

She nodded. It looked like she'd be getting quite an immersion in art this season. "Of course, Frances. We can go this afternoon if you like."

Annabel felt more than a little guilty for sneaking into the Exhibition without paying the entrance fee. But it would be much easier to wrap Frances and herself in shadow before entering it rather than after. She promised herself to send a shilling anonymously through the post that afternoon and guided Frances toward the quiet darkness behind the staircase leading up to the Great Room. Taking her arm, she drew as heavy a shadow as she dared around them; today was bright and sunny, and too thick a shadow would be conspicuous.

"Keep close," she murmured. "It's much easier for me to do this if we are touching."

Frances nodded solemnly. "I understand," she whispered. They made their way cautiously up the stairs. Annabel scarcely dared to breathe as they ascended; keeping out of others' way on stairs was much more difficult to do than it was in a room, since there was little space to dodge a chance contact. But they made it safely up and into the Anteroom. It was more crowded than it had been on Saturday, so she concentrated on steering them away from viewers and left it to Frances to survey the pictures.

"There. I think I can reach that one easily," Frances said, tugging on her arm. Annabel looked up: *Titania, Puck, and etc.* showed the well-known figures from Shakespeare...except that Nick Bottom bore not only an ass's head, but a strong resemblance to Sir Henry Hebbly.

They shuffled closer to the painting, waiting for a pair of quizzing-glass-wielding elderly ladies to complete their examination of its brushstrokes before coming right up to it. Frances drew off her gloves and reached up to touch it, then hesitated. "I don't know if I can do it. My old governess would be horrified if she saw me touching a painting!"

"I know. Remember, it's for a good cause," Annabel whispered back. "But we must hasten, before someone else decides they need to look at it as closely as those ladies did."

"Yes, of course." Frances drew a deep breath and gently placed her fingertips on the canvas. "Oh, yes," she breathed. "Magic has definitely been used here. It's...angry. Someone is out for revenge."

Annabel scribbled that on the notepaper she'd

brought. "Revenge. That makes sense. Any indication of what it's revenge for?"

Frances touched another section of canvas, a distant look on her face. "Not really. It's not clear…I get the feeling whoever did this has done so because they can't think of what else to do. There's a—a powerlessness about it, a sort of desperation. It's…I'm not certain, but I think it's a woman doing the magic."

Hmm. That made sense too. If a woman bore a grudge against Sir Henry, she couldn't precisely challenge him to a duel. "Anything else?"

Frances shook her head. "We ought to look at another one."

They made their way to *Lowther Castle, Westmoreland: Evening*, which still bore its Lady Hebbly-resembling cows. Frances didn't sense anything new there, except for one detail: the anger wasn't directed at Lady Hebbly herself. That made Annabel feel both better and worse; it had been difficult to imagine anyone being angry with Lady Hebbly, but it seemed dreadfully unfair that she should be so treated because someone had a quarrel with her husband.

They moved into the Great Room, avoiding the strolling pairs and groups; fortunately, most of them seemed more intent on each other than on the pictures around them. That was scarcely surprising; the Exhibition had always been as much about meeting and greeting, seeing and being seen, as it was about viewing modern art. Again, she felt heartened—perhaps no one was noticing how Lady Hebbly was being caricatured because they were too wrapped up in each other.

On the less heartening side, several new pictures had been tampered with. In the *Portrait of Sir Ronald Timsbury*, painted in the sitter's library, it could just be seen that the titles on the spines of the books in the shelves behind Sir Ronald all read, "Henry Hebbly is an ass" in tiny gold and black letters.

"Well, that's reasonably unequivocal," Annabel said, making a note.

"What do you think we should do?" Frances looked up at Sir Ronald, her forehead wrinkled.

"As much as I hate to say it, I think we need to set up a watch. It's the only way I can think that we'll catch anyone in the act." Annabel tried not to think about the fact that she would be spending the next several days here, trying to keep her friends concealed in shadows as they looked for the culprit. "Do you think he—or she, I suppose—has to touch the pictures to change them? If she can do it without actually being present, there's no way we'll ever catch her—"

"Oh!" Frances gasped.

"Hmm?" Annabel glanced up from her notebook just in time to see Frances push through the shroud of shadow concealing them. "Frances, stop!" she hissed...but it was too late. She was hurrying across the Great Room, darting through the startled groups of people around them. Following her erratic trajectory, Annabel saw why: Frances' brother, Lord Glenrick, was there...along with, much to her surprise, the Marquis of Quinceton.

They were standing before a painting, and Lord Glenrick was speaking almost in the other man's ear, holding his arm. She could not see Lord Quinceton's face, but something about the set of his back and shoulders all but shouted his desire to be anywhere but there.

"Alex! Quin! I didn't know you'd be here today!" Frances said loudly. "Annabel and I were just—" She gulped, obviously remembering that no one was supposed to see them.

"Frances!" Lord Glenrick looked startled. "What are you doing here?"

"Fellbridge?" Lord Quinceton's dark head jerked up.

Annabel sighed and waited for a moment when the doorway between this and the Anteroom was clear, then hurried over to it. Once there she took a cautious look around, then shed her shadow and made her way over to them, just as if entering from the other room. "We meet again, my lord. I do believe you are an art lover after all, despite your disavowals," she said with a smile to Lord Glenrick.

"I am if it brings me into proximity with certain other art lovers of my acquaintance," he promptly returned. "Frances did not say you two would be here today."

"It was a—a last minute decision," Frances said, shooting her a desperate look. "I happened to mention to Annabel I had not yet seen the Exhibition, and she insisted we come after our Almack's meeting. Isn't that so, Annabel?"

"Yes, indeed." Annabel agreed quickly and hoped Lord Glenrick didn't pay close enough attention to his sister's comings and goings to know it was an outright lie; Frances of course had been here several times already, making observations for the Lady Patronesses.

Mercifully, though he raised his eyebrows, he did not say anything. But Lord Quinceton was regarding her with a faint frown between his brows. "Are you an art lover, Fellbridge?"

"Lord Quinceton." She nodded in greeting. "I did not know you were back in town."

"I returned yesterday. Answer my question, if you please."

Why hadn't she'd known he was back? She buried that plaintive thought beneath indignation at his highhandedness. And then Lord Glenrick answered for her.

"I believe I can say that Lady Fellbridge is an admirer of art. I had the pleasure of seeing her before this very picture just two days ago." He smiled at her.

Had he? Annabel glanced up at the picture before them and saw with a small start just which one it was. *The Mother's Plight* had stirred up no little controversy when it was chosen for the Exhibition; it showed a destitute woman wrapped in a ragged length of plaid, an emaciated child in her arms, begging by a Scottish roadside as a luxurious carriage passed her by, its obviously wealthy English passengers looking through her as if she weren't there. Though the last uprising of supporters of the Stuart monarchy against the Hanoverians had been more than sixty-five years ago, feelings still ran high in some quarters over how the Scots had been treated by the English. She recalled suddenly that Frances and Lord Glenrick were Scottish...but since their family had retained its dukedom, they must have supported King George. They surely didn't bear a grudge against the English, did they?

Then she saw that Lord Quinceton was regarding her with an even deeper frown. "Did you, in-deed?" he said.

"Oh, yes," Lord Glenrick smiled enigmatically, and Annabel had the feeling that quite another conversation was taking place underneath their words—one she was not privy to. She opened her mouth to speak, but he went on, "I am looking forward to our outing to Hampton Court on Wednesday," he said to her, his expression warming.

"Are you going to Hampton Court, Alex? I have not been there in forever!" Frances's eyes lit up.

"Then perhaps your brother could be convinced to alter his plans and bring along companions," Lord Quinceton put in. To Annabel's surprise, he was smiling at Frances.

She blushed a deep red. "Me? R-really?"

"Unless you'd rather not go, madam."

"Oh!" Frances tapped his arm playfully. "Of course I want to! Alex, will you bring Quin and me as well?"

Lord Glenrick hesitated, and Annabel thought he was about to say no. Then he shrugged. "I should have no objection whatsoever. But I had planned on driving my curricle."

"Then I shall drive mine as well. We'll make a party of it," Lord Quinceton said.

For just a moment, Annabel wanted to protest. The thought of Lord Quinceton accompanying her and Lord Glenrick on their drive was off-putting, somehow. Lord Quinceton would probably do his best to put her out of countenance whenever possible, just from a spirit of perversity...or else he'd do the same to poor Frances, which would be even worse. Why on earth had he asked to join them?

But when she met his eyes, expecting to see mischief or mockery in them, all she saw was a certain guardedness. "A party sounds delightful!" she said instead of protesting, and leaned toward Frances. "Well, shall we go see the rest of the pictures? Good afternoon, gentlemen."

Lord Quinceton bowed without speaking. Lord Glenrick touched her arm. "I've taken the liberty of sending you a book I've very much enjoyed. I hope it will provide you a few hours of entertainment," he murmured.

She smiled. "You are very kind. I shall look forward to receiving and reading it."

He bowed. She took Frances's arm and turned away.

"I beg your pardon!" Frances whispered when they were barely out of earshot. "I forgot!"

"Don't worry. No harm done," she said soothingly. "We were mostly done with our examination anyway."

Frances sighed. "Annabel, you're so kind. Shan't we have a lovely time on Wednesday?"

"Of course," she replied. Without turning, she knew that both men were watching them. This was the second time she'd seen the pair of them together *tête-à-tête*...and yet it was very clear, if one paid attention, that the pair of them were not friends. There was definitely something afoot here, and she intended to find out what it was.

Frances came home with her, and they sent notes

around to all the other Lady Patronesses informing them that a further watch on the Royal Academy Exhibition would have to be commenced at once. Frances stared dubiously at the list of hours that Annabel drew up. "But you can't be there every single day," she protested. "That's not fair! And what about Wednesday? Why can't some of us go to watch without being hidden?"

"Some of us can. But I expect that it will be easier to eavesdrop on potential culprits when hidden, don't you think?"

"I suppose so. I feel *dreadful*, Annabel. I didn't mean to do this to you when I asked for your help! Really I didn't—"

"Pooh." Annabel patted her hand. "I shall only be there part of each day. I promise I won't permit it to take over my life."

Frances dabbed at her eyes with a dainty lace handkerchief. "I'm glad to hear that." She paused, then said, "It was very kind of Quin to ask me to drive with him to Hampton Court, wasn't it?"

Kind was perhaps not the first word that came to mind. But she could not say that to Frances. "I am certain we'll all have a lovely time," she said instead.

"You don't think he would have asked me if he didn't...*like* me, do you?"

"Of course he likes you. You've been friends for years," she said bracingly. "A man doesn't invite a female to whom he's not related to drive with him if he doesn't like her very much—" She stopped, recalling that Lord Quinceton had taken her driving. Several times. But surely that was different...

"Just as Alex asked you." Frances turned back to their list. "Thank you for drawing this up for me—

I'm terrible at this sort of thing. I'll make copies and send them around to everyone."

Annabel saw her to the door, directing her coachman to drive Frances home. This had certainly been an interesting day, between the new investigation and now the inclusion of Frances in the planned outing to Hampton Court...not to mention Lord Quinceton. She thought of the odd note in his voice and manner toward her and wondered what they meant...and whether Wednesday would provide any answers, or just more questions.

Chapter Two

Annabel was at the Exhibition shortly after it opened the next morning. "I fear I shall soon grow heartily sick of looking at these pictures," she murmured to Emily, who had agreed to help keep watch today despite the short notice. They'd taken up their station in the Anteroom for now, with the plan of moving back and forth between it and the Great Room if they spotted any visitors behaving suspiciously.

"I fear I'm heartily sick of them now," Emily murmured back. "Except for the fish-girls. I've grown rather fond of them." She nodded toward *Nausicaä and Her Handmaidens.* "Why do so many artists love to paint naked, fearful females clutching shamefacedly at their own bosoms? No, don't bother telling me. I already know the answer."

Annabel smiled. If she had to spend long hours lurking in a shadow with anyone, it was Emily. The Exhibition Rooms were filling up fast that morning, so they could chat a little, so long as they kept their voices low, and their conversation would be absorbed in the general, louder hum. However, more people meant having to pay closer attention to keeping out of their way. This would undoubtedly be a *long* day.

"I wonder if we shall see Lord Glenrick here today?" she said idly.

"Why should we? Annabel, you sly puss—are you making assignations with him?" Emily sounded—it was difficult to see facial expressions under their cloak of shadow—vastly amused.

"No, you goose! It's simply that I've seen him here twice in the last few days—once when I was here with Eliza Denton, and once with Frances. That time was awkward, as we were in shadow. Frances forgot, because she saw Lord Quinceton."

"And leapt across the room to accost him, I assume." Emily snorted. "Frances and her infatuation with him. When will she give him up as a lost cause?" Then she grinned. "Maybe she has. I stopped at Thomas's on my way here to pick up some stockings and saw her buying black gloves and ribbons. She's either going into mourning for her late, lamented love, or somebody died."

"Really? That's odd." Frances hadn't said anything about a death in her family, and no court mourning seemed imminent despite continuing rumors of the King's ill health. "Perhaps Lord Quinceton isn't so lost a cause, though. He asked her to join Glenrick and me on a drive to Hampton Court tomorrow."

"He did? You must be joking!"

"Why? I admit that at first I thought it a trifle presumptuous to invite himself to go with us, but

Frances was so delighted that I'm glad he did."

"Hmmph." Emily was silent for a moment. "I'll wager Glenrick wasn't so delighted. How is his courtship of you progressing?"

Usually, Annabel would have protested at such a question. But today she hesitated, buying herself time by surveying the viewers wandering past them. None seemed to be behaving in a suspicious fashion. "He sent me a book yesterday. A new poem by Mr. Scott," she said at length.

"Oh, I'd heard about that. Was it any good?"

In fact, she'd stayed up long past her usual hour for retiring reading *The Lady of the Lake*. It was very dramatic, with disguised kings and rival suitors, pagan seers and battling clan chieftains, though not anywhere as fevered as a Marjorie Banks Gilbert novel. The most striking part had been the poem's settings: the highland forest, the remote island in Loch Katrine where James Douglas hid, the proud ramparts of Stirling Castle. It had made Scotland, which she'd never spared much thought for, sound mysterious and romantic.

"Yes, it was. I liked it very well," she said.

"And its donor?"

Annabel was glad her countenance was muffled by shadow. "I...like him as well."

"Ah. Then it was deucedly awkward of Quin to have invited himself to your jaunt with him. Why do you think he did?"

"I don't know. Frances—"

"Oh, hang Frances!"

"Emily!"

Emily sighed. "Well, not truly, but you know what I mean. Annabel, are you being willfully blind, or have you honestly not noticed that Quin is just as interested in you as Glenrick is—perhaps more?"

Annabel shook her head, then remembered that Emily probably couldn't see her. "I am persuaded you're imagining that. I won't deny that he—that he has *some* interest in me." She recalled once again the odd way he'd looked at her yesterday. "But I cannot believe his interest can be regarded as tender. If anything, it's a—a fellowship. Well, it makes sense," she replied to Emily's skeptical silence. "He once implied he regarded me as an honorary man. Why else would he call me 'Fellbridge' and engage to discuss with me our farms and crops?"

"Anyone who could regard a female with a figure like yours as an honorary man needs a pair of strong spectacles. Maybe he's decided it's the best way to get in under your guard? You've always been dreadfully prickly toward him."

"I doubt my prickliness would serve to put off someone of his lordship's mettle," Annabel said. "And besides—"

Emily grabbed her arm. "Over there," she whispered. "In front of *Nausicaä*."

Annabel looked. A young couple—though on observing their identical dark, waving hair, deep blue eyes, and pointed chins, she guessed them to be siblings rather than lovers—stood before *Nausicaä and Her Handmaidens*, heads together as they conversed in low tones. They appeared to be much amused.

"They look familiar. I think I've seen them here before," Emily muttered. "Last week, when I was here taking notes on pictures."

"We must try to approach them," Annabel said.

If only Clementina were here with her exquisite senses! She would certainly have been able to hear what the two were whispering about. But she had been excused from watch duty and long hours on her feet on account of her delicate condition.

They shuffled carefully along the wall, but the groups of loitering, chatting people prevented them from getting much closer than they already were. "Do you think you can read them from here?" she asked Emily. Proximity was necessary for Emily's mind-reading ability to accomplish much.

"I can try," Emily said, and narrowed her eyes as she gazed at the couple.

The young woman stiffened and looked around the room as if she were a fox scenting hounds. She said something to the young man, and they moved quickly to the door.

"Come on!" Annabel said, giving Emily's arm a tug. These two were too interesting to lose sight of. Anyone who could sense Emily's gentle touch on her mind had to be someone worth investigating.

But evading the crowds in the room took too much time. By the time they reached the door and looked down the great staircase, the couple had vanished.

"Bother!" Emily muttered. "I almost had her."

"Did you get anything?"

"Not really. We were too far away. It's interesting that she felt me, though."

"I know. I was thinking the same thing." Annabel leaned against the wall and began to write in her notebook.

"What are you doing?"

"Writing a description of them for the others to

look out for when I'm not here. That pair may not have anything to do with this, but we need to make certain of that."

Emily nodded. "If they do have something to do with this, they'll probably be back."

"Precisely. And one of us will be watching for them if they do."

The following morning dawned bright and sunny and promised fair all day. Annabel carefully chose a hat with a generous brim to wear and carried a parasol with her for the trip to Hampton Court when Lord Glenrick came for her.

"You come prepared," he commented as he handed her into his curricle, then swung up beside her, tossing a coin to the boy who held the horses' heads.

Annabel settled her skirts and raised her parasol. "My mother always says that an ounce of prevention is worth a quart of sunburn lotion. I'm quite convinced she has the right of it."

He laughed. "May I say that you are one of the cleverest women of my acquaintance?"

"Or the one least willing to spend good money on doubtful sunburn cures."

"Ah, but frugality is a time-honored Scottish virtue. I am doubly charmed. Are we ready?" he called over her head.

She turned. Lord Quinceton's curricle was behind them, with Frances happily ensconced in it. For a brief moment, Annabel felt unaccountably cross at the sight. Then she recalled herself—what foolishness! Why should she care who sat in Lord Quinceton's curricle?—and smiled and waved. "Good morning, Frances!"

"Annabel!" Frances waved back. "Won't this be diverting?"

"That was the intention," Lord Quinceton said. He barely nodded to Annabel, a short, cool greeting which she returned in both degree and temperature...and unusually, he barely met her eyes. Hmmph. Emily was imagining things if she truly thought he had any kind of interest in her.

Annabel was delighted to see on their arrival that the palace's gardens were at their late spring peak. After they had settled the horses in the shade of a tree, she set out on Lord Glenrick's arm to inspect the formal beds.

"There's not enough color in London, outside of silk warehouses," she said, eagerly drinking in the purples and golds of alliums and late tulips.

"Do you prefer the country to the city, then? A Lady Patroness of Almack's, the very center of fashionable London?"

Annabel smiled. "I shan't tell them if you won't."

"My lips are sealed, madam," he said, all mock solemnity.

"Good; that means I can shamelessly indulge myself in gardens and flowers without fear. Isn't there a bluebell wood in the Wilderness here?"

"I believe there is. Shall we find it?"

"Yes, please! The bluebells ought to still be in bloom. At least they would be at home."

"Oh, the Wilderness!" Frances exclaimed. "Isn't

that where the maze is? We must see that!"

Annabel jumped. She hadn't realized Frances and Lord Quinceton were so close behind as to be able to overhear their conversation.

"Then the Wilderness it is," Lord Glenrick declared. He hailed a passing gardener to ask for directions, and they turned their steps in the direction the man indicated.

"Thank you," Annabel spoke quietly. "If it's shady enough there, I might even venture to lower my parasol and avoid the danger of putting out one of your eyes."

"I thank you for that. Being a Cyclops is not on my list of life ambitions." He made a wry face.

"No, I would imagine not. What *is* on your list, then?"

He hesitated, then returned her smile. "Oh, many things. You would be surprised at some of them, I think."

Annabel wondered if his reticence was due to the audience of two not far behind them and tried to hurry their steps a little. "You must tell me some of them some day."

"I intend to." His voice was almost caressing. "Tell me, did you enjoy *The Lady of the Lake*? Or no—you cannot have had time to read it so soon."

"Oh, but I have. I was going to thank you again for it. It kept me up far too late last night. In fact, I think I liked it even better than *Marmion*. The setting was almost a character unto itself. It's made me quite eager to visit Scotland."

He drew her arm a little closer. "I would count it an honor to show you my country someday. The King James in *The Lady* was one of my ancestors, you know. There's more—quite a bit more—than a drop of royal Stuart blood in the Carrick line. It was only because my great-grandfather was such a—shall we say, *convincing* fellow—that my family held onto our lands and titles after the Forty-Five...but that's a story for another day. Though sometimes, in idle moments, I can't help wondering what might have been." He sighed. "It is a fool's game, thinking about might-have-beens. I hope it isn't one you play very often, my dear."

This was not the path she'd expected their conversation to take. Of course, she often thought about what might have been if the limb on that wretched tree Freddy had climbed had not broken: might she have had another child by now, as she'd longed to? And beyond that was the might-have-been she only rarely allowed herself to contemplate: what if someone other than Freddy had offered for her first—someone who had wanted her for more than her dowry and expected ability to produce an heir?

"I—I try not to, but it isn't always easy, in my circumstances," she said, hoping she'd achieved the unconcerned tone she'd tried for.

"Maybe there are might-soon-bes that you could think about instead. That is what I do when regrets over the might-have-beens raise their ugly heads." His voice dropped. "I have an idea for a might-soon-be that I very much wish to discuss with you."

Annabel met his eyes and a little thrill of uncertain pleasure fluttered through her at the warmth in his expression...and then she couldn't help glancing self-consciously behind them. Frances was chatting happily away to Lord Quinceton...who was staring directly at *her*.

She looked away hastily. Had he been listening to their conversation? Could he even hear it, above Frances's prattle? Then she straightened her shoulders and lifted her chin. What if he had? Lord Glenrick had said nothing he—or she—must blush for...or that was any of Lord Quinceton's business. But nudging the conversation onto a slightly different tack might be more comfortable.

"I cannot help being intrigued by your might-have-beens," she said. "Do you think the nation would have been better off with one of your relations on the throne?"

"Instead of His Royal Highness the Prince of Whales?" Lord Glenrick enunciated the 'h' with dry precision. "Or any of his estimable brothers?"

They came across a copse of bluebells then, and the conversation was subsumed in cries of admiration from Frances. Annabel admired them more quietly; there was nothing more serene and soothing than a bluebell wood, the hazy purple-blue veil that covered the sun-dappled greenery under the shade of the trees. Lord Glenrick seemed to have caught her mood; he too was silent as they wandered the mown path through the flowers. She could have lingered there for much longer, but Frances, despite her initial pleasure in the bluebells, soon grew bored.

"Can't we go to the maze now? I'm aching to see it! Aren't you, Annabel?" she asked plaintively.

Annabel smiled to herself. For a woman in her thirties, Frances could be very *young* sometimes. "I think it would be great fun," she said. Lord Glenrick raised an eyebrow at her, but obediently turned to follow Frances and Lord Quinceton toward Hampton Court's famous hedge maze.

"Oh, this is so exciting!" Frances said as they came to its entrance. "You won't get us lost, will you, Quin?"

"I'll endeavor not to," he replied. "Except that I thought that doing so was the point of the exercise."

She giggled. "Well, yes, but no one's supposed to admit it. And anyway, the man up there can direct us out if you can't." She waved at a bored-looking groundskeeper, ensconced on a tall platform above the maze to help direct the hopelessly lost to the exit.

"That sounded like a challenge, Quinceton!" Lord Glenrick called after them. "Do you indeed think mazes are 'great fun?'" he added more quietly to Annabel as they waited for Frances and the marquis to get a head-start down the green passage.

She had thought that attempting the maze might indeed be amusing. But now, in the moment, the idea of trailing through it behind Frances and Lord Quinceton had lost its appeal. "Not particularly, but I don't want to disappoint Frances," she murmured back. "She was so looking forward to coming here."

"You are a darling, you know," he said, abruptly turning and leading her away from the maze's entrance. "But if you're not as eager to get lost in there as she is, then we shall leave it to her and Quin. She won't miss us. Not with her present company," he added.

So Lord Glenrick was aware of Frances's obsession with Lord Quinceton, then. There was probably no way he could not be, after all these years. Yes, Frances would be quite happy to wander the maze without them...but how did Lord Quinceton feel about this arrangement?

And why, for heaven's sake, was she even thinking about them?

Lord Glenrick steered them down a quiet path shaded by trees, and they ambled along for some time in solitary peace. For such a pleasant day, the gardens were remarkably thin of visitors, which suited her quite well after all the crowds she'd been among whilst on watch at the Exhibition. Sally and Maria and Dorothea and Emily were all taking turns today to watch there; would any of them see the handsome young couple that she and Emily had observed behaving so oddly yesterday? It was a pity that Clementina could not help—she would have the best chance of hearing just what they were whispering about—

"A penny for your thoughts, Annabel?"

She glanced up at him, startled at his use of her given name. He smiled back. "I beg your pardon, my dear. Perhaps I should not have done that. But it's how I think of you, you know. And I think of you a great deal."

Oh. Annabel fought to ignore the fluttery sensation that rose once again in her midsection. "I doubt my thoughts are worth as much as that. I'm just enjoying the day."

"So am I." Their steps had slowed; now he halted them completely in the shade of a great holly tree. He gazed at her for the space of a breath or two, then with great deliberation raised his hand to her cheek, allowing his fingertips to trail lightly across it before bending his head and touching his lips to hers.

She closed her eyes as a jumble of thoughts and reactions tumbled through her: gratification and excitement (wouldn't Emily be pleased to know she'd been right?) followed by nervous disapproval (wouldn't Grandmother Shellingham be appalled?) and finally...just a whiff of disappointment.

She'd wondered how it would feel to be kissed by a man who sincerely wanted to kiss her, unlike Freddy and his good-natured but perfunctory salutes. But Lord Glenrick's obvious desire—it was plain in his quickened breath and the increasing eagerness of his mouth—had called forth no answering physical response in her. Was she, after all, one of those chilly women incapable of passion? Perhaps if she *tried* to enjoy it, just as she'd dutifully tried to enjoy Freddy's occasional conjugal visits—

"Annabel," he whispered, his other hand reaching up to grip her shoulder. "Oh, Annabel, I could just *devour* you—"

That send a bit of a shiver through her. She made herself unstiffen under his hands and tried to kiss him back, but could not help feeling relieved when he finally drew back to look at her.

"You've completely bewitched me, you know." He traced the outline of her mouth with one finger.

"Oh, no, Lord Glen—"

He pressed the finger over her lips. "You must call me Alec, my dear."

She took a breath. "Alec, I—"

"Ssh. There's nothing to discuss. Only tell me that you did not find that repugnant."

"No, of course I didn't." She hadn't, really. Not *repugnant*—

"Then might I do it again sometime soon?"

How Emily would crow if she'd heard that! She lowered her gaze. "I—yes, you might."

His hand tightened on her shoulder...but just then a voice called, "*There* you are! Why didn't you follow us?"

Lord Glenrick—could she make herself start calling him Alec?—quickly dropped his hands and turned. "What, through the maze already?"

Frances and Lord Quinceton were coming down the path toward them, Frances still clinging to his arm. "Quin marched us directly to the center and out again in no time at all. He's so clever!" she said, looking up at him through her eyelashes.

Lord Quinceton did not rise to Frances's compliment. He was once again looking fixedly at her, Annabel realized with some discomfort, his expression unreadable. What had he and Frances seen as they rounded the corner and come upon her and Lord Glenrick? Had it been obvious that he'd been kissing her? She raised a hand involuntarily to her mouth, and he looked away.

Frances was still happily chattering away. "I'm so glad we found you. I need to borrow Annabel and sit down for a moment."

Lord Glenrick's brow furrowed. "Are you well, Frances? You haven't overexerted yourself, have you?"

Frances waved a careless hand at him. "Quite well. Go away, you two. We'll go sit on that garden seat for a few minutes." She indicated a bench set a little bit further down the path overlooking a pretty little copse of bluebells and the last of the primroses.

Her brother looked at her with concern but took Lord Quinceton's arm and continued past them.

"How kind your brother is!" Annabel said when they were out of earshot. "Are you quite well?"

"Alec's always been a most considerate brother," Frances agreed. "And I'm perfectly well—it's just that I've torn a ribbon off my slipper. Do you think you could fix it for me? Our nanny never permitted me to properly learn to do anything but embroider because she didn't think a duke's daughter ought to know how to sew. I just about *died* when I felt it come loose while Quin and I were in the maze."

Annabel strove to keep her countenance. Evidently it was permitted to a lowly marquis's daughter to do something as menial as wield a needle. "Certainly, Frances."

"Oh, thank you! You're such a dear! I've a needle and thread in my reticule—isn't it the silliest thing? Nanny wouldn't permit me to sew, but always insisted I carry them."

She kept up a stream of talk as they went to the bench, in a very good mood indeed. Annabel wondered if Lord Quinceton was in an equally exalted frame of mind after their walk through the maze and glanced after him and Lord Glenrick, strolling slowly down the path. Lord Glenrick still held Lord Quinceton's arm; Lord Quinceton held himself stiffly, and Annabel remembered that they'd stood the same way in front of the picture at the Exhibition. There was definitely something odd between the pair of them—

Frances plonked down on the bench, fumbled with one of her shoes, and handed it to Annabel. "See? I was right—one of the ribbons is off." She rummaged in her reticule and pulled out a tiny cork with a needle stuck in it, wrapped in thread. "Did you have a nice time with Alec on your walk?"

Annabel took the needle, knotted the thread,

and began to tack the end of the ribbon into the kid slipper with quick stitches, her face bent over her work to hide her blushes. If Frances hadn't seen them kissing, she'd eat her hat, feathers and all. "He is a charming companion," she said.

"That's what he says about you." Frances touched her arm. "He cares for you a great deal, Annabel. I do hope he and you—well, I think it's high time he married, and I can't think of anyone I'd rather have for a sister...oh! What tiny stitches you make!"

Annabel had drawn in her breath, but Frances was busily peering down at her handiwork, exclaiming over her small stitches, so a response seemed unnecessary...which was a good thing, as her head was awhirl. Was Frances exaggerating, or did she truly think that her brother's thoughts were drifting toward a proposal? What would she say if he did make her an offer? It would be tremendously flattering, of course—after all, he was a future duke. But she'd promised herself that if she married again, it would be for love. And she wasn't at all convinced that she was ready to fall in love with Lord Glenrick, even though Freddy had been gone for over two years...which reminded her—

"Frances, pray forgive me—I forgot to ask you." She took a final backstitch and knotted the thread. "You haven't had a bereavement, have you?"

Frances's head snapped up. "What?" she asked sharply.

"I was just curious—Emily saw you in Thomas's buying black gloves the other day."

For some reason, she paled. "Oh. N-no, no one's died...that is, I received a letter from my cousin—my great-aunt Mary is not in the best of health, it seems, and I—I thought it wise to be prepared."

"Oh dear, how sad. Is she very elderly?"

"Quite. You know, I think I must learn to do practical sewing—what if you had not been here today?" she said, accepting the needle back from Annabel and sticking it back into the cork in her reticule.

The two men returned not long after. The drive home was a quiet one, aside from Frances's chatter in the carriage behind them.

"Will I see you at Almack's this evening?" Annabel asked as Lord Glenrick escorted her to her door.

He hesitated. "Alas, no—I have a previous engagement. I wish I did not. But I trust I shall see you very soon." He lifted her hand to his lips and kissed it, meeting her eyes as he did.

Annabel blushed and smiled...but couldn't keep from glancing back at Lord Quinceton's curricle. Frances was, amazingly, still talking; but once again, Lord Quinceton was watching her, his expression unreadable.

Annabel arrived at Almack's that evening bubbling over with good spirits. A letter from Soames, her farm bailiff at the Abbey, was awaiting her when she came home from the afternoon's expedition with Lord Glenrick. It contained the very welcome news that not only did the season's corn crop appear very forward in the recent sunny weather, but also that he'd already arranged the sale of their fleeces barely a week after the sheep had been shorn...and for a very good price. Now she'd be able to afford a few additional improvements she hadn't budgeted for this year, and if the autumn's crop was as good as it bid fair to be, she'd be able to re-roof several tenants' cottages this year rather than next. She felt as if she could breathe more deeply, all of a sudden, from sheer relief.

Sally pounced on her as soon as she arrived, tucking her arm through Annabel's and drawing her to the Lady Patronesses' seats. "How was your visit to Hampton Court with Glenrick?"

Oh, dear. Emily had obviously been talking. "It was very enjoyable." Then, when Sally opened her mouth, no doubt to ask for details, she put in quickly, "Did you see anything of note today at the Exhibition?"

Fortunately, the distraction worked; Sally's brow furrowed. "No—apart from more attacks on the Hebblys. It was disgraceful, Annabel—worse than the baby pig. I just hope Lady Hebbly hasn't seen any of them. It would be enough to send anyone into a decline."

Annabel sighed. "I cannot compass how one keeps the wife of the head of the Hanging Committee of the Exhibition away from it. Perhaps one of us should call on her, though I fear that might just distress her more, if she's seen the pictures."

"Maybe she hasn't recognized herself," Sally said hopefully. "One doesn't go to the Exhibition expecting to see one's features superimposed on livestock—ah, Quin! How pleasant to see you here this evening."

Annabel fought to keep her expression under control as Lord Quinceton, debonair in a midnight blue coat, strode up to them. She hadn't known he'd be here tonight—not that she'd had the opportunity to exchange more than two words with him today.

"I wondered if anyone else had noticed that bit of nastiness," he said, acknowledging Sally's greeting with a nod. "I should have known that you would, Fellbridge. I don't believe that much gets past you." There was something unpleasantly pointed about his words, which mystified Annabel.

"I've no notion what I've done to deserve such praise—if praise it is," she said.

"Why, what have you noticed, Quin?" Sally asked. Annabel smothered a smile. Watching Sally—Sally!—switch on such an innocent, unknowing air was most amusing.

"The pictures at the Exhibition being altered so abominably, especially the ones being made to look like Lady Hebbly. I would give a great deal to know how it's being done." He cocked one eyebrow at Annabel. "Another investigation, Fellbridge?"

"Ooh, does Annabel investigate things? How exciting!" Sally burbled. "Annabel, you never told me! What do you investigate?"

Annabel heartily wished the marquis at the bottom of the sea—and hoped Sally didn't think she had somehow compromised the Lady Patronesses. "Nothing, really. Lord Quinceton is pleased to make his little jokes," she said coolly.

To her relief, Sally flashed her an understanding look, then said, "I shall leave you to enjoy your joke, then—I see that Maria is trying to catch my eye." She nodded to them both and left.

Annabel wished she could go with Sally and leave him standing, but no good reason to do so occurred to her. Instead, she remained resolutely silent after Sally's departure. The odious marquis would have to speak first!

"I've told you before, Fellbridge—if you ever need my help with your investigating, I am at your service," the odious marquis said softly.

"And I have told you that your offer, though kindly meant, I do believe—" she drew the last words out till they negated their own meaning—"are misguided. I am engaged in no such activities."

"Ah, yes. So you've said." He paused. "Why Lady Hebbly, do you think? I cannot imagine anyone might have cause to attack her; a vendetta against her husband is much more likely. Will you call on her? I would instead talk with Sir Henry—it would probably be more to the point and less distressing to her. If I should happen to see him at Brooks's, I would be happy to make some inquiries on your behalf."

"That would be very kind of you if the matter were of any interest to me, but I believe I have already said it is not," she said. It wasn't a lie; this was Frances's investigation, officially.

He sighed. "You did mention that, didn't you? My memory grows worse daily. Then we shall speak of something else. Did you enjoy Hampton Court? Those secluded paths in the Wilderness seemed to meet with your approval."

For a moment she wished she could hide; he *must* have seen Lord Glenrick kissing her. But then she grew angry. The effrontery of him! She was an adult. What business was it of his if she chose to permit a man to kiss her? "As did the maze with yours, I am certain," she snapped.

One corner of his mouth quirked. "Indeed. The groundskeeper up on his platform overlooking it has his uses beyond directing the lost. Not that his chaperonage was required."

"Nor was any in the Wilderness!"

"No?" He paused, just long enough to allow the skepticism in that one syllable sink in. Then he said, abruptly, "Tell me, madam—what did you think of *The Mother's Plight*?"

"The *what*?" She stared at him. Talking with him tonight was like conversing with an eel.

"One of the few pictures at the Exhibition that has not had Lady Hebbly's countenance incorporated into it. The Scottish picture—I was told by one whom I presume is a reliable source that you had seen it and admired it greatly."

Which picture? What was he talking about? Then she remembered: the Scottish woman with her infant. "Oh, that one. It was—er—"

He was watching her intently. "'Er?' Is that all you have to say about it?"

"I didn't look at it very closely, if you must know," she said crossly. "I was rather more concerned about Lady Hebbly."

"In the pictures which you aren't investigating," he said drily, but his expression had cleared.

Annabel dearly would have liked to stamp on his foot in sheer annoyance, but one simply could not do that, no matter how strong the temptation. "Lord Quinceton, I was in an excellent mood when I arrived here, and I will not allow you to ruin that."

"Far be it from me to dampen your mood. What has happened to put you in alt?" He took her arm and tucked it under his. "You must tell me about it."

"I don't want to walk with you—" she began furiously, but he had already drawn her along beside him.

"We have some catching up to do since I was away. I regret not being able to converse with you earlier today," he said, ignoring her protest.

"No, you seemed quite happily occupied," she couldn't help retorting. "I wish you would not trifle with Frances, sir! She is my friend."

"Not as happily occupied as you were—" he began, then shook his head. "No, that isn't fair. You were Glenrick's guest, after all, much as I might deprecate that fact. I beg your pardon."

Annabel swallowed, deflated by his apology. She should not have said what she had, either. "Why *did* you invite yourself to Hampton today?" she heard herself ask.

"Can't you guess?" he said, smiling grimly. "Now, why the excellent mood?"

For some reason, she suddenly felt shy. This was probably the oddest of the many odd conversations she'd had with him. "I received some good news from my bailiff this afternoon. Nothing you would find of interest."

"On the contrary, I find it of absorbing interest. What was his news?"

She made her voice as off-hand as she could. "Just that the wool from our spring shearing has already sold. If the fall crops come in as well as they're promising, I shall find myself more beforehand with the world than expected and can take care of some matters I did not think to be able to attend to for another year."

"Ah. What matters?"

"My lord, you cannot really—oh, very well," she hastily amended when he frowned. "I've been wanting to repair some pensioners' cottages on the estate for some time. I know I should put any profits back into the land, but I'd promised myself a bit of a treat if this were a good year."

"And repairing tenants' cottages is your treat." The muscles of his arm tightened where her hand rested on it, as if he were clenching his fist.

"Is there anything wrong with that?"

A long moment passed before he answered, in a slightly constrained voice, "Not a thing, Fellbridge. Not a thing."

She didn't believe him for an instant. "Well then, how would you spend a windfall like mine?"

He paused again, and then to her surprise laughed softly. "How would I spend it? If the world were a perfect place, probably at Rundell and Bridge, buying something gorgeous and outrageously expensive with which to bedeck my wife. Pearls, quite possibly. Or pink diamonds."

Definitely the oddest conversation! "But you aren't married!"

"No," he agreed. "I said 'if the world were a perfect place.' Regrettably, it is not."

Chapter Three

Annabel sneaked into Somerset House the next day before the Exhibition had officially opened even though her partner for the morning, Georgiana, would not arrive for another hour. Perhaps observation duty would give her something to think about beyond the curious events of the day before, events that a restless night had done nothing to clarify.

At first, she had been pleasantly ruffled yesterday by Lord Glenrick's kiss and by Frances's comments. After her conversation with Lord Quinceton at Almack's she felt even more ruffled—but less pleasantly so. The man had a positive genius for putting her off balance, in notable contrast to Lord Glenrick, who never challenged or riled her.

On the other hand, Glenrick did not make her feel so...*alive.*

Glenrick and Quinceton...as much as it went against her grain (after all, Shellingham women were not brought up to think of themselves as attractive) she was forced to admit that Emily might be right: both men had an interest in her. The question was, what were those interests? Lord Glenrick might be "smitten," as Eliza had put it; did that mean he was thinking of her as a possible future wife, as Frances had implied? What about Lord Quinceton? She had assumed he merely enjoyed fencing with her as one would with an amusing acquaintance. But there had been a definite whiff of anger in his not-so-subtle digs about Glenrick's conduct at Hampton Court and her implied complicity in it (goodness, that made her sound the veriest criminal!)—anger that could well be explained by jealousy. Was it jealousy at the thought of losing a flirting partner to another man, or something more?

And what was the pair's relationship with each other? Several times now she'd seen them in close conversation; yet Lord Quinceton had warned her to avoid Glenrick that first night at Almack's. And then there was what happened last night...

She had not lingered long at Almack's, tired after all the activity of the day. Lord Quinceton found her as she was calling for her carriage and remained with her until it arrived, saying very little. He accompanied her into the street, ignoring the footman and handing her into it himself.

"Thank you. Good night," she'd said politely, not in a mood to brangle with him further.

"Good night," he replied, but did not step away from the landau. Instead, he remained there, one hand on the door, looking at her with a faint frown on his face. In the light of the torches by the door, his hair and eyes were nearly black, yet caught unexpected glints of fire.

"Was there anything you wished to say, my lord?" she said, pointedly looking at his hand.

He gave a small start, as if her words had recalled him to himself. "Yes, actually."

"Well?" she said, after a moment's silence.

"Just...be careful, Fellbridge." He'd paused again, then added, "Please."

She'd found herself turning to look at him as her carriage moved down King Street toward St. James. He returned her look, until she had turned the corner and he was lost from view.

Be careful of whom? Or of what?

But it was the *please* that had kept her awake last night. She could not spend her life wondering just what he wanted from her. It was almost as bad as spending her life in this wretched Exhibition, waiting for something to happen.

Just then, something did happen—though it was not by any means a welcome event. Annabel saw a short, stout woman in a dark gray pelisse sidle around the doorway into the Great Room. She wore a veil over her elegant black hat, but Annabel knew her immediately...and her heart sank. She waited until the small figure was out of sight, then slipped off her shadow and followed it.

Antonia Hebbly stood before *Death of the Leviathan*, in which a group of Laplander hunters were savagely harpooning (in a most realistic and sanguinary manner) a large whale—which somehow bore Sir Henry's features. She appeared as transfixed as the whale...but when Annabel reached her side, she saw that her shoulders were heaving, and heard a muffled sniff escape her.

"Lady Hebbly," she murmured, and gently

touched her arm. "This is...simply dreadful."

Lady Hebbly stiffened, but relaxed when she turned and saw Annabel. "Oh, my dear child," she said, and collapsed against her.

Annabel patted her back and made soothing sounds as Lady Hebbly wept into her shoulder. Thank heavens the Exhibition had not yet opened for the day; the clerk must have known who Lady Hebbly was and allowed her in. "I wish you had not had to see it, ma'am," she said.

"It's h-h-*horrible!*" poor Lady Hebbly managed to say, between sobs. "That awful picture...my poor Henry—what has he done to deserve this?"

Oh, good—maybe she hadn't seen *Lowther Castle, Westmoreland: Evening* or any of the other pictures that bore her likeness. But Lady Hebbly went on, dashing her hopes.

"I d-don't care about the ones of me. I know my face is—is easy to mock. But *this*—it is so *hateful.*" She found her handkerchief and lifted her veil to dab at her eyes. "I beg your pardon, Annabel. I did not intend to trouble you. Please forget my lapse—how are you? I have not seen you since the beginning of the season. And the boys? Have they settled into Eton? I know your mother is well—I received a letter from her on Tuesday and have been very remiss in not yet answering it."

It was Lady Hebbly all over to make light of her distress. Annabel had known her forever—she was related to half the nobility of England and had been one of Mama's closest friends since they were young girls, both of them daughters of important earls. But her lofty origins had not made her proud; she was the kindest and most considerate of women...hence her concern at not having replied to Mama's letter two days after having received it.

"The boys are having a splendid time at school, and I'm very well. Busy, of course, with Almack's and everything." She tucked Lady Hebbly's arm in hers and tried to steer her away from the picture. But Lady Hebbly would not be distracted.

"Who is doing this?" she asked plaintively. "I am terrified that Henry will see them, even though as a rule he avoids the Exhibition once it is installed because he says he can no longer stand the sight of the pictures. But he has in the past come back to check that all is as it should be, and I must keep him from doing so this year. I only came because I overheard a conversation at a rout-party last night. I know I should not have eavesdropped—it was very wrong of me—but I could not help it. Oh, how shall I keep Henry away? He does not need to see this after all he's been through—" Her lips quivered.

Annabel looked involuntarily down at Lady Hebbly's hand on her arm, still clad in black gloves though it had been nearly a year and a half since their only son was killed at Corunna. Again, how typical of her to think of her husband's grief above her own.

"You didn't say anything to Sir Henry about this, did you?" she asked.

"Oh, no. I wanted to see it first, to see if it were really true. I only hope no one else tells him. How is this happening? I cannot believe they were like this when they were hung or Henry would have seen immediately."

Annabel hesitated. "I don't know, ma'am—but I am hopeful it will end soon."

Lady Hebbly looked up at her, her regrettably

cow-like eyes still swimming with tears. "Do you think so? Oh, Annabel, I hope you're right."

"I'm convinced I am." Annabel steered her toward the exit to the stairs. The clerk must have opened the doors, as viewers were starting to drift in. She wanted to be able to watch them...which meant encouraging Lady Hebbly to leave.

But Lady Hebbly stopped at the doorway. "You're so certain—do you know something about this, my dear?"

"Er...no." Lying to Mama's oldest friend was particularly trying, especially when those gentle brown eyes were fixed on her face. "But it can't go on. Someone will catch whoever is responsible and make him or her stop."

Lady Hebbly studied her for a moment, then smiled her sweet smile. "Thank you, my dear. I hope that will be the case." Her smile faded. "You will tell me if you learn anything about this?"

"I doubt that I will," Annabel said quickly. "But if I should, I will certainly tell you." She bent and kissed Lady Hebbly's plump cheek and watched while she slowly descended the Great Staircase... then hurried over to look at *Death of the Leviathan* again to study it.

There was a deeper quality of anger evident in it—deeper than had been seen in the earlier alterations—that was disquieting. And not far away, Sir Henry's portrait of Lady Hebbly had been rendered so hideous that she could only hope that Lady Hebbly hadn't seen it. She made a circuit of the room, the hairs on the back of her neck prickling. Sally had been right last night: this was the worst yet.

"Annabel?" Georgiana had come up beside her.

"What are you doing not in shadow? Is everything all right?"

It was a huge relief to not have Georgiana hostile any longer. "I'm so glad you're here!" Annabel took her arm and led her to *Death of the Leviathan*. "Lady Hebbly was here and saw that."

Georgiana looked at it and gasped. "Good heavens! Should we warn them? That feels almost a threat."

"I know. It's troubling." Annabel found them an unobserved spot in a corner of the Anteroom and pulled a shadow over them both. "I think we should watch that picture carefully today," she murmured. "The changes were new as of yesterday according to Sally, and whoever did it will surely be back today to gloat."

"I expect you're right." Georgiana glanced up at the canvas as they took up their station to one side of it. "What a dreadful thing. I expect Antonia was very upset. She adores Henry, for some reason. I remember when they were first betrothed." She sighed, and Annabel felt her shake her head.

"Yes?" she murmured encouragingly. She had heard hints about the Hebblys, which of course Mama had loyally refused to discuss. "Was it a... noteworthy occasion?"

"Well, we all thought Antonia was desperate. She was well into her twenties and hadn't had one proposal despite her fortune. She didn't show to advantage in tight-waisted gowns and powdered curls, poor girl. When Henry Hebbly offered for her, Lord Ferrington nearly suffered an apoplectic fit—an impecunious artist seeking his only daughter's hand! But Antonia had fallen head over heels with him—he *was* a good-looking young man, I'll admit—even though it was clear to everyone else that he was chiefly interested in her dowry."

Poor Lady Hebbly! "I suppose they both got what they wanted," Annabel said.

Georgiana snorted. "Henry got the better end of that bargain. I doubt he would have been as successful if he hadn't had Antonia as well as Antonia's money. He's always been far too arrogant for his own good; she's the one who smooths things over with the people who commission his work. I expect she's the one who gets most of his commissions in the first place."

That was more or less the truth; Annabel remembered Sir Henry—he was plain Mr. Hebbly then—painting her older sister the winter before she came out into society. She'd received the impression that Mama had done it as an excuse to have the then-Mrs. Hebbly (she refused to use her courtesy title of Lady Antonia after her marriage) stay with them for a few weeks.

"Thank you for coming here today. It's monotonous duty, I'm afraid," she said after a while.

"Pish," Georgiana said. "You've had to put up with more of this than anyone. Where, may I inquire, is Frances? It is her investigation, is it not?"

"She'll be here on Saturday." Annabel watched a pair of women approach *Death of the Leviathan*, then hastily turn away with little *moues* of disgust. "And I did spend all of yesterday elsewhere."

Georgiana sniffed. "And so did she."

Annabel began to protest, but stopped. "You're very kind."

"Hmmph." Georgiana sounded embarrassed.

"Speaking of Frances, Glenrick is spending a great deal of time in London this year. I wonder if he has finally been driven to accepting his fate?"

"His fate?" Annabel strove to sound no more interested than she ought to. "What fate is that?"

"To find himself a wealthy wife, and the sooner the better."

"Oh, indeed it cannot be as bad as that!"

"No? From what I understand old Carrick's mortgaged everything that can possibly be mortgaged—what he hasn't broken the entail on and sold outright. The only thing for it is for his son to marry well."

Annabel thought of her conversation with Frances about the identity of Glenrick's possible future bride. Was she aware of her family's precarious financial state? She had to be...so why had she said that she hoped Annabel might become her sister-in-law, when she knew her to be struggling with her own money problems?

Georgiana was still speaking. "Though it does seem odd," she said musingly.

"What does?"

"Well, for a man whose family is all but at a stand-still, he seems very comfortably situated. His horses and that new curricle of his—a box at the opera—not to mention actually living in Carrick House rather than renting it out for the season."

That *did* seem odd, except— "Perhaps the rumors of their debts are exaggerated?" Annabel asked—hopefully, she realized.

"I wonder. My husband says that Glenrick is doing a great deal of entertaining at his clubs this year—dinners and private parties, quite lavish at times. He's either determined to go further into debt, or there's something we don't know. Maybe they found a gold mine on their property up in Scotland and haven't told anyone."

Annabel was glad that Georgiana was unlikely to be able to see her face, concealed as they were by shadow. What *was* going on with Glenrick? How much interest should she take in his affairs? How much interest did she *want* to take?

"Annabel," Georgiana muttered, grasping her arm. "There. That couple. I've seen them here before."

Annabel looked up sharply—she should stop brooding about her own affairs and pay attention to the Exhibition!—and examined the nearby viewers. Not too far away, in front of a canvas of Cincinnatus with his plow, stood the same dark-haired young man and woman she and Emily had seen on Tuesday—the attractive pair that bore enough of a likeness to be siblings and who had seemed to feel Emily's seeking their thoughts.

"Yes—Emily and I have seen them here too, and the girl definitely sensed Emily trying to read her," she said. "Do you think you can follow them without being seen? And listen to what they're saying? They may be perfectly innocent, but they might not."

Georgiana watched them for a moment. "I'll do a moth and light on one of them," she said. "It's the best way to remain unseen—flies buzz too much. Shall I listen just while they're here, or stay on them?"

"Whatever you think best. If what they say makes you think they're the culprits, then yes, please stay with them when they leave so we can get their address. I'll come to your house at about three to hear what you've learned, and we can go on to Frances's from there."

"Very well." Georgiana drew in a deep breath. A moment later, she was gone. Annabel could just see the small moth that fluttered for a moment under the shadow where Georgiana had stood before it moved into the room. Annabel admired how she darted this way and that in the random way of moths rather than moving in a straight line toward the pair. She flitted aimlessly above their heads for a moment, then circled around and settled delicately on the back of the young woman's shoulder.

Annabel had just breathed a sigh of relief when the girl leaned forward and said something to the young man. To her horror, he pulled a handkerchief out of his pocket and clapped it over the girl's shoulder—and directly over Georgiana. He carefully— thank heavens it was carefully!—cupped his hand around the moth, then drew it back and twisted the edges together so that she was trapped in a small bag of fine linen. He handed it to the girl, who held it up to peer at it in the light from the skylight above them.

"No!" Annabel breathed. She could just see Georgiana fluttering in the cambric prison, undoubtedly panicking—it was impossible for her to change back into her human shape here in the middle of the Summer Exhibition, yet as a moth she was horribly vulnerable. She had to convince them to release Georgiana.

"It's far too crowded in here," the girl said loudly. One or two people glanced at her. "I should prefer to be where we will be less jostled." She made a great show of tucking the handkerchief into her reticule, and Annabel guessed she suspected that Georgiana was not acting alone: her speech and action were for the benefit of Georgiana's unknown accomplice. Very well then; she would follow them and demand Georgiana's release...and find out if they were the ones responsible for defacing the pictures. And even if they weren't, the Lady Patronesses would want to know who they were; it was part of their business to keep an eye on people in London known to have powers.

The pair moved slowly toward the stairs, the girl still talking loudly about the crowds. That was reassuring; it meant that she had not actually seen or sensed Annabel but hoped to draw out anyone who had accompanied Georgiana. She followed them as closely as she dared, trying to decide her next step.

She was so intent on following them that she almost walked into the Marquis of Quinceton lounging at the top of the stairs, his negligent posture proclaiming his boredom...but she saw at once that it was a pose and that he was closely watching the Exhibition-goers climbing the staircase. Good heavens, why was *he* here? Almost involuntarily she looked around for Lord Glenrick—was he here as well?

And then it occurred to her—since he was here, she might as well make use of him. She dodged and wove and managed to slip down the Great Staircase ahead of the young woman and man, ducked behind a statue and cast off her shadow, and went to the foot of the stairs where she waved up at Lord Quinceton.

He saw her almost immediately and came down the stairs to her. "Why am I not surprised to see you here, Fellbridge?"

"I haven't the faintest idea," she said, a little

crossly. "But since you're here, you can make yourself useful."

"I am at your service, madam. What do you want me to do?"

"We need to follow them." She nodded toward the pair, slowly making their way to the doors leading to the Strand.

"And then?" He proffered his arm.

Annabel took his arm but didn't respond at once. She would have to be very careful. "We—or rather I—must speak with them. I must ask you to leave any talking to me."

"Hmm. I take it that I have been included in this venture in the role of bodyguard?"

Annabel didn't take her eyes off the young woman. "Does that trouble you?"

"Not in the least. Though you might not credit it, it's why I'm here."

"What, to watch over me?" She was so surprised that she glanced up at him involuntarily.

"Your quarry is escaping," he said calmly, nodding toward the just-closing door.

Annabel silently cursed herself and practically pulled him along with her to the door. But she need not have worried; her quarry stood on the pavement below the door, as if waiting for someone. She took a deep breath and called, "Excuse me!"

The young woman turned, and Annabel saw that she was younger than she'd initially appeared despite the striking, almost foreign loveliness of her sapphire eyes and shining black hair. Those sapphire eyes were examining her with great interest just now, and a not-entirely-pleasant smile hovered on her lips. "Madam? Were you addressing us?"

"I was." She made herself smile pleasantly; it wouldn't do to give away how anxious she was. "Please excuse my interruption, but I believe that you have in your possession something of interest to me."

The girl's smile grew wider. "Do I?" she said softly. "May I ask who you are?"

Lord Quinceton stirred uneasily. Annabel pressed his arm, either in warning or reassurance. "Certainly. I am Lady Fellbridge."

She raised her eyebrows. "And him?"

"The Marquis of Quinceton."

"Oh!" For a moment, the girl looked apprehensive. Then she straightened her shoulders. "Who sent you? Sir Henry?"

"Ange," the young man murmured.

Ah ha! She thought about playing ignorant and asking why she should mention Sir Henry, but the girl looked skittish enough to say—or do—something foolish if she were pushed too far. Better to avoid such games. "No, Sir Henry didn't send me. No one did." She mentally willed Lord Quinceton to continue to hold his tongue. "But my...friends and I are aware of certain, ah, activities in connection with Sir Henry's pictures at the Exhibition—"

"I thought there was someone watching us. Didn't I say that, Philippe?" The girl spoke the name with a decidedly French pronunciation, Annabel noted. "How many are there of you? What do you want? Why are you spying upon me, unless Sir Henry sent you?" The girl's voice rose in pitch with each question.

Annabel chose her words with care, both so as not to further antagonize this rather alarming young woman, and not to say anything that the Marquis shouldn't hear. "I will be happy to discuss this matter with you—after we discuss what you are holding in your handkerchief."

"My handkerchief?" The girl produced one from her sleeve and waved it negligently almost in Annabel's face. "Why, there is nothing here, as you can see!"

"Angelique, that's enough." Philippe frowned at the girl, who pouted and tucked her handkerchief away once more. "So it isn't just a common moth," he added. "My sister was certain it wasn't."

Oh, dear. Annabel shot a quick glance at Lord Quinceton. His face was impassive, but she knew he had not missed a word. Perhaps bringing him along had not been such a good idea after all. But it was too late to try to get rid of him; just now, she had to ensure Georgiana's safety. "You will draw a great deal of hostile attention upon yourselves if any harm befalls it," she said firmly.

Angelique opened her mouth to speak, but Philippe scowled at her again. "Allow me to talk to her." He turned back to Annabel. "Why should we release it? How do we know you won't go straight to Hebbly and tell him you know who's responsible for changing the pictures?"

Annabel pushed away a quick surge of triumph—she'd caught them! "That is a fair question. But as it happens, I don't believe that Sir Henry is even aware of what is going on. Lady Hebbly is, however, and—"

"Then he does as well," Philippe interrupted, looking disgusted. "How can she not tell him, after what my sister has done to her likeness?"

So it was only Angelique who was changing the pictures. "Lady Hebbly doesn't *want* him to know. She's generous enough to ignore the insults to herself to keep him from knowing and becoming upset."

"Oh." He looked down at his feet, obviously abashed. Annabel was glad to see some signs of a conscience in *one* of them.

"Will you tell me why you are doing this?" she asked in a gentler tone. "I gather that your difficulty is with Sir Henry rather than his wife. If that is so, can we not continue to—ah—involve Lady Hebbly? I would rather she were not further hurt. She is a close family friend."

Again she felt Lord Quinceton move slightly as if in reaction to her words, but he remained silent. The young man, who had brightened at the first part of her speech, looked downcast by the end. "I don't think we can do that. Our quarrel with Hebbly is of a—a *particular* nature—"

"Never mind, Philippe! She's in no place to be able to make demands of us. If she does not leave us alone, then we can't promise her stupid little moth won't get eaten by a bird or swatted by a housemaid. Or—" She opened her reticule and pulled out the handkerchief. Annabel could just see a faint movement inside it. "Or maybe I'll just..." She started to close her hand around it, watching Annabel in a manner unpleasantly like a spoiled child intent on breaking a valuable out of sheer spite.

But before her fingers had closed completely, Lord Quinceton's hand shot out, grabbing her wrist and twisting it. Angelique cried out and dropped the handkerchief, and Annabel had the presence of mind to swoop down and scoop it up.

"Unhand my sister, sir!" Philippe cried angrily.

"Certainly," the marquis replied, and released Angelique's wrist.

She glared at him, tenderly cradling it against her breast. "*Canaille*! You have broken my hand, I am certain!"

"If I had done you any real injury, you would be in no doubt of the fact," Lord Quinceton said calmly.

Annabel turned her back to them and unfolded the linen, holding her breath...and was enormously relieved to see that Georgiana was unharmed. She bent over the handkerchief and whispered, "If you can fly, go home. I'll come to you later as we planned."

Georgiana's wings tentatively opened and closed once, twice. Then she lifted into the air above them, well out of reach, and fluttered away.

Annabel watched for a moment to be certain that she was strong enough to fly, then turned back to the others. Angelique and Philippe were still glowering at Lord Quinceton, who looked supremely unconcerned.

"Now then," she said briskly. "I suggest we hail a hackney and go to someplace where we can discuss what is to be done in a little more privacy. Though you may not believe me, I wish to help you."

"I do not choose to ride in a carriage with such a one as *him*," Angelique declaimed, drawing herself up and inclining her head haughtily toward Lord Quinceton.

"I do not choose to allow Lady Fellbridge to ride unaccompanied in a carriage with such a one as *you*," Lord Quinceton countered.

"Oh!" Angelique's hauteur turned to outrage.

"Why, you—you—"

"Are we in agreement that we must speak?" Annabel ignored Angelique's sputtering and spoke to Philippe. "My offer stands—I do want to help you resolve your quarrel with Sir Henry."

Philippe, who had been looking glum, turned to her. "You'll help us? Truly?"

"Of course." She guessed that he as well might be younger than she'd initially thought. "But you must promise to leave the pictures at the Exhibition alone while we work on your problem."

He hesitated, then nodded. "That seems fair. I'll undertake to see that Ange behaves herself. Er, I apologize for what happened—with your—you know—" He fluttered his hands in imitation of a moth's flight. "We weren't going to hurt it—truly we weren't—but my sister gets carried away—"

"I'd noticed," Annabel said, her voice carefully neutral. "Do you wish to come to my house, or do you prefer we meet elsewhere?"

"Fellbridge, do you think it advisable that this pair of miscreants be permitted to know where you live?" Lord Quinceton put in.

"I don't care where she lives!" Angelique cried. "I don't ever want to—"

Philippe ignored her. "If you don't mind, ma'am, I think you ought to come to our house. It will be easier to explain the matter there."

"Certainly." Annabel turned her attention back to Lord Quinceton and Angelique. She was still upbraiding him, drawing curious looks from passersby, while he stood by and listened with an unruffled and even slightly appreciative air. "Perhaps we should take separate carriages?" she said to Philippe.

He grimaced and nodded, then tore a leaf from a small notebook and wrote down the address for her. She recognized it as being in a part of London that had seen better days but still clung to the edge of respectability. Hmm.

"Shall we go?" Annabel broke in when Angelique finally paused for breath.

"Your timing is impeccable as always, Fellbridge. Miss Termagant had just started to repeat herself, which is fatal if one wishes to have the most blighting effect on one's adversary. It is, I have noticed, a common failing in the young and not very clever." Lord Quinceton again held his arm out to her and led her to the edge of the pavement, ignoring the small furious shriek behind them.

"Was that quite necessary?" she asked in a low voice, listening to Philippe trying to calm his sister.

"It was the best way to keep her occupied while you spoke to her brother," he said, still unruffled, flagging down a passing hack and handing her into it. "Where are we going?"

Oh, drat! She hadn't intended for him to come along as well; Angelique would be far too inclined to quarrel with him rather than talk sensibly. "I have been invited to their house to discuss this matter," she said, and told him the address.

He raised an eyebrow but said nothing beyond giving the driver their destination. Annabel spent the first few minutes of the drive trying to think of a way to get rid of him once they arrived.

"I—ah—do not think that your presence would be helpful while I speak with them," she finally said, when no polite fiction presented itself.

"I had no intention of staying for your

interview, though I would feel more sanguine if the meeting were elsewhere. I suppose I could remain with the hack until you are through."

"Why?"

"Was I not engaged to serve as your body-guard?"

"Oh. Yes, quite." She hesitated. "I—thank you, but I don't expect that I am in any danger."

"As you wish." He inclined his head.

They rode without speaking for another few minutes until Annabel couldn't stand it any longer. "Why did you do that?" she asked abruptly.

"Do what, Fellbridge?" There was a definite edge of amusement in his voice.

"The—the handkerchief." She didn't trust herself to say anything about the handkerchief's contents.

"Oh, that? Because it seemed important to you that the creature it contained come to no harm." He shrugged.

Annabel was silent for a while, absorbing that. *Creature*, he had said, not moth—though he must have seen what was in that handkerchief and had heard Philippe's comment about it not being just a common moth. Might he suspect it was much, much more than a moth?

She still wasn't certain what to think when the hackney turned a corner and stopped in front of a red brick house. Someone had once taken good care of it, but now the wrought-iron railings were spotty with rust and the brass knocker dull. Lord Quinceton got out and handed her onto the pavement.

"Thank you," she said. "I—I appreciate your help today."

"You're welcome." He looked at her for a moment, then said, "By the by, Fellbridge, I thought you said that you weren't investigating anything?"

Annabel felt herself flush. "I'm not." When he frowned skeptically, she added, "It isn't my investigation. I'm just helping Frances."

His expression didn't alter, but she almost felt his sudden alertness. "I see," he murmured. "And her brother? Are you helping him as well?"

"No! Just—just Frances." She met his eyes, her chin raised not a little defiantly. Though his name had not been uttered, Lord Glenrick suddenly seemed to loom between them.

Lord Quinceton continued to study her face until their hackney driver harrumphed impatiently and the hack containing Philippe and Angelique pulled up. Then he turned away abruptly, went to pay their driver and speak to him briefly, and got back into the hackney that brought them, without another word. Annabel watched as it rumbled down the street and wondered what had just happened.

Chapter Four

"Oh, good," Angelique said, practically in Annabel's ear. "You got rid of him. I was afraid we would have to invite him in as well."

Annabel started. "No. This is between us. Lord Quinceton was only…assisting."

Angelique frowned and opened her mouth, but Philippe none-too-gently moved her aside. "Please come in, Lady Fellbridge," he said, moving to open the door, which was in need of a coat of new paint.

Annabel cast one further look at the hackney carrying Lord Quinceton down the street, then sighed and turned to the door. Deciphering Lord Quinceton would have to wait until later.

"Why is *that* still here?" Angelique jerked her head back toward the other hackney. "Did not your rude friend pay him off?"

"I'm to wait for 'er ladyship," the driver said, unperturbed. "'Is lordship said I must." He fixed a stern look on Angelique. "An' the sooner you stop flapping your gums out 'ere and do wha'ever yer s'posed to do, the sooner I can take 'er ladyship 'ome and go get me other guinea."

Good lord—the marquis was paying the man *two guineas* to wait for her? "In that case yes, I shall go in at once. Thank you, er, mister..." Annabel smiled at the driver, who blushed furiously.

"I hain't no mister, yer ladyship," he said, removing his hat. "Jes' plain Bob Carter."

"Well, thank you for waiting for me, Mr. Carter. We'll try not to keep you waiting long."

"Take yer time, mum." He accompanied this about-face with an airy wave. "I'll jest catch me forty winks while I wait." He wrapped the horse's reins around his wrist, settled himself more comfortably in his seat, and tipped his hat over his eyes.

Angelique gave a sniff and swept through the door that her brother held open. "Ma'am?" Philippe said quietly to Annabel.

"Thank you." Annabel followed after her.

As had the outside of the house, the inside had seen better days, or at least had once known a caring hand. Philippe cast an embarrassed glance at the entrance hall's spotted mirror and dusty table cluttered with scraps of paper, bits of discarded clothing, and not a few dirty dishes and muttered, "This way, please."

He led the way into a salon, where Angelique had already thrown herself down on a faded blue sofa, one arm flung dramatically across her eyes. "He is rather handsome, I suppose," she said as Philippe led Annabel to a chair.

"Who is?" Annabel asked when Philippe did not seem inclined to respond but went to stand by the empty hearth, frowning.

"That hateful marquis." Angelique shifted her arm slightly and surveyed Annabel with one eye. "Are you going to marry him?"

Annabel felt herself blush a fiery red. "Good heavens, no!"

"Is he rich?"

"Quite, from what I understand."

"Hmm. If you're not going to, then maybe *I'll* marry him."

Philippe sighed. "Go right ahead. Who cares if you haven't actually made your come-out yet?"

Angelique propped herself up on her elbows to scowl at her brother. "That's only two years from now. Why shouldn't I plan ahead?"

"I beg your pardon—you're only sixteen?" Annabel was surprised into asking. No wonder she'd felt as though she were dealing with a naughty child.

Angelique's scowl deepened, but she wouldn't meet her eyes. "Well, I will be soon enough."

"While we're waiting for you to grow up, can we talk to Lady Fellbridge about helping us?" Philippe asked in a long-suffering tone.

His sister sat up. "Ooh—will you tell us who that moth really was?"

Annabel was beginning to understand the young man's long-suffering air. "Yes, please do tell me why you need my help. You said that Sir Henry Hebbly has done you some injury?"

"Not us," Philippe said earnestly. "It's—"

"Yes, it is too us, because if he weren't being so horrid and keeping Papa out of the Academy, then Papa could sell his pictures for lots of money, and we could have things comfortable again the way they were when *Maman* was alive," Angelique interrupted. Her eyes practically flashed blue sparks.

"Will you please be quiet and allow me to tell this my way?"

"Not if you're going to be all prosy and boring about it!"

"Your father is a painter?" Annabel asked loudly, before the argument could escalate. If she were not careful, the temptation to smack this child would get the better of her. "But not a member of the Royal Academy?"

"You do not know our Papa's work?" Angelique demanded. "But he is a genius! How can you not know him?"

"As you haven't yet told me his name, I scarcely find it surprising that I don't know him."

Angelique closed her mouth. Philippe rolled his eyes at her and said to Annabel, "His name is John Ronderley, and while he isn't a member of the Academy, he's every bit as good as any artist there. Mr. West says his portraits are most admirable, and Mr. Turner and Mr. Owen have been trying for years to get him voted in. If he were an Academician, he would receive more commissions. When our mother was alive, she was good at bringing in work for him. But with her gone—" He looked away, obviously fighting back strong emotion. "That's her," he added, gesturing at the wall above him.

Annabel rose and went to examine the masterfully painted portrait hanging over the chimneypiece. The woman it depicted looked so much like the pair behind her that there was no mistaking her identity; she could almost have been Philippe's older sister, or Angelique in a few years' time. "She was a beautiful woman," she said gently. "How long has she been gone?"

"Two years." Philippe took out a handkerchief and blew his nose. "She was French—that's why we have our names. I'm called after her father, who died in the Terror."

"How did your parents meet?"

"*Maman*'s family sent her to England early in '92 when the food riots began in Paris—her father was a wealthy merchant and could read the writing on the wall. But her parents never made it here, and she had to take work as an artist's model when her money was stolen. Our father met her and fell in love with her at first sight."

"It was *extremely* romantic," Angelique added. "I shall have a romantic marriage too. Perhaps I'll pretend to be a page and go work in the marquis' house, until he sees through my disguise and kneels at my feet, pledging his eternal devotion."

Philippe snorted. Annabel was glad she was still facing the picture, so that Angelique could not see her expression. "And you think that Sir Henry is somehow keeping your father out of the Academy?"

"We *know* he is!" Angelique burst out. "Papa's friend Mr. Thomson told us so—that whenever Papa's name is presented, Sir Henry ensures that he is voted down. And so we don't have enough money because Papa isn't any good at finding people to paint pictures for, so he just stays in his rooms and paints what he wants and forgets about us, and we're—" she gestured around her.

"We can't get him commissions," Philippe took up her thread. "And I'm—" He swallowed. "I'm not old enough to get more than an apprentice's position somewhere. Papa's sister's husband is taking me to work for him next month—he's a grain merchant—but I can't support us on an apprentice's salary. And he'll be wanting me to travel with him, which means there won't be anyone to look after my sister any more—"

"I told you that I can take care of myself!"

"Yes, just as much as a kitten can!" he retorted. "We need a respectable housekeeper to take care of both you and Papa, but we can't afford one. We can barely afford food and fuel, much less any servants." He met Annabel's eyes straight on, but it was obviously an effort to do so. "I know it won't fix things right away, but getting Papa into the Academy will be a start. Between that and my working for Uncle Barker, we can maybe manage."

These poor children—at fifteen and—what, eighteen for Philippe?—trying to work with the hand an unkind fate had dealt them. "So how is changing the pictures at the Exhibition meant to accomplish getting your father voted into the Academy?"

"Well, isn't it obvious?" Angelique's voice made it clear she thought Annabel a little dim. "I shall make Sir Henry's pictures hideous until he stops being such a beast and permits Papa to enter the Academy."

"Oh. So, in short, you're blackmailing him."

Philippe looked a little shame-faced but nodded. "It was the only thing we could think of."

"He deserves it! And after all, we warned him first. We thought it only fair," Angelique said, the picture of righteous virtue.

"You warned him?"

"We sent him a note. We said that unless he

allowed Papa into the Academy at once—only we didn't say it was our Papa, of course—then he'd regret it."

"I see. Was there a membership vote taking place?"

Philippe's brow furrowed. "Er—"

"Who cares?" Angelique interrupted. "I'll bet Sir Henry could have got him in to the Academy if he really wanted to, but he didn't. And we waited a whole week, too—"

"Because I made you. You only wanted to give him two days—"

Angelique ignored him. "—so I started changing the pictures! Just a little at first, but more and more each time."

"Yes, I should like to talk about that." Annabel went back to her chair and sat down. "How do you change the pictures?"

The girl shrugged. "I don't know. I just do."

"She's always been able to change how things look," Philippe put in. "She can make her dresses different colors—"

"Here." Angelique rose, an impish look on her face. "Give me your handkerchief."

Annabel removed it from her reticule and gave it to her. Angelique held it up and examined it for a moment—and suddenly it was no longer her cambric handkerchief, but a square of black velvet. She handed it back to Annabel. "There. Feel it."

Annabel did—and raised her eyebrows. "It looks like velvet, but it still feels like my handkerchief. So you are changing its appearance, but not its substance. Do you have to touch it to do this?"

"It's easier if I can, but no." Angelique looked at

her, suddenly suspicious. "Why aren't you shrieking and fainting, the way most people would if I'd just done that to them?"

"Because she's obviously not like other people, you goose, or she wouldn't be here talking to us about this." Philippe turned to her eagerly. "Can you turn into a moth too, like whoever it was did in the Exhibition?"

"No, I can't. Have any other members of your family had this ability as well?" she asked quickly before they tried to question her further. "Your mother or father?"

"No, just me. And no one in Papa's family. My aunt nearly had hysterics when I changed the ribbons in her hat from pale pink to scarlet once when I was little." Angelique smiled reminiscently.

"We don't know about *Maman*'s family, of course," Philippe added. "Maybe someday we can look for them if the war ever ends. *Maman* talked about going to look for her brothers and cousins when the Peace of Amiens happened, but then it fell apart and we couldn't go."

"I see." The Lady Patronesses would be interested to hear about Angelique's ability...once this matter was taken care of. "What happened when you sent Sir Henry the note demanding that your father be admitted to the Academy? Did you tell him what the consequence would be if he did not?"

"Certainly not!" The girl tossed her head. "We told him he'd regret not listening to us. Wasn't that enough?"

"It doesn't seem to have been, since according to Lady Hebbly, he doesn't visit the Exhibition once it's installed." Annabel ignored Angelique's gasp of indignation. "So unless someone's told him about the pictures, he doesn't know what you've done and probably just assumes the note was from a crank."

"He'll pay attention to the note we're sending in a day or two." Angelique's smugness had returned. "I'm going to turn all his canvases black if he doesn't admit Papa to the Academy. I thought one each day, till it's done."

"Oh, no!" Annabel exclaimed. "You don't know that he alone can arrange for a new member to be admitted." She sent a look of appeal to Philippe, but he shrugged.

"To be honest, I don't care. We don't have any other choice," he said.

"But *why* is Sir Henry doing this? Does anyone know?"

Philippe shook his head. "Mr. Thomson said he tried to ask Hebbly about it, but he wouldn't say—only looked angry and walked away."

"We're tired of waiting, Lady Fellbridge." Angelique had dropped all her affectations and suddenly looked old and tired. "There's nothing else we *can* do."

Annabel looked from her to Philippe. Strictly speaking, this was Frances's investigation—*she* should be the one making decisions. But something had to be decided now; there was no time to bring Frances in to discuss the matter or to convince these two that she could be trusted to help—she still wasn't certain that they fully trusted *her*. It was perfectly acceptable for a Lady Patroness to act on her own when events required it, but doing so made Annabel uncomfortable. Well, it appeared that she would have to live with that discomfort.

"Yes, there *is* something we can do," she said firmly. "We can talk to Lady Hebbly. If anyone can find out why Sir Henry is blocking your father's acceptance as an Academy member, she can. And she is the kindest person in London; I expect she'll be eager to help you."

Philippe was the one who, to her surprise, looked dubious. It was Angelique who said, "Truly? She would help us?" There was an unexpectedly wistful note in her voice.

"I think she would."

"Philippe?"

His brow furrowed, but after a moment he sighed. "Oh, very well. I don't care for it, though."

Annabel guessed his reluctance to speak to Lady Hebbly had something to do with how they'd done such unpleasant things to her image. "It will be all right," she said gently. "Now, I shall write her a note right here, so that you can see what it says, and ask her if we can meet tomorrow. Does that suit you? And Philippe can deliver it if he wishes, so that you know she has received it and that I haven't altered it."

He blushed. "I wouldn't accuse you of such a thing."

"I didn't expect you would. But I want you to be able to be certain that all is being done as it should. Might I have use of paper and ink?"

"I'll get them." Angelique jumped up from her sofa and ran from the room.

Annabel took advantage of her absence. "I would not suggest we call on Lady Hebbly if I didn't think it was the best way to resolve this," she said, going to Philippe and touching his arm. "She really is the best and most charitable of women." She'd had a lot to be charitable about, but Philippe did not need to hear about that.

He hunched his shoulders. "I just feel bad that we...did what we did to her."

"She'll understand. Ah, thank you, Angelique," she said as the girl galloped into the room. She sat down at the table that Philippe led her to (after he shamefacedly dusted it off with his handkerchief) and wrote the note. "I believe she is usually at home on Friday afternoons, fortunately for us. Is two o'clock agreeable?"

"Two o'clock can be agreeable in summer, but in winter the light is not in the least so," said a voice from the doorway. "However, September is probably the best time of year for two o'clock. *Early* September, mind you."

"Papa!" Angelique straightened from where she'd been hanging over Annabel's chair.

Annabel looked up. A man in shirt and waistcoat liberally daubed with streaks of paint stood vaguely peering at them. He had a kindly face and mild blue eyes, just now enhanced by a blob of blue paint on his forehead. "I always know what time it is, by the light," he said conversationally. "It's just what happens in my line of employment. Do I know you?"

Philippe stepped forward. "Lady Fellbridge, this is our father, John Ronderley. Lady Fellbridge is, er, helping us with something," he added to his father.

"That is very kind of her." Mr. Ronderley bowed, then looked at her consideringly. "I should like to paint you someday. In autumn, I think. Your colors would be good for early autumn. At two o'clock, even." He smiled.

"Thank you, Mr. Ronderley. Someday I hope you will." It was too bad she didn't have the money to commission a picture; her mother would love to have one, and it would help this family at least a little.

Angelique went to him and took his arm. "Did you need me, Papa?" she asked, leading him away from the door and back into the passage.

"Did you get that madder lake for me yet? I need it to finish the landscape," Annabel heard him say, a little peevishly, before a closing door somewhere in the back of the house put a period to their conversation.

Next to her, Philippe sighed. "He doesn't always seem to remember that we can't aff—" He flushed. "Angelique sits with him sometimes and adjusts his colors when he's done for the day, so that in the morning he decides that the picture is all right after all and he doesn't need a more expensive pigment."

Annabel finished writing, blew on the paper to dry the ink, folded it and wrote the Hebblys' address on it. "It must be very difficult for her." She handed him the note. "Will you deliver this for me?"

He took the note reluctantly. "You don't have to give it to me. I trust you."

"Yes, but you will be doing me a favor if you bring it round to her." This would be a busy afternoon; she still had to call at Frances's and Georgiana's today. She rose and drew on her gloves, which she'd removed to write. "Two o'clock tomorrow, then? You won't forget?"

He grinned. "Or allow my sister to change her mind and weasel out of it? No ma'am, we'll be there."

Bob Carter, the hackney driver, looked relieved when she emerged from the Ronderleys' house.

"So yer all right and tight, mum? I didn't care fer the looks o' that chit who I drove 'ere," he said, jumping down from his perch to hand Annabel into the hack. "I was thinkin' she could use to 'ave 'er bottom tanned to remind 'er to keep a civil tongue in 'er 'ead."

"She's not as bad as she seems to be, I think. Thank you for your concern, at all events—I'm quite well." She settled in the seat and gave him Frances's direction. "Once you've brought me there, you may go to Lord Quinceton's to collect your guinea."

He frowned. "But that ain't where you live, mum."

Annabel raised her brows. How did he know that? "No, but I can walk home from there."

He shook his head. "Eh, that won't do. My d'rections was to take you 'ome when you was done, to Chesterfield Street. I don't dare go to 'is lordship till you're safe there."

She opened her mouth to protest, then closed it. Whatever highhandedness Lord Quinceton had chosen to perpetrate upon her wasn't this poor man's fault. "Very well, Mr. Carter. I'll try not to take long."

As they rumbled down the street, she sat back and stared unseeing out the window, reliving in her mind the morning's activities...and Lord Quinceton's behavior over its course. He had been almost docile when she had demanded his assistance. His method of dealing with Angelique Ronderley had been unexpected but effective. He had done everything she'd asked of him, had never asked inconvenient questions—until, that is, they had stood on the pavement outside the Ronderleys' house.

He had been so...so *vehement* at her mention of helping Frances—and had jumped to the conclusion that Lord Glenrick was somehow involved, which just seemed odd. He knew full well that she and Frances were both Lady Patronesses of Almack's; why had it not occurred to him that her assistance to Frances might be connected to that? One day, she would *make* him tell her what lay between him and Lord Glenrick...and smiled at the ludicrous notion of making the Marquis of Quinceton do anything he didn't choose to do.

The hackney drew up in front of Carrick House a few minutes later. But when she plied the knocker, the footman who answered shook his head when she presented her card and asked for Frances. "She ain't here, your ladyship. Been gone all day, her and his lordship too."

"Oh dear." Annabel wondered if the sickly great-aunt had died, but it would not do to question a servant about a family matter. "Could you ensure when she returns that she knows I called to see her? It's on a matter of some urgency."

The footman promised to do so, and she returned thoughtfully to her appointed bodyguard waiting in his hackney.

At a few minutes before two o'clock the next day,

Annabel arrived alone at the Hebblys' house. She'd not heard from Frances—not a word—though Georgiana had sent a note to say that she was shaken and sore, but otherwise unharmed after her brief captivity.

She hesitated on the doorstep. Frances's absence was troubling: this was supposed to be *her* investigation, yet here Annabel was. Granted, she knew Lady Hebbly better than any of the other Lady Patronesses, and Sally would not fault her for stepping in to resolve the matter if Frances had been called away. But it still felt as if she were trespassing somehow.

"Lady Fellbridge!" Angelique's voice called her out of her reverie. The Ronderleys were hurrying up the pavement toward her, looking a little out of breath, and her conscience smote her. Had they walked all the way from their house? She should have picked them up but had wanted to ascertain that they came of their own volition.

"Exactly on time!" she said cheerfully. "Shall we?"

Angelique was unwontedly subdued and merely nodded. Philippe straightened his back and said, "Yes, please."

Lady Hebbly's butler knew her and gave her an avuncular smile as he ushered them through the door. "Madam will be pleased to see your ladyship," he said. "It's been a good day for visitors for her."

Annabel hesitated. "Is anyone else here?" She certainly couldn't talk to Lady Hebbly about Sir Henry's blackballing of John Ronderley if there were other callers present.

"Just her ladyship's cousin." He led them to the

main salon's door and announced, "Lady Fellbridge is here, madam, and her friends."

Annabel walked into the room, trailed by Philippe and Angelique—and froze. Seated on one of the sofas was Lady Hebbly...and Lord Quinceton.

Behind Annabel, Angelique gasped. *"You!"* she cried.

"Annabel!" Lady Hebbly rose and held out her hands. "I was so pleased to receive your note. Are these your friends that you wished me to meet?" She smiled at Angelique and Philippe in the friendliest fashion—then paused, a puzzled look dimming her smile. "Have—have we met before?"

Angelique curtsied prettily, but her expression would have frozen the Thames. Philippe bowed. "I don't believe so, Lady Hebbly."

Annabel kissed Lady Hebbly's cheek, then glared at Lord Quinceton over her head. *"He's* your cousin?" Yes, she knew that Lady Hebbly was related to half of the noble families of England...but why had *he* had to be one of them?

"I have that honor, Fellbridge." He had risen as well and was grinning openly. "You're just jealous that I have nicer cousins than you do."

"My cousin Medea has been practically human since—since—" She closed her mouth and glowered at him. Saying anything further about the topic was quite impossible, as he well knew.

"Poor Fellbridge. An unfair riposte, was it not? I offer my apologies." He did not, however, appear to be in the least contrite.

Lady Hebbly looked from one to another of them, smiling. "I see that you two are already acquainted. Won't you please sit down? Come." She nodded at Angelique and patted the cushion beside her.

Annabel went to the sofa opposite, still glowering at Lord Quinceton. Phillipe sat beside her. "I had hoped that we could speak to you alone, ma'am," she said.

Lady Hebbly turned to look at Lord Quinceton, her expression troubled. "I know, my dear. But Geoffrey asked if he could be here as well, if you came to speak with me."

"I have not yet given up my role as bodyguard, Fellbridge," Lord Quinceton added.

"You don't have to guard Lady Fellbridge, you horrible man. She is our friend!" Angelique declared.

Annabel concealed her surprise. Evidently she *had* won their trust.

"But I might have to guard my cousin," Lord Quinceton replied smoothly. "Antonia, perhaps we should change places so that you are not seated next to this young lady. Her temper is very uncertain."

"Geoffrey, don't tease the child! Annabel, I wish you would tell the purpose of this visit. I know that anything you say will not leave this room," Lady Hebbly said.

Annabel sighed. Lady Hebbly was probably right—Lord Quinceton had never gossiped about Gilbert Marjoribanks's demon or her cousin Hartley's future wife who just happened to be a siren. Still...she turned to Philippe. "I believe that Lady Hebbly is correct in her assumption that this conversation will remain confidential, but it is not up to me to decide. What do you wish?"

"Never!" Angelique declared. "I should rather die on the rack than have That Man hear what we have to disclose!"

"That could doubtless be arranged, given a little time and ingenuity," That Man murmured. Lady Hebbly frowned at him.

Philippe gave Annabel an agonized look and leaned toward her. "Do you really trust him?" he asked in a low voice.

Annabel was aware of Lord Quinceton's gaze upon her. "Yes," she said, firmly if reluctantly. "And not all the...details of the matter have to be discussed here."

"Fellbridge, you never cease to surprise me," Lord Quinceton said. "Thank you for that."

She looked at him quickly—and saw that there was no gleam of mockery in his eyes. He nodded to her; reluctantly, she nodded back.

"No, Philippe!" Angelique cried. "Not in front of him! Do you not recall how this monster nearly broke my wrist?"

Lady Hebbly gasped...but Philippe shook his head. "Ange—*shut up!*"

There was a moment of stunned silence. Annabel stole a quick glance at Lord Quinceton and saw that he was pressing his lips firmly together... and all at once she too was perilously close to bursting into laughter.

Fortunately, Philippe provided no further reason for her to do so. "Will you explain to Lady Hebbly why we're here, Lady Fellbridge?" he said, ignoring his outraged sister sputtering on the sofa across from him.

Annabel took a breath, hoping her voice would be steady. "Certainly, Philippe. Lady Hebbly, my friends here are the children of an artist, John

Ronderley. It seems that Sir Henry has been blocking his admission to the Royal Academy for many years without ever making clear what his objections are. It has affected Mr. Ronderley's ability to make a living, and his children wish to know why he has been denied membership when so many prominent Academicians have supported his candidacy."

Lady Hebbly's brow furrowed. "Ronderley... that name sounds familiar..." She shook her head, and turning to Angelique, took her hand. "Oh, you poor dears. This is a terrible thing that has happened to you and your papa. Of course you are upset!"

Angelique's ire seemed to evaporate before Lady Hebbly's sympathy, and Annabel guessed she was remembering *Lowther Castle, Westmoreland: Evening*—among others—and not proudly. "We just want to know *why*," she said, with a small sob.

"There, there, my child. I should think you would." Lady Hebbly put an arm around her shoulders. "I'm afraid I have no idea, myself. Sir Henry does not discuss Academy matters with me— but if you say other members have supported your father—"

"Mr. West and Mr. Turner and Mr. Owen all have," Philippe said earnestly. "And not just them."

"My goodness." Lady Hebbly paused. "Does... this have anything to do with what is happening to the pictures at the Exhibition?"

Angelique began to cry in earnest. "We didn't know you were so kind! We did it because we thought it would make Sir Henry allow our papa into the Academy!"

"We sent him a letter," Philippe said in reply to Lady Hebbly's bewildered look. "We said we would stop altering the pictures if he stopped opposing our father's election. Lady Fellbridge found us out but said she would help us. We promised her we would not change any more of the pictures till we'd spoken to you."

Lady Hebbly had grown pale, but her arm stayed firmly around Angelique's heaving shoulders. "I see. I think that I should perhaps—"

But they never found out what it was that Lady Hebbly perhaps thought because the loud *bang!* of the front door slamming startled her into silence.

"Antonia!" a loud, angry voice shouted. "Antonia, where the devil are you—oh."

Sir Henry Hebbly stood in the doorway, his handsome face below his artistically waving gray hair just now an angry shade of puce. He coughed slightly and tried a smile, but it appeared more like a gritting of his teeth. "My apologies—I didn't know you had company. Is that you, Quinceton? Haven't seen you about in a while. Please excuse me." He began to turn away.

"Henry, what is the matter?" Lady Hebbly still kept her arm around Angelique, but now it looked more like a restraint than a comfort.

"Nothing I would discuss just now—good God!" Sir Henry was staring at his wife—no, at the tear-stained girl at Lady Hebbly's side who had lifted her head and was staring back at him with brimming eyes. The angry color in his cheeks faded to pasty white. "Angelique," he said hoarsely. "No—it cannot be—"

And he fell to the floor in a faint.

Chapter Five

A short while later, the chaos had calmed. Lord Quinceton and Philippe had lifted Sir Henry's inert form onto a sofa, and Lady Hebbly had loosened his cravat, called for tea, and produced a vinaigrette, which she now waved under her husband's nose.

Sir Henry's head jerked, and he coughed and brought up a hand to push the tiny silver box away from his face. Then he sat up, squinting into Lady Hebbly's anxious face. "Where is she? Where is Angelique?"

"How do you know my name, you—you—" Angelique had recovered as well, and stood a few paces away, clutching Philippe's arm.

Sir Henry stared at her, and then at her brother...and his eyes rolled back into their sockets as he collapsed again.

"Henry!" Lady Hebbly applied the vinaigrette once more.

"I suspect the next several minutes might be

difficult ones. Especially for Antonia. Watch out for her, will you?" said a voice in Annabel's ear. She jumped; Lord Quinceton had come up behind her.

She turned to look at him. He was watching Sir Henry and Lady Hebbly, and his eyes were somber. "Why? Do you know what is going on here?" she asked.

"Not precisely, but I have a suspicion we'll find out shortly." He went to help Lady Hebbly ease Sir Henry into a sitting position and pile cushions behind his back. Annabel saw the butler, who was hovering anxiously in the doorway with a tray of tea things and a decanter of brandy and went to take it from him and set it on a side table. Behind her, Lord Quinceton firmly closed the salon's doors.

"Annabel, will you pour Henry some tea?" Lady Hebbly was still kneeling at her husband's side.

"Of course." Annabel poured a cup, added liberal amounts of milk and sugar, and brought it to her, after which she withdrew to the far side of the sofa.

Lady Hebbly smiled her thanks and turned to Sir Henry. "Do you think you can drink some, my dear?" she said tenderly, holding the cup to his lips.

Sir Henry dodged it. "I don't want any of your damned cat-lap now." He craned his neck to stare again at the Ronderleys, but Annabel thought his eyes lingered on Philippe, even as he once again murmured, "Angelique."

The girl scowled at him. "You still have not said how you know that is my name!"

"It was also our mother's name," Philippe said slowly. "And my sister resembles her greatly."

"As do you, young man," Sir Henry said. A little color had returned to his face, but there was now a queer gleam in his eyes.

Lady Hebbly drew in a sharp breath. Annabel looked over at her and saw that her eyes had widened.

"If you know who we are, then you know my father, John Ronderley. How can you live with yourself, after what you've done to him? He is as worthy as anyone—worthier than *you*—to be a member of the Academy!" Angelique came closer, dragging her brother with her, till she stood almost over Sir Henry. "My papa is more worthy to be a member than you because he would never blackball another artist for no good reason." She turned and buried her face in her brother's shoulder.

Philippe held her, patting her back as she sobbed, and met Sir Henry's gaze steadily. "My sister is right. I don't know why you've done this, but—" he lifted his chin. "It was *not* the act of a gentleman. Perhaps that is the difference between you and our father."

Sir Henry stared at him for the space of a few breaths, then closed his eyes, his forehead creasing as if the sight of Philippe pained him.

"Oh, Henry." Lady Hebbly's voice was sad. "Have you really done that to this poor girl's father?"

"I had my reasons," he muttered, eyes still shut ...until they flew open. He looked up at his wife, and Annabel wondered if he would not faint again. "Antonia?" he whispered. "You...know?"

Annabel looked from one of them to the other— Sir Henry's face guilt-stricken, Lady Hebbly's deeply sorrowful—and all at once understood why Lady Hebbly had phrased her question to him in that way. She stole a glance to see if Philippe had understood it as well.

Lady Hebbly sighed. "I guessed. I should have done so as soon as these children walked through the door—they're the very image of the portrait in your study that you keep behind a curtain, but I could not place the resemblance till just now. That poor young woman—and her poor child!"

Sir Henry grabbed for her hand. "You don't understand—it was less than a week till our wedding when Angelique told me she was breeding. What could I possibly do? What if it had come out that I'd seduced some French *émigrée* and got a bastard on her? Your family was unhappy enough about allowing you to marry an artist."

"So you just...abandoned her?"

"No! I left her a note!"

Annabel winced. But she could not do as Lord Quinceton had asked and go to support Lady Hebbly just now; all of them in the room were frozen in place, watching the tableau being enacted before them between husband and wife. Lord Quinceton looked serious and more than a little sad; Angelique confused; and Philippe—Annabel looked away.

Lady Hebbly's face was almost as devastated as his. "Why did you not help her once we were married and you had the money? I would not have minded."

"I couldn't. She'd already gone to Ronderley. He'd *married* her, for God's sake." Sir Henry's hands clenched on his wife's.

She stifled a grimace, but her voice was calm when she said, "What else could she do? She was in a far worse position than you were. John Ronderley *was* a gentleman to marry her and give her unborn child his name—no, he was more than that. He was a good man—unlike you." She extracted her hands from his and tried to struggle to her feet. Lord Quinceton stepped in quickly and helped her up, then led her to the other sofa.

"Thank you, Geoffrey." She sat for a moment, trying to master her breath, then looked up at Angelique and Philippe. "Come sit with me, my dears," she said gently, patting the cushion next to her.

"Would you truly have helped our mother?" Angelique took a step toward her. "Even though your husband had—had—"

"Yes, I would," Lady Hebbly said. "The poor girl —she must have been terrified."

"Oh," Angelique said softly. She crossed the rest of the distance to Lady Hebbly and sat down, leaning against her as if she were a weary child.

Lady Hebbly put an arm around her shoulders. "Philippe?" she said.

He shook his head, his face pinched and white.

"Brandy?" Lord Quinceton went to the table and poured some out. "I find it helpful when one has had a shock."

"Thank you, Quinceton." Sir Henry, who had collapsed back against the cushions, held out his hand.

Smiling faintly, Lord Quinceton walked past him and handed the glass to Philippe. "Toss it back. It'll help." He went to stand by Annabel. To her surprise, she found his presence reassuring.

Philippe hesitated, then swallowed the brandy —and promptly went into a coughing fit. But when he'd caught his breath once more, the suffering in his eyes was a little less obvious. With a visible effort, he raised them to look at Sir Henry. "Lady Hebbly's right. My fath—" He stumbled over the word, then shook his head. "No, he is still my Papa, no matter what, and he is the best of men. He never allowed me to know by word or deed that I wasn't truly his son." He took the other seat by Lady Hebbly.

"Henry." Lady Hebbly's voice was as gentle and modulated as always, but under it was a thread of steel. "I believe you owe these children an explanation."

"Here? Now?" Sir Henry's eyes shifted from her to Annabel and Lord Quinceton.

"Yes, now." She took Philippe's hand. "I assume that their mother posed for you and that you seduced her."

"I loved her!" he retorted. "She was the most beautiful woman I had ever seen, and still is. I worshiped her!"

"But not enough to marry her and acknowledge the child she carried—*your* child!"

"It was impossible! I told you..." He trailed into silence as she shook her head.

"So she went to Mr. Ronderley, who did what you would not and gave her a home and the protection of his name and raised your son as his own... and you thank him by obstructing his membership in the Academy. For the love of God, why?"

Sir Henry's face had gone a mottled red. "Because he had Angelique, and I did not! If he could take from me what I'd wanted, then by God, I could keep from him what he'd wanted!"

Lady Hebbly stared at him, and for the first time, Annabel saw that there were tears in her eyes. "Henry, are you truly so—so broken? Have I ever known who you are?" A tremor ran through her. "It almost makes me glad that Richard died at Corunna, so he would never have discovered what I have learned today about his father."

"Your son is dead?" Philippe covered her hand with his.

She nodded. "He was an aide-de-camp to Sir John Moore—and—and your half-brother."

"My half-brother." Philippe swallowed and bowed his head.

"By God," Sir Henry whispered. He sat forward and swung his feet to the ground. "I still have a son, don't I?"

"No, Henry." The tears overflowed and ran unheeded down Lady Hebbly's plump cheeks. "You do not. You gave him up a long time ago."

"But—"

"Enough!" she barked.

Sir Henry recoiled as if he'd been struck. Lady Hebbly waited a moment to ascertain his silence, then continued. "If Philippe chooses to acknowledge you in private, that is his decision. But he is John Ronderley's son, both by affection and by law, and there is nothing you can do about that. There is one thing, however, that you *will* do." She leaned forward and caught his eye. "I have never asked you for anything, Henry. Never. But I am going to ask you now for something, and you will give it to me." Her voice was now calm and assured—and relentless. "You will see that John Ronderley is made a member of the Royal Academy as soon as possible."

He stared at her, unable to look away. "Antonia, I cannot simply—"

"You can, and you will. It is the least—the

least—you can do for this young man."

Sir Henry stared from her to him, and his handsome face suddenly looked old. "Philippe—my boy—"

"No." Philippe leapt to his feet. "I am *not* your boy. You decided that before I was born." He stalked from the room. A moment later, they heard the front door slam.

The room was silent after his abrupt departure. Then Angelique straightened, though she did not leave Lady Hebbly's side. "Are you going to stop persecuting my Papa and make him a member of the Academy?" she demanded.

Sir Henry was staring at the carpet between his feet. "Yes," he said dully.

"Good. And are you going to be kinder to Lady Hebbly?"

"Angelique!" Lady Hebbly started.

"I'll bet he's perfectly horrid to you. La, he puts me in mind of a spoiled child half the time when he opens his mouth."

Annabel felt rather than heard Lord Quinceton's chuckle.

"And if he isn't kinder to you, then I won't pose for him," Angelique finished triumphantly.

"I do not recall asking you to do so!" Sir Henry said, all injured dignity.

She lifted her chin and looked down her nose at him. "Don't be silly. I know you want to paint me, but I won't permit you to do so until you promise to be kinder to Lady Hebbly. She's my friend, and she's worth a—a *million* of you. If I were her, I certainly wouldn't forgive you for being such a horrid, mercenary scoundrel who married her for her money instead of facing your responsibilities."

Sir Henry's brow had darkened and an explosion seemed imminent. But when he looked at the pair on the sofa opposite him—Angelique magnificently indignant next to his pale, sorrowful wife—something seemed to shift inside him. "I—she's right," he said heavily. "I don't deserve you, Antonia."

Lady Hebbly sighed. "I know you don't. But you could begin to try to."

That evening found Annabel at a rout-party. She'd almost sent her regrets; the afternoon's events at the Hebblys' had been exhausting and depressing. But she needed the distraction—though on seeing the Marquis of Quinceton purposefully approaching her, she had at first quailed.

"Fellbridge," he greeted her. "I'm glad to see the events of the afternoon didn't get to you."

"They nearly did," she confessed, rather to her surprise. But there was no one else with whom she could talk about what had happened today. "I cannot stop thinking of poor Lady Hebbly and Sir Henry."

He took her arm and steered her toward an unoccupied corner. "What about them troubles you?"

"Sir Henry, mostly. Do you think most marriages are made in such—such bad faith?"

He looked at her, and for a moment she feared he would ask her whether her own had been...but no, he very likely already knew the answer to that. After all, he'd been one of Freddy's great friends.

"A great many are, I think," he said after a

moment's consideration. "But not all of them. I believe it quite possible to have a marriage in which the principals share strong affection and respect. I do not intend to have mine be any other way."

Annabel blinked. "I did not know you were contemplating matrimony. Do I know the lady in question, or is it a secret?"

"Don't you?" There was a strange edge to his smile. "Why, Fellbridge—and I had always admired your powers of observation."

It was on the tip of her tongue to ask if he intended to propose to Frances...but no, she would not. Still, the idea of him marrying only seemed to exacerbate her low mood, which made no sense. "I beg your pardon for disappointing you, Lord Quinceton. I shan't tease you for her name, then, but wait for the general announcement."

That strange smile widened, then was gone. "Did you see young Philippe when you brought the redoubtable Miss Ronderley home?"

Ah, this was a safer topic—she hoped. "No. I expect he still had several miles to walk before he could contemplate talking to anyone."

He nodded. "It was prodigious difficult for him. Hebbly could not have been more cow-handed, could he? But I expect Antonia will find him somewhat humbled from now on."

"I hope she does." She would have to write to Mama to encourage her to invite Lady Hebbly to visit Belsever Magna later this summer, the poor dear. A few weeks away from Sir Henry would probably do her good—

"I hope to do myself the honor of taking you driving on Sunday if you are not already engaged,"

Lord Quinceton said suddenly, interrupting her thoughts.

"I'm afraid I am. Sunday is the Fourth of June." The twins would expect to see her at Eton for the school's unofficial annual celebration of the King's birthday, with its boat parade, picnics, and fireworks.

"Ah, the Fourth of June. I had almost forgotten." He hesitated, then said, "Tomorrow, then? Unless you're already engaged with Glenrick."

"I have no engagements." Funny that he should bring Lord Glenrick up; she hadn't thought about him at all over the last day...and then remembered that she had. Perhaps it was because she was tired and still a little frazzled by the day's revelations that she found herself saying, "If I ask you a question, will you answer it?"

He smiled, but there was a hint of wariness about it. "It depends on the question."

"Yesterday, when we were at the Ronderleys' house—why did you take exception to the thought of me helping Lord Glenrick with anything?"

To her surprise, he threw back his head and began to laugh—actually laugh out loud.

"I don't see what is so amusing about my question," she said coldly. People nearby were regarding them with raised eyebrows. "Your behavior was most peculiar. I wish to know why."

He subsided into chuckles, shaking his head. "Oh, Fellbridge, my incomparable Fellbridge—"

"I am no such thing!"

"Ah, but you are. And you relieve my mind infinitely. If you have to ask why I take exception to your helping Lord Glenrick with anything, then you don't need—or want—to know why I do."

"That makes no sense!"

"It makes a great deal of sense. I shall come for you at three tomorrow if that will suit." And to her astonishment, he took her hand and lifted it to his lips. Though he still smiled, the expression in his eyes utterly transfixed her. He released her hand, then left the room.

Annabel tottered to a nearby chair and sat down. She'd been thoroughly shaken, not by Lord Quinceton's laughter or his cryptic reply, but by herself—and her reaction to the warmth of his lips on her gloved hand.

To her surprise, Lord Quinceton arrived for her the next day in a hackney, driven by none other than Bob Carter, who greeted her cheerfully. "Afternoon, yer ladyship!" His horse had been brushed till it gleamed, and the doors of the carriage blacked and polished.

"Good afternoon, Mr. Carter," she replied, then in a lower tone said to Lord Quinceton, "A new fancy of yours? Hackneys instead of curricles for driving? The *ton* will be aping you yet."

He smiled. "You overestimate my credentials as a leader of fashion. We're not going driving. We're going to the Exhibition."

"Hence Mr. Carter. Must we, really? If I have to look at another art exhibition for the rest of the year, I may have the vapors."

"You? I didn't think you knew the meaning of the word 'vapors.' And yes, we must. I want to see if that hideous child has kept her promise and returned the pictures to a semblance of their original selves."

"She's not hideous—well, not *really*," Annabel protested, but within she was alert. Angelique had indeed promised that she would set the Exhibition pictures right as they were leaving the Hebblys' house...and Lord Quinceton had scarcely blinked. Perhaps after brushes with literary demons and Sirens, a girl who could change paintings was nothing startling. But his calm acceptance of these things was unnerving. It might be necessary to inform the Lady Patronesses that because of her, he had learned about Titivillus and been drawn into catching the Siren who was robbing the *ton* at concerts as well as this. Would they blame her?

She was also very, very aware of Lord Quinceton as he handed her into the hackney and climbed in beside her. Despite her weariness she had tossed and turned for a good portion of the night after returning from the rout-party. Good heavens, the man had merely brushed his lips across her gloved hand, and she'd been ready to swoon. Yet when Lord Glenrick had kissed her—quite thoroughly, too—she'd barely felt a thing. It was disconcerting, to say the least.

And yet...and yet, it was also exciting. Perhaps she wasn't the cold, passionless woman she'd feared she was. But the fact that had it been Lord Quinceton, of all men, who'd had such an effect on her...

She turned her head to examine his profile. Emily had once called him a fallen angel, which wasn't an inapt description; from the side he did rather resemble a piece of handsome but especially fierce Renaissance sculpture—St. Michael with his sword, perhaps? What would she do if he kissed her

the way Lord Glenrick had at Hampton Court? The
thought made her shiver.

"Chilly, Fellbridge?"

"Not a bit." She hesitated, then blurted, "Who is
she?"

He turned to look at her. "Who is who?"

"Your intended bride."

"My—ah, yes." His lips twitched. "I thought you
said you would not tease me to reveal her name?"

"I'm not teasing! I'm just...curious."

"Why, Fellbridge. I did not think you took any
interest in my affairs."

"As you seem to take an interest in mine, I do
not see why the reverse should not be permitted."

"Permitted? On the contrary, I positively encourage it. I am not at present affianced to any lady,
if you wish to know the truth. I am merely contemplating it. Does that satisfy your curiosity?"

"You make me sound as if I were a dreadful
busybody," Annabel said, trying to sound miffed instead of relieved.

"Not at all."

They arrived at Somerset House, which Annabel was pleased to be able to enter not wrapped in a
shadow, and ascended the Great Staircase...and
there, emerging from the Anteroom, were Angelique
and Philippe.

"Lady Fellbridge!" Angelique rushed to her and
flung her arms around her. "I've just finished changing everything back! Did you come to see?" She
lowered her voice and said, "Though I think some of
my changes made the pictures more amusing, especially the Nausicaä. What a daub that one is! When
Sir Henry paints me—he called this morning to beg

me to sit for him, by the way—he says he'll show it at next year's Exhibition. I'll have to make certain he gets it right and fix it if he doesn't."

"I am certain he will be most grateful for the assistance," Lord Quinceton commented.

She cast him a superior—nay, pitying look. "Ah, poor Lord Quinceton. I am afraid that you shall have to resign yourself, once my portrait appears in the Exhibition next year and Lady Fellbridge has presented me at court, to an inferior role in my entourage. I expect that I shall have proposals from at least four dukes, and as a mere marquis, I am afraid you will be sadly out of the running. Sir Henry says—"

"I don't want to hear another word of what that man has to say," Philippe interrupted her. "You're making a perfect idiot of yourself—what do you know about dukes? I doubt there are four of them in the kingdom in the market for a wife, much less a school-aged chit such as you. I beg your pardon, sir—and you too, Lady Fellbridge—"

Angélique scowled. "He's been the most horrid grump ever, and it's been even worse since Sir Henry called this morning—yes, you have!" she added when he protested. "All he wanted to do was talk to you alone for a few minutes, and you wouldn't even shake his hand—"

Annabel got a strong impression that Philippe would have happily murdered his sister on the spot, but the young man showed admirable restraint. He imprisoned her arm in his and began to retreat. "Good afternoon—and thank you, Lady Fellbridge. Oh—and thank you for your note, my lord—we'll definitely consider it. I may need to get my sister out of the country eventually, if she isn't driven out at bayonet-point first—"

"Philippe!" Angelique stamped her foot, then nearly fell over when he propelled her away.

Annabel was proud of herself for not smiling till they were well out of sight. Then she sighed. "I am disappointed to hear Sir Henry is being so ham-fisted with the poor boy."

"Does it surprise you?" Lord Quinceton led them through the door into the Anteroom.

"No, not especially. But it is such a delicate situation. If Sir Henry is not careful, he will drive Philippe away completely by being too eager to clasp him to his bosom."

"Perhaps Antonia will be able to rein him in a little."

"I hope so—oh." *Lowther Castle, Westmoreland: Evening* was there where it had always been... but the cows now looked only like cows and not like Lady Hebbly. "It appears that she kept her word," she said.

They circled the room. The Bishop of Bath and Wells and his lady wife were as they should be, as were Nausicaä and her maids and Nick Bottom. In the Great Room, the whale being dispatched by Laplanders was merely a whale, and the volumes in Sir Ronald Timsbury's library were now clearly seen to be a complete set of Virgil. And the portrait of Lady Hebbly—

Annabel gazed at it for a long time. It was recognizably Antonia Hebbly, but Angelique had *not* returned it to its original condition. The woman gazing out from the canvas was beautiful, even with Lady Hebbly's regrettable features; the faint curve of her lips and the soft smile in her eyes somehow communicated the sweetness and kindness of her nature and transformed her. "Well," she said at last. "Perhaps Angelique will turn out all right after all."

They continued to stroll around the room, but Annabel was no longer looking at the pictures. What would Sir Henry say when he saw Lady Hebbly's portrait? Would he even notice the difference? He mercifully had not had the chance yesterday to ask how the pictures had come to be changed. With any luck, he would continue to be so distracted by the revelations of the day that he never would, and the Lady Patroness's investigation could be closed—and not a moment too soon for her tastes.

"What did you write to Philippe Ronderley, if I may ask?" she asked Lord Quinceton as they once more descended the stairs.

He gave a deprecating cough. "Oh, nothing of great importance. I merely offered to introduce him and his sister to friends of mine in the War Office. It occurred to me that they might be able to help them search for the whereabouts of their mother's family in Paris...if Angelique would be willing to perform her services on the art in the *Musée Napoléon*. The effects would be most...amusing."

It was too much for Annabel; she began to giggle, then laugh, there in the middle of the Great Staircase, and had to pause until she had caught her breath. "Oh, you are a bad man!" she said, when they had resumed their descent. "Imagine what she could do to the Emperor's portraits!"

"That had been my thought as well," he said calmly. But when Annabel glanced up at him, she saw he was watching her face with some amount of concentration.

"Sir Henry has quite the wrong idea," he said as they left Somerset House.

"About what?"

"About worthy subjects for painting. Angelique—what is she? A pretty face, with nothing behind it. But you—now that would be a picture worth painting. If he could catch you, that is." He halted by the door of Bob Carter's hackney, and turning her to face him, took her chin in hand and tilted her face toward his.

For an instant, Annabel thought he would kiss her, and remembered how the thought of his doing so had sent a wave of warmth through her. It did so again, and she took a quick breath through parted lips, waiting, wondering—

He gazed down at her, a smile lurking in his eyes—and something else that she could not quite decipher. "No, I am not at all persuaded that Sir Henry would have the skill to do you justice," he finally said, and released her. "You're too elusive, Fellbridge. It will take a more cunning hand than his to capture you." He opened the hackney's door and held out his hand to help her in.

⁂

I hope you enjoyed the fourth installment of The Ladies of Almack's! There's more—much more!—to come. If you'd like to keep up with the news from King Street, sign up for my newsletter for new release announcements, extras, and more about the ladies: https://marissadoylenewsletter.link/

Also, if you enjoyed reading *The Cursed Canvases*, please consider telling your friends who might also enjoy it or posting a review on the site where you purchased it or on your favorite social media site such as Goodreads or LibraryThing.

Author's Notes

The Royal Academy of Arts

Founded by a petition to King George III by architect Sir William Chambers, the Royal Academy of Arts came into being in 1768 with the mission of promoting the art of design in Britain, both through the establishment of a school of art and through the exhibition of the work of British artists.

Thomas Gainsborough, Joshua Reynolds, and Benjamin West were all founding members, as were two women artists, Angelica Kauffman and Mary Moser. After a few years in Pall Mall, the Academy moved to more spacious, specially-designed quarters in the newly rebuilt Somerset House, where it remained until 1837. After another move or two, the Royal Academy is now located in Burlington House, Piccadilly.

The Summer Exhibition, Somerset House

The annual Summer Exhibition put on by the Royal Academy at Somerset House on the Strand was an accepted part of the London Season by the late eighteenth century; it gave the fashionable (and not-so-fashionable) a chance to see and be seen, all while pretending to be very knowledgeable about modern art. To my delight, I found that my dear Ackermann's Repository, one of the leading magazines of the period, published an annual article on the Exhibition, and I greatly enjoyed reading the oh-so-snide critiques of several prominent works from 1810's show. And while I didn't use actual pictures as mentioned in the article, I used them as a guideline for creating my own works of art for Angelique Ronderley to vandalize.

The Lady of the Lake and the start of the Scottish craze

Sir Walter Scott's first narrative poem, *Marmion*, had been fairly well received on its publication in 1808...but with *The Lady of the Lake*, released in late May of 1810, his popularity soared...and as a result, a craze for all things Scottish swept the country, growing until it touched even the Prince Regent, who visited Scotland and had his portrait painted in a kilt. It eventually led, in later years, to Queen Victoria's obsession with the country and her building of her Scottish retreat, Balmoral, still beloved by today's royal family. This was kind of a big deal because for most of the previous century, Scotland had been regarded with at best derision and at worst, outright hostility. Why? Well, read the next note.

The Stuarts and the Forty-Five

The Stuart dynasty ruled England from 1603 (when James I, son of Mary Queen of Scots, inherited the throne from his Tudor cousin Elizabeth I) until 1714, on the death of Queen Anne...with time out for Oliver Cromwell and the English Civil War and the Glorious Revolution that put William of Holland and his wife, Mary of England (and Anne's big sister) on the throne. On Queen Anne's death, the throne of Great Britain went to distant cousins in the female line, the Electors of Hanover, despite the fact that Anne's half-brother, son of her deposed father James II, was alive and well. But James II and his children by his second wife, Mary of Modena, were Roman Catholic—and by law, a Catholic could not (and still cannot!) sit on the throne. The next thirty years saw several attempts by supporters of a Stuart monarchy to reinstate the dynasty, the most serious being that which occurred in 1745; fans of Outlander will find this familiar territory! After the failure of Charles Stuart to retake the throne and his defeat at the Battle of Culloden, harsh reprisals were enacted against his supporters, especially in Scotland—hence, the Exhibition picture I invented, *The Mother's Plight*, which seems to hold such fascination for Lord Glenrick.

The Terror

The Reign of Terror (September 1793-July 1794) was the bloodiest period of the French Revolution, during which over forty thousand met their deaths, many via the guillotine. It began as a power struggle between two factions, the Girondins and the Jacobins, and quickly turned into a systematic purge by the

Jacobins and their leader Robespierre to remove all "enemies of the revolution"...which was often used as an excuse to settle personal grudges. The clergy in particular suffered heavily; it was the mass execution of an order of nuns that may have been the tipping point that led to Robespierre's downfall and the end of the Terror.

Rundell and Bridge

Established in 1787 by Philip Rundell and John Bridge, within ten years this London firm had been appointed jeweler and goldsmith to the king, and a few years later Principal Royal Goldsmiths & Jewellers. Where royalty went, of course, the fashionable followed, and Rundell and Bridge was *the* place to go for one's jewelry, silverware, and other expensive baubles in the way of snuffboxes, vinaigrettes, and so on. The Prince Regent/King George IV was an enthusiastic customer: pieces made for him and for his successor William IV, including the Sovereign's Ring, the Sword of Offering, and the Diamond Diadem, are among the Crown Jewels today. The firm closed in 1843, having also been goldsmiths to George IV, William IV, and Victoria.

As an amusing side note (because historical side notes are the best), Mr. Rundell's sister-in-law Maria is well-known in her own right as author of one of the best known early English cookbooks, *A New System of Domestic Cookery*, first published in 1805.

Madder lake

Maybe it's just my inner history geekiness rising to

the fore once again, but I happily lost a couple of hours trolling through a website called Pigments through the Ages (https://www.webexhibits.org /pigments/) looking at the history of how tints of paint were created from plant and mineral sources. Madder lake is a pinkish red pigment derived from the roots of the madder plant (Rubia tinctorum) and was used as far back as ancient Egyptian times.

Peace of Amiens

Great Britain and its allies and France were in a more or less continuous state of war in the years between 1793 and 1815...except for the period between March 1802 and May 1803, a time known as the Peace of Amiens after the treaty that brought it about. The English took advantage of the peace to rush over to Paris to do massive shopping, visit the Louvre (soon to be renamed the Musée Napoléon) and catch a glimpse of the First Consul, Napoleon Bonaparte, who was almost as curious about them as they were about him. Unfortunately, their upset over Napoleon's rearranging of the map of Europe overcame their shopping lust, and the war resumed, not to end for another twelve years.

Vinaigrette

No, it's not salad dressing, though it does involve vinegar. It's actually a small silver box, usually not more than an inch and a half long, with a tight-fitting lid covering a perforated lid inside, which in turn holds a bit of sponge in place. The sponge was soaked in an aromatic vinegar and sniffed at when its owner felt faint. Similar to smelling salts, but much less nasty—the main ingredient in smelling salts is ammonia crystals, which are just painful to sniff!

The Battle of Corunna, January 1809

A dress rehearsal for the Battle of Dunkirk 130 years later. As it would at Dunkirk, the British Army had its back to the sea at Corunna in northern Spain, facing an oncoming enemy—in this case Napoleon's army under Marshal Soult—and had to fight while evacuating onto ships. The Commander-in-Chief, Sir John Moore, was killed, but not before hearing that the French had been repulsed and the evacuation of his army (as well as some Portuguese and Spanish troops) would be successful. Despite the evacuation's success, this was a low point in British fortunes in the war against Napoleon.

TURMOIL ON THE THAMES

Chapter One

Chesterfield Street, London
Early June 1810

Annabel knew she was being shameless. Indeed, she was quite certain her behavior verged on decadence. And she was enjoying every minute of it.

She lifted the spoonful of sliced strawberries dripping with sugared cream to her lips. Ah, heaven. Now a sip of chocolate, accompanied by a blissful wriggling of her toes under the counterpane. Lying abed till half-past ten whilst drinking chocolate and eating strawberries and cream was abandoned behavior indeed for a Shellingham. Thank goodness the portrait hanging over the chimneypiece of Grandmama—given last year as a special mark of her approval of Annabel's continued chaste widowhood—was just canvas and paint. Poor Grandmama would be scandalized if she truly were present.

But really, didn't she deserve a half-hour or so

of regret-free dissipation? Last week's investigation of the mysterious alterations to the pictures at the Royal Academy's Summer Exhibition had been especially tiring, both physically and emotionally. She'd *earned* a little relaxation this morning. And this afternoon—she smiled in anticipation.

Today was the Fourth of June and the birthday of the dear old king. While few people outside court circles would pay much attention to the date, in one place it would be celebrated as a high holiday.

Because of its proximity to Windsor Castle, the king's favorite residence, Eton College and its students had always enjoyed a firm friendship with his majesty. The king took a deep personal interest in the school and was a frequent visitor, and Eton's boys responded by turning his birthday into an unofficial day of celebration. The "unofficial" part was because the headmaster and staff of Eton did not sanction or participate (at least openly) in the day's events, turning an indulgently blind eye to the annual boat race—ahem, procession—upon the Thames, followed by a picnic and evening fireworks.

Their presence wasn't missed. The event had become part of the social season, and the *ton* turned out in force for it even if Eton's masters didn't. Dukes and earls and even the king's own sons came to be taken as guests on the boys' boats and to drink champagne in the field across from Surly Hall, a well-known riverside pub, where the race ended.

Today Annabel would be among their number, for Will and Martin had demanded that she come—bringing a suitably magnificent picnic, of course—to join them for their first Fourth of June. Annabel had agreed at once; in another year or two her presence might not be so welcome. She and her cook had conferred over the contents of the picnic box last week after Martin sent another note entreating her to bring *lots* of sandwiches and cakes—especially his favorite iced cakes that only Mrs. Dailey could bake.

Annabel smiled at the memory of her son's earnest note. In a little while she would rise and dress and pay a visit to the kitchen to see how Mrs. Dailey was getting on. Or... or perhaps she'd just pour herself another cup of chocolate and—

An urgent scratch at her dressing room door made her sit up. Before she could respond, her maid Winters had thrown open the door, her pale face even paler than usual. "Madam!" she gasped. "Lord and Lady Shellingham are here!"

"What?" Annabel stared at her. Mama and Papa here in London, at this time of year? "Right now? Where are they?"

"Hanscomb put them in the salon and is bringing them coffee." Winters hurried to remove the tray from Annabel's lap. "Lady Shellingham says she will come up to see you in a few minutes. I have your water for washing."

"Oh, heavens!" Annabel jumped out of bed. So much for her peaceful morning in bed! What could have brought her parents to London? Papa hated being away from Belsever Magna in spring and only came to town when there was a question being discussed in Parliament that he cared about. Perhaps that was it—but why hadn't they told her they were coming?

With Winters' help she was washed and hastily arrayed in a dressing gown when a firm knock sounded on her door and Mama's voice called,

"Annabel?"

"Mama!" Annabel rose from her dressing table as Winters opened the door. "What a lovely surprise!"

Sarah, Lady Shellingham was a small, plump woman with dreamy blue eyes whose vague manner was completely spurious—except when it wasn't. "Is it?" she said. "Didn't the boys tell you we'd be coming with you to Eton today? We got the sweetest letter from Will begging us to come."

"No, they didn't—not that I'm not delighted to see you." Annabel bent to kiss her mother's soft cheek.

"Well, since the new barouche he ordered was ready and his roses were still a week from their full display, your father thought we could manage a few days in London. We came down Friday. We're staying at Grillon's—it didn't make sense to open the house just for a few days—"

"You could have stayed with me," Annabel interrupted reproachfully.

"No, we couldn't. Papa was afraid you'd try to make him go to Almack's."

"But Almack's is only on Wednesdays."

"I know, dear, but he doesn't always listen. I don't know what we'll do next year when little Sarah is ready to make her curtsey to the queen. Your sister will want us here in town, of course, but tearing Papa from his roses will be next to impossible." Mama sighed and took off her hat, then seated herself at Annabel's dressing table to pat her hair smooth. "You aren't still wearing that disgraceful thing, are you?" she added, glancing at Annabel through the mirror.

Annabel flushed. Her dressing gown was old—and looked it. "It's not as if anyone ever sees me in it but Winters."

"*I'm* seeing it, right now...and you never know who else might at some point."

"Mama!" Annabel could not decide whether to be scandalized or amused.

Mama turned away from the mirror and peered more closely at her. "You do look tired, darling. Perhaps you need to cut down on your social commitments? I shall have a word with Sally Jersey before we go home. If Almack's is wearing you down this much—"

"Mama, I'm not twelve! And anyway, it's not that—" Annabel began, then stopped. Mama of course had no idea about her extra duties with the Lady Patronesses. "This was just a—an especially busy week."

"Hmm." Mama turned back to the mirror, this time carefully *not* looking at her. "Are there, ah, any specific persons keeping you busy of late?"

Annabel restrained a sigh. For the last year and a half Mama had been dropping delicate and not-so-delicate hints about her marital status, or lack thereof. Unlike Grandmama Shellingham, she thought it long past time for Annabel to remarry.

She opened her mouth to reply in the negative to Mama's question, then stopped. Someone *had* been occupying a great deal of her attention—two someones, in fact. But she winced at the idea of telling her mother about Lord Glenrick's kissing her. And Lord Quinceton of course did not even belong in this conversation, no matter how much time she had recently spent in his company. "If anyone begins to keep me busy in that fashion, Mama, you shall know at once," she said with a bright smile.

"Oh, darling." Mama shook her head. "You are still the worst liar in all England, aren't you? Who is he?"

How did Mama always know? She hesitated, then said, "Um—Lord Glenrick. He's been, ah, most attentive."

Mama gave up any pretense of primping at the mirror and turned in her seat to face her. "Glenrick? Good heavens!"

Annabel looked away. "He seems to think me attractive."

Mama waved her hand. "Of course he does. You're a very attractive girl. But haven't you paid any attention—no, I don't suppose you have over the last few years. Everyone knows that the Carricks are practically at a standstill and that Glenrick would be a fool if he married anyone but an heiress to shore up the family fortunes. Regrettably, you are *not* an heiress. So why is he dangling after you, unless—" She frowned. "Has he tried to kiss you?"

"Er, yes."

Mama's frown deepened. "In that case, I expect he wants to make you his mistress. There's nothing wrong with that if it is agreeable to you, so long as you're discreet about it. However, considering how quickly you were breeding after you married Freddy, I would worry about unintended consequences—"

"Goodness, Mama!" Being a Shellingham for forty years had not repressed her mother's straight-forwardness.

"—still, I could wish better for you." She sighed. "Papa and I *would* be pleased to see you married again." She rose and wandered over to the window. "I had hoped Freddy was going to be a better husband than he turned out to be. He seemed to quite dote upon you when he asked us for your hand, which was why Papa agreed to overlook the fact that his finances weren't as solid as we would have preferred."

Annabel looked sadly at her back. "It—it all turned out well enough, Mama. I have Will and Martin, after all."

"True." Mama's shoulders relaxed—but not entirely. "Speaking of whom, isn't it time you were dressed? We have an enormous picnic waiting in the carriage for two hungry little boys."

Annabel paused on her way to ring for Winters. "What? Did they ask you for food as well?"

Mama laughed and turned from the window. "The way Will phrased it, they're positively wasting away. I expect they'll grow six inches over the summer. Your brothers were the same way—two months of insatiable appetite, and then I had to order all new clothes for them because they'd outgrown everything in their wardrobes."

"I hope they're getting enough to eat," Annabel said. Was Mrs. Poltrey, who ran their lodging, feeding them properly? They had looked well enough when they were home at Easter, but perhaps this was a more recent problem. She would have to question them this afternoon. She went to the bell and rang for Winters.

"Annabel." Mama had followed her; now she touched her arm. "About Glenrick. Do you return his regard?"

Annabel paused, still holding the bell pull. Did

she? She had been so wrapped up in being flattered by his obvious preference and by Frances's marital hints that she hadn't truly considered that question. She thought of his kiss on that quiet wooded path at Hampton Court and what she'd felt—or not felt.

"I don't know," she said, looking down at the toes of her slippers. "I can't help feeling a little...well, he's the next Duke of Carrick, after all. And I've never felt *desired* before. I hadn't realized what a heady sensation that could be. But now, thinking about it without him before me—I don't know."

"Oh, my poor dear." Mama folded her in an embrace. "I could just *smite* your lout of a husband."

Annabel had been inclined to teariness, but Mama's indignation made her laugh instead. "That's already happened if you recall—the poor old dear. And I'm quite well. Just...confused."

"Men. The world would be a much simpler place without them, wouldn't it, Winters?" Annabel's maid had appeared, bearing a bronze muslin walking dress trimmed with bands of brown silk.

"That it would, your ladyship." Winters had been a maid at Belsever Magna before becoming Annabel's maid. "Perhaps not as amusing, however."

"I'll take simple over amusing any day," Mama said firmly. "Is that a new dress?"

"No, an old one we remade. Don't you care for it? I think it's one of Winters' best efforts." Annabel smiled at her maid. "One does not dress up too much for this event, so I understand."

"Hmm." Mama eyed the dress as Winters laced Annabel's stays and helped her on with a petticoat. "Very pretty, but—" She pressed her lips together and said, more firmly, "Very pretty."

Mama herself was, as always, beautifully turned out, today in cream-colored muslin with a high-necked lilac sarsenet mantle. Annabel knew that her straitened circumstances and limited dress allowance troubled her fashionable parent, but Mama had sufficient delicacy to not make too great a fuss about it.

While Winters dressed her hair in a simple style, Mama wandered around the room, examining her treasures: miniatures of the boys when they were three by Richard Cosway, a pair of Limoges vases Freddy had given her when the boys were born, the small but exquisite watercolor of an orchid that the boys' friend Augustus Blackburn—Gus—had painted for her.

"That's a pretty thing," Mama commented, peering at it closely.

"Isn't it? You'll probably have the opportunity to meet the artist later today." Gus would almost certainly be there with the boys this afternoon—or at least with Martin, while Will rowed.

"I'll look forward to it—good heavens, darling!" Mama said, pausing before the portrait of Grandmother Shellingham. "Do you really want a picture of Grandmama in your *bedchamber*?"

"Why? What's wrong with it?"

"It's so—unconducive!"

Winters gave a strangled sort of cough but heroically maintained her countenance; upper servants never betrayed that they'd heard a word uttered by their superiors unless directly addressed. Annabel, however, had no such constraints. "Mama!"

Mama shrugged. "All I can say, dear, is that if

I'd allowed your grandmother's portrait in *my* bed-chamber, you and your brothers and sister might not be here today. Poor Papa!" She surveyed it a moment longer, then shook her head.

"How is Grandmama, anyway?"

"Oh, very well. There are still fifteen chairs in the dining room that need new covers. I think she's signed a pact with the devil to stay alive until she's done embroidering them."

Annabel grinned. Why didn't that surprise her? Grandmama sometimes seemed to forget that her eldest son was himself a grandfather now.

"You're ready, milady," Winters said, setting down her comb and handing Annabel her earrings.

"Thank you, Winters." Annabel slipped them on. "Speaking of Papa, shall we go down and join him for coffee before he thinks we've forgotten him?" She stood up, took Mama's arm, and led her from the room. As the door closed behind her, she heard poor Winters giving way to her pent-up mirth and smiled in sympathy.

Two hours later, after not only coffee but a hastily-improvised nuncheon Annabel called for after Papa's pointed complaints about the inadequacy of break-fast at their hotel, they were off to Eton in Annabel's landau.

That had taken some negotiating. Just the day before, Papa had taken delivery of a new barouche of which he was very proud, lacquered in the Shelling-ham maroon and gray and with new matching liveries for his coachman and groom that he had designed himself. But Mama had put her dainty lilac kid half-boot down and declared that they would drive with Annabel. "I have not seen my daughter in months," she said firmly, "and I intend to drive with her. You may take the new barouche, but you will look very silly being driven to Eton all alone, no matter how much you want to show it off."

Papa glowered. "I don't want to show it off. I want to ascertain that all is as it should be before we drive it home. *A stitch in time saves nine.*"

"Nonsense. You and Ambrose drove it around London for an hour and a half yesterday. If there were something wrong with it that required the carriage-maker's attention, you would have found it then." She fixed him with a stern look. "*Pride goeth before a fall.*"

He sighed. "Your point, Sarah."

Annabel tried not to smile. Mama lately had taken to countering Papa's beloved maxims with her own, often more aptly chosen. She twined her arm in his as Mama rang for Hanscomb to have the carriage brought around. "I'm glad we're going all together, Papa," she said, and kissed his cheek.

He continued to glower despite the corners of his mouth having turned up. "Trying to turn me up sweet, are you, you artful puss? Well, I won't have it." But he squeezed her arm and sent the new barouche back to the hotel's stables and climbed into the landau without demur when Thomas drove it up. "Do we have quite enough food, d'ye think?" he commented, eyeing the large wicker hamper in the seat next to him. A similar hamper had been stowed in the boot, along with a folding table and campaign stools to sit on.

"I hope so." Annabel adjusted her sunshade; the early afternoon sun was bright. "The boys were emphatic about it."

He folded his hands on the expanse of waistcoat covering his comfortable belly. "*Man cannot live by bread alone.*"

Mama snorted. "*Boys will be boys.*"

Papa tried to frown but failed. "They will, won't they? Your point, my dear."

"Yes, I know. Now, Annabel, perhaps you know—what is this dreadful story we've heard about the Duke of Cumberland? Did his valet really try to murder him?"

"That's what they're saying. I haven't heard much else," Annabel said. Gossip had begun circulating on Thursday that the king's fifth son, the Duke of Cumberland, had been attacked and nearly killed by one of his valets, a Sardinian named Joseph Sellis, that previous night. But she had been in the thick of the Summer Exhibition investigation and had not paid much attention to the whole sordid matter.

"Doesn't surprise me in the least. Cumberland's a bad 'un," Papa said. "Always has been. Of course, that's not to say he deserved to be attacked in his bed in the middle of the night. And the valet slit his own throat, it seems. They say Cumberland had been far too friendly with the man's wife. Or with Sellis himself. Place looked as if a pig had been slaughtered in it, evidently."

"Really, George, must we?" Mama wrinkled her nose. "I wondered what had you as thick as thieves with our waiter at breakfast. You were gossiping."

"I was gathering information," Papa said loftily. "Men don't gossip."

Mama snorted. *"Heed not what a man says, but what he does."*

"How are your roses faring, Papa? Did they survive the winter unscathed?" Annabel asked before he had finished sputtering. Talking about his roses was guaranteed to divert Papa from just about anything.

It worked. Papa happily spent the next hour discussing each of his bushes in detail, including the number of buds set in some cases. Annabel privately resolved to have the boys invite Gus to Belsever Magna during one of their summer holiday visits to paint a few of his favorites.

As they approached the village of Eton, the roads grew crowded. Papa sighed as he waved to the sixth carriageful of his acquaintances, and Annabel knew he was regretting not having taken his new barouche. She saw many acquaintances of her own and was pleasantly surprised when a carriage containing Maria Sefton, Lord Sefton, and a pair of gentlemen pulled alongside them.

"Annabel!" Maria exclaimed. "I'd wondered if you would be here to visit the boys." She smiled and nodded at Mama. "Lady Shellingham, it's a pleasure to see you."

"Yes—Will is rowing." Annabel couldn't keep a note of pride out of her voice.

"Oh, that's splendid. I'm glad to see one of us here," she added in a slightly lower voice. "There's something I might need your help with—"

"Hoy, Shellingham! Where's this new barouche I've heard about?" Lord Sefton boomed, drowning out his wife's words.

Papa smiled through gritted teeth. "I'd be happy to take you around Hyde Park in it tomorrow, sir."

"That's done it," Mama murmured to Annabel. "We'll be in London till your father's done showing off his barouche to all and sundry."

"Ha! I should enjoy that, sir! Drive on!" Lord Sefton called to his coachman.

"I'll find you after the procession!" Maria called as their coach drew ahead.

"I shall look for you," Annabel replied, but they had already passed. What might Maria need her help with? It must be special Lady Patroness business, or she wouldn't have been so circumspect. Heavens, was there a new investigation looming already?

In another half hour they'd finally reached the Brocas, a large, south-facing meadow directly on the Thames with a lovely view of the towers of Windsor Castle to the southeast. Thomas left them off near the road to make their way toward the river where the race would be starting. The field looked so cheerful, its green breadth milling with excited boys (some on horseback) and strolling sightseers, that Annabel regretted that they could not picnic right here on the sunny grass. But any such thoughts were banished by the sight of the Honourable Martin Chalfont running toward them at full tilt, his beaver hat in hand.

"You're here!" he shouted and flung himself at her. Before she could begin to give him the briefest of hugs, he'd already caromed off her like an errant billiard ball to give his grandparents a similar greeting. "Did you bring a *huge* picnic?" he demanded.

"Yes, two of them, you jackanapes!" Annabel answered. "Why didn't you say you'd written to your grandparents as well?"

He looked at her as if he doubted her intellectual capacity. "Because I wanted them to come and bring a picnic too. Twice as much. I *can* do maths, you know."

"Isn't Mrs. Poltrey giving you enough to eat?" Annabel examined his figure anxiously. He didn't look particularly thinner—

"Oh, yes, she feeds us good and proper. We just wanted a bang-up feast today." He grinned up at her angelically.

A faint warning bell sounded in Annabel's mind. She knew that grin...and from experience, distrusted it.

"Where is your brother, Martin?" Mama asked before she could question him further.

"Oh, down by the boats. Gus is somewhere too. You'll see 'em at Surly's after the race. Give me a minute to gather everything, and we can get going. Where are your carriages?"

"What 'everything' requires gathering?" Annabel asked.

His smile remained, but his gaze slithered away from hers. "Just a few things we wanted to bring along."

Annabel looked past her offspring and saw a quintet of boys who bore a strong resemblance to pack donkeys, loaded with what appeared to be several planks, four sawhorses, and a bundle of tall naphtha torches. "What do you need those—"

"Can I go with *you*, Grandpapa?" Martin interrupted, inserting just the right note of hero worship in his voice.

Predictably, Papa melted. "I should say you can —except I doubt there'll be room enough in your mother's carriage what with the extra picnic hamper—"

"You came together?" For the first time, Martin's smile faltered. "But how am I supposed to get our stuff there?"

"Martin, what is all this for?" Annabel asked in a firm voice.

"Just for—for a thing we're doing tonight. It's—it's in honor of the king's birthday," he added, with the air of a relieved magician who finds he has not flubbed his trick after all. "I didn't know you'd be coming in just one carriage, though. You should have said so!"

Papa examined Martin's retinue with a practiced eye. "You might fit all that in your mother's carriage if none of us had come," he said. "No notion how you'll get it there, my boy."

"But I have to!" Martin's face crumpled, and he seemed alarmingly close to tears.

"It is very simple," a familiar voice said from behind Annabel. "Lord and Lady Shellingham will drive in my curricle with my groom, and Fellbridge and I shall walk to Surly's. The river path is only a couple of miles. That will leave the landau to Master Chalfont and his, er, accoutrements."

Chapter Two

Of course. She should have *known* he would turn up here today. "This is an unexpected, er, pleasure, sir," Annabel said as she turned to face the speaker.

Lord Quinceton swept off his hat. She just caught the mischievous gleam in his eyes before he made her a low bow. "A pleasure indeed. But I don't see why it should be so unexpected, as I happen to be an Old Boy myself." He bowed again to Mama. "Your servant, Lady Shellingham. Sir," he added, nodding to Papa.

"How d'ye do, Quinceton," Papa greeted him affably. Of course Papa was acquainted with him from the House of Lords.

Martin fixed Lord Quinceton with a suspicious stare. "Who're you?"

"I don't presume to call myself a friend of your mother's, Master Chalfont, but perhaps I can lay claim to being her devoted acquaintance," he replied. "I am Quinceton."

Annabel snorted. "You, sir, presume precisely as much as you want, when you want."

"I beg you not to speak so, madam! You'll give your family a bad impression of me." He shook his head in mock distress.

"No worse than the one you're giving yourself. You're being quite ridiculous, you know." And so was she. No, the day was *not* suddenly brighter and more exciting just because he had arrived. Not in the least.

"My apologies." He inclined his head. "I've told you before, you do bring out the worst in me."

"Only because you permit it!"

"But the temptation, Fellbridge! The temptation!" Did he have to smile at her in that fashion, so that the corners of her own mouth could only turn up in response?

Martin was not satisfied. "Why'd you call my mother Fellbridge? That's my brother's name."

"It is indeed—or it will be when he's old enough to do it honor," Lord Quinceton said, now all seriousness. "In the meanwhile, your mother is performing that task heroically."

"Hmm," Mama said to no one in particular.

Papa appeared much impressed by this statement. "By God, she is, isn't she? Since Freddy was fool enough to cock up his toes as he did, he should be deucedly grateful to have married someone who was able to pick up the pieces he left behind. Thank you for the offer of your curricle, Quinceton, but I believe I fancy a walk as well. What do you think, my dear?"

Martin's face uncrumpled. "Then *I* can drive the carriage there?"

"No, you may not, young man. Thomas will

drive you," Annabel said firmly. She turned to Mama. "Unless you would care to go with him?"

"No, I shall walk as well," she said. "It *is* a lovely day, and if I grow tired, your father will carry me."

"What?" Papa's eyes widened.

Mama smiled at him sweetly and took his arm. "Come along, dear. We'll see you all soon!" She propelled him gently toward the river.

"Fellbridge?" Lord Quinceton murmured. That mischievous twinkle was back.

Too late she realized that she'd fallen in with his plan without even having considered otherwise. "Oh, very well," she said, perhaps not as graciously as she ought. The man was possibly even better than her mother at arranging situations to his liking. "I must tell Thomas that he should drive Martin and his friends. Would Gus care to go with you?" she asked her son.

Martin shot one more suspicious look at Lord Quinceton, then shook his head vigorously. "No, he can't. No room," he added, at her surprised look. "Come on, men!" He began to march toward the road, leading his crew of boys in the manner of a nabob with his retinue of native bearers.

Once the doubting Thomas had been assured that yes, she really did want him to drive Martin and his baggage to the field opposite Surly Hall and that she herself truly did want to walk there, Annabel took Lord Quinceton's proffered arm and allowed him to lead her toward the river to see the boats. The sun sparkled on the water, but a soft breeze kept its warmth from becoming oppressive. "I will admit that it is a perfect day for a walk," she said as they strolled down the field.

"That is what I appreciate about you, Fellbridge —one thing among others, I should say. You're always gracious in defeat."

"I was not aware there had been a contest."

"Perhaps not a contest, but I concede that I did rather take over your plans for the day. Well, your son and I. However, everyone seems content with the results. At least I hope they are." He glanced at her sideways.

"Surely the fact that *you* are is enough?"

Instead of laughing and agreeing, which was what she expected him to do, he shook his head. "No, not at all. Do you take me for such a selfish fellow?"

"I take you for one determined to get what he wants."

"Fair enough. At least you are forewarned."

Annabel felt herself color and was grateful for the concealing brim of her hat. "Why didn't you say you were coming today when I mentioned I would be here?" she asked, to change the subject.

"Does it perturb you that I did come?"

"Are you waiting for me to say, 'Fie, Lord Quinceton, indeed I am delighted to see you here!'"

He grinned. "It would be very gratifying if you would. I didn't say I would be here because I was not yet certain that I would be. I did not know whether you were coming with Glenrick and couldn't think of a delicate way to ask. It is not much of a pleasure to see you in his company."

He was determined to make her blush today, wasn't he? "Confessing yourself at a loss? I *am* astonished, sir!"

"You're supposed to be. It's all part of my fiendishly devious plan to keep you off balance."

She looked up at him, truly astonished this time. "Why do you want to do that?"

He smiled. "I am somewhat surprised my lord Glenrick did not undertake to accompany you to-day," was all he said.

Ah. So he was in one of *those* moods. She would endeavor not to play into it further. "I have neither seen nor heard from Lord Glenrick since Wednesday," she replied, then added, more slowly as the thought had not previously occurred to her, "Nor Frances, for that matter."

"Nor have I."

She tried not to allow that response please her too much. "Frances said something about an elderly great-aunt who was in failing health."

"Here in London?" His tone was skeptical.

"I don't know." Had Frances even said? She could not remember. Perhaps they *had* left for Scotland—but it seemed unlikely that Frances would make such a journey at the height of the season to attend the sickbed of a relative she had never before mentioned in all the years of their acquaintance...not to mention not leave any word for any of the Lady Patronesses.

"Hmm," the marquis said.

His steps slowed until they ceased altogether. He was silent for so long, his brow creased, that after a long minute Annabel asked, "Are you well, sir?"

He started and resumed walking. "I beg your pardon. I am not being a very entertaining companion, which is most remiss of me after I basely extracted you from the bosom of your family in order to monopolize your attention."

She laughed. "You do talk the most complete

nonsense. Was that something you learned at Eton, or is it a natural ability?"

"What nonsense? I am always quite serious, Fellbridge. I have every intention of monopolizing your attention whenever possible."

She stole a glance at him to try to gauge his expression, but his face was bland and unrevealing. What had got into him today? She was used to his teasing, but this was different. If anything, she would call it *flirting,* which left her feeling very off balance indeed.

Two months ago, she would have said that Lord Quinceton was the last man she would ever set up a flirtation with—in fact, she'd spoken those very words to Emily. And then he'd somehow insinuated himself into her life and thoughts till—till now she had to admit that she found his company...well, exhilarating. And perhaps more.

She took refuge in changing the subject. "Very well. If we are to talk nonsense, then what is this I am hearing about the Duke of Cumberland? My father was very full of it this morning, thanks to a waiter at Grillon's."

"You don't know?"

"I know only the smallest bit. I was otherwise occupied last week with the Ronderleys, if you recall."

"Yes, I suppose you were. There's not much to say; the duke is said to have been attacked by his valet, who then seems to have changed his mind and ended his own life instead. Is that what your father said?"

"More or less, with a little extra sordid speculation as to why such a thing had happened." She shook her head. "I pity the king. He's a good man, I think—why are most of his sons so prone to trouble and scandal? I am reminded of the fairy story where the bad fairy who wasn't invited to the christening comes anyway and curses the king's child—or children in this case—out of sheer spite. First there was that dreadful business last year with the Duke of York and his mistress that made him resign from the Army, and now this."

Again to her surprise, he didn't laugh. "I've thought that myself," he said slowly. "Not so much a bad fairy but something else—or perhaps I should say someone."

Annabel was not a Lady Patroness for nothing. Lord Quinceton did not miss much, as she'd learned to her occasional dismay. If *he* thought something peculiar was going on... "Whom do you suspect?" she asked sharply.

"Oh no you don't, Fellbridge. This investigation is not for you."

"But you think there is something worth investigating?"

"I don't know yet. I may be dragged into it against my will—no," he said firmly, as she opened her mouth. "If there *is* anything going on, I do not wish to see you of all people mixed up in it."

It was on the tip of her tongue to ask why not her of all people, but his expression was so forbidding that she did not argue further. She would, however, report this conversation at tomorrow's meeting of the Lady Patronesses. In the meanwhile, they had reached the river's edge, and just now she wanted to put these discomfiting thoughts aside and simply enjoy the day and her sons' pleasure in it.

On the river, all the boats had been bedecked with flowers in honor of the king, and the boys wore the most outlandish collections of clothing they could manage by way of festive costume; even their hats were garlanded and beribboned. Will's boat was close enough to the bank that he saw Annabel waving and nearly dropped his oar waving back; a friendly cuff to the back of his shoulder from the older boy behind him just made him grin.

"I've not seen your sons before. They're ludicrously like their father," Lord Quinceton commented.

"Yes, aren't they?" Annabel replied. It felt decidedly odd to be discussing Freddy with him.

"I suspect, however, that they have their mother's brains. Your late husband may have been the best of good fellows, but he could be thick as a plank at times, regrettably."

Annabel glanced up at him, but there was no ironical quirk to his expression. How was she supposed to respond to such a statement, especially as she was in complete accord with it? "His intentions were good," was all she could think of to say.

"You are kind enough to not speak ill of the dead. I have fewer such compunctions. I don't know that I can ever forgive him—" He stopped speaking, instead staring into the distance across the river, his lips compressed.

Annabel blinked at the bitterness in his voice. Forgive what? What could Freddy have ever done to him? She waited for him to finish, but he remained unwontedly silent, so she sighed and tried to think of something else to say. "I do hope the boys will be careful. Those boats look so fragile."

"The river should be past its spring spate by now," Lord Quinceton said in a much more normal tone. "Nothing to be concerned about." He smiled reminiscently. "I remember being out in one when it wasn't. Fortunately, my mother was not there to see me."

"Why am I not surprised to learn that you were an incorrigible child?"

"I beg your pardon, madam, but I was no such thing. In that particular instance, in fact, I was victim rather than perpetrator—and a fortunate one. The river was in a forgiving mood that day, and we made it to shore unharmed if in a damper condition than when we were launched by a group of fourth form boys who thought it would be a capital joke to send a group of first years out without oars."

"Good heavens. I hope that sort of behavior is no longer permitted." Annabel shuddered as she gazed out at the river. Although Will and Martin might not mind such japes—they were, in that respect, very much their father's sons—*she* certainly found them alarming. She looked again at Will's boat and frowned; was the water flowing a little faster than it had been moments before? But no, that could not be.

"It wasn't permitted then, either. If it makes you feel better, I am under the impression that that sort of tomfoolery has lessened somewhat since my day."

"I should hope so! Well, Gus, and how are you?" she said kindly as Augustus Blackburn hurried over to them, his eyes fastened on her worshipfully.

"I'm very well, Lady Fellbridge." He bowed. "Is Martin with you?"

"I'm afraid Martin has gone to the picnic field in my carriage."

"Oh." His face fell, and she wondered if he and the boys had indeed had a falling out. Was that why Martin had insisted on leaving without him? But Gus straightened his shoulders and said, "Never mind. I ought to get started." He started to turn away, then hesitated. "Will—will you be there, ma'am?"

"Yes, Gus, and I hope you'll join our picnic. Will and Martin's grandparents are here as well."

"Oh, thank you!" For a moment she thought he would fling his arms around her. Poor creature, he probably did not receive many hugs. Then he bowed again, grinning happily, and joined the surge of boys streaming toward the river path.

"A friend, I take it?" Lord Quinceton said.

"My sons' friend, Gus Blackburn." She didn't elaborate, hoping he would not recall Maria's rashly blurted explanation about Gus's being the culprit in the voucher-forging incident several weeks ago. The boy had already grown since April; Annabel remembered their conversation about affording new coats and was glad that for a few years at least his basic wants would be met. Perhaps his father could be recalled to his responsibilities before the money Gus had accumulated ran out.

"Ah. So that is young Master Blackburn," Lord Quinceton said. "I trust the child has avoided further criminal activity?"

Drat it, he remembered. "He didn't commit a crime. Well, not an actionable one anyway," she amended. "And what he did was understandable under the circumstances."

Just then, a shouted "Oy!" made her look up—

and gasp. The boats already on the river (some were still drawn up to the bank awaiting guest passengers) were rocking and heaving as if under a heavy swell. Boys frantically worked their oars, trying to keep the narrow craft from capsizing in the sudden waves rolling down the river.

"William!" She pulled away from Lord Quinceton. What had happened to roil the river so suddenly? A moment ago it had been calm and sparkling gently in the sun—

A hand closed on her shoulder, halting her. "Be still, Fellbridge," Lord Quinceton said in her ear.

"My son is out there!"

"And just what do you think you can do for him?"

Her breath caught in her throat. Oh, a pox on him for being right!

But as she watched, straining despite herself against Lord Quinceton's iron grip on her arm, the river quickly subsided, looking once more like a river and not like the Channel in a tempest, and the boats stopped threatening to capsize. She anxiously scanned them until she spotted Will, still safely seated if a little scared looking. "I thought you said the river was past its spring spate?" she said, her voice shaky.

Lord Quinceton released her arm. He was watching the surface of the river closely. "It is. What did you see?"

"Wasn't it obvious?"

"I have a reason for asking. Be precise, please."

She restrained an impulse to argue and reviewed the images in her mind. "I...don't know. It—it's foolish, but...it looked almost as if the surface of the water was trying to shake the boats off as a horse does a fly. But that's—" She shook her head. "What did *you* see?"

He was still watching the river. "More or less what you did."

"I didn't know rivers did that sort of thing."

"They don't, usually."

"Then what—"

"I don't know. Unless..." A frown drew down his brows. "No. They couldn't have forgotten," he muttered.

"Who?" Again, perhaps it was being a Lady Patroness, but she had the distinct impression that there was something odd going on here...and that he knew something about it. "Forgotten what?"

He stared out at the river for a moment longer, then seemed to come to a decision. "Are you up to a brisk walk?"

"What, immediately? Can't we watch the start of the procession?"

"I think it would be best if we leave now, so that we may keep the boats in view."

Ah. So there *was* something going on. She looked again at the boats full of laughing boys, already recovered from their scare a moment before. "I am, if you will tell me what is concerning you about the river."

He smiled as he led her toward the path Gus had taken. "But my dear Fellbridge, you have not been very forthcoming when I have asked similar questions recently."

"I—I have not always been at liberty to answer questions that concern other people's affairs."

He looked down at her and raised an eyebrow. "Nor am I."

She took a breath. "Lord Quinceton, I must ask you to tell me if there something amiss with the river. If there is, I think I deserve to know about it. My elder son is in a boat upon it as we speak."

They had overtaken a rowdy knot of fifth form boys on the path, a couple of them on what looked like borrowed cart-horses. The marquis steered them past the boisterous, incongruously flower-bedecked group without speaking. When they were no longer in earshot, he said quietly, "I fear that there's something amiss with the Tamesian Potamides."

"The *what*?"

"Tamesian Potamides." He looked at her sideways. "Also known as the river nymphs of the Thames."

Annabel was careful not to allow her expression to change. *River nymphs?* Was he hoaxing her?

But no: she had always been truthful with him, even if she hadn't always been forthcoming with *all* of the truth. She guessed that he was according her the same courtesy. And if he believed—no, if he knew that there were river nymphs in the Thames, it would explain why he'd been so accepting of the book demons and Sirens she'd discussed with him. *How* he knew about these river nymphs—now *that* would be an interesting topic for discussion.

"I was not aware that the Thames had resident nymphs," she said—remarkably calmly, she thought.

"All of Britain's rivers have them. They only become of concern when the river is navigable. There is a crown officer whose duty it is to"—he paused—"to maintain cordial relations with the inhabitants of rivers upon which human commerce takes place, most specifically the Thames. If the Thames nymphs are happy, it seems their sisters in other rivers are as well. With the occasional exception, of course."

"Really? Which officer is that?" She examined him carefully; from the lack of a certain look in his eye, she was reasonably certain he was not hoaxing her. Did the Lady Patronesses know about this? There were a number of crown officials whose duties and titles went back hundreds of years, the reasons for their existence now almost lost in history. Perhaps this was one of those.

"It's not one you'll have heard of. The royal office of the King's Maintenancer of the Tamesian Potamides is not frequently discussed, for obvious reasons."

The King's—heavens, that was a mouthful. "How do you know about it, then?"

"My grandfather held it under George II. It's not a sinecure as are some of the other old offices. The King's Maintenancer is an envoy. He is supposed to meet with the Thames nymphs sometime in early spring and negotiate an annual tribute to avert excessive spring flooding and guarantee human safety on the rivers for the year. Within reason, of course. If some drunken lout falls off a bridge on his way home from the pub and drowns, that's his affair. But the nymphs promise not to prey on humans who happen to be on or near a river, minding their own business." His eyes grew distant. "Grandfather took me to a meeting with them on one occasion when I was a boy."

Annabel tried not to think of nymphs preying on people on the river. "That must have been interesting."

"Quite, as they took a fancy to me and wanted to keep me as part of the annual settlement that year."

They were passing another group of boys at that moment, or Annabel would have demanded a further account of that meeting. But just now there were more immediate matters to discuss. "And you think that what the river did just now is a sign that something is upsetting the river nymphs?"

"I don't know. I worry that it might be."

"Might the present, er, Maintenancer not be fulfilling his office properly? Who is he, anyway? Or are you allowed to know?"

"The House of Lords is aware of the King's Maintenancer and what he does, since he's traditionally drawn from our ranks. The present incumbent is Lord Rossing."

Rossing...when had she run across that name recently? Then she remembered. "I saw him not so long ago—at the Summer Exhibition with Lord Glenrick." And he'd not looked pleased at her and Eliza's interruption of their *tête-à-tête*. "What can be done if he's not properly fulfilling his duties?"

"I don't know. It's never happened before." His voice had gone oddly flat.

"Why should a crown officer not do his job, anyway?"

Lord Quinceton did not reply for a long moment. At last he said, "That is a very good question."

They hurried along the path, overtaking several groups of boys and other holiday makers, including her parents. Approaching them, Annabel was struck by how content they looked. Mama's face, just visible past the edge of her parasol as she turned her head to say something to Papa, wore a sunny smile; Papa's responding laugh as he patted her hand resting on his arm was warm and happy. It had always been so between them, no matter how much Papa pretended to bluster and Mama to tease him in return, and below it was a bedrock of affection and devotion that Annabel couldn't help envying. Perhaps it was because they were closer in age than she and Freddy had been and had more in common...or perhaps it was simply that Freddy had not wanted such a relationship with her.

She touched Papa's sleeve as she and Lord Quinceton drew even with them. "Dawdlers," she said, wrinkling her nose at him.

"*Slow and steady wins the race*, minx," he said cheerfully.

"*The race is to the swift,*" Mama intoned.

Papa frowned. "I don't think that's how that one originally goes, m'dear, although I can't help suspecting you've got the right end of it. Do you see how it goes with me, sir?" he said to Lord Quinceton. "I am beleaguered from all sides. Beleaguered, I say!"

Lord Quinceton inclined his head. "I have heard it said, sir, that what is sauce for the goose is sauce for the gander."

Annabel was startled into laughing out loud. "Oh, Papa, he has you there!"

"Hmmph. So much for masculine solidarity in the face of feminine onslaught," Papa replied in a grumpy tone, but his eyes were twinkling. "Why are you two in such a hurry?" he added as Lord Quinceton led her past them.

"Oh—we, er, need to keep Martin from eating all the food before we get there. We will see you shortly," Annabel called over her shoulder.

"Leave them be, George," Mama said. "Four would definitely be a crowd."

"Oh ho! Sits the wind in that corner?" Papa said, and then they were too far behind for any further conversation to be heard, thank heavens. Oh, Mama—was she so eager to see her younger daughter remarried that she saw potential suitors in every man Annabel chanced to speak with? If only she could convince herself that Lord Quinceton had not heard that bit of conversation…but she knew too well how observant he was—

A glance to the side quickly banished any thoughts of Mama and suitors: the river had grown darker, the water grayer and more turbulent even in the golden light of late afternoon. "Look," she said quietly to Lord Quinceton.

He was already looking. "Damnation. We should have taken my curricle after all."

Annabel did not care for the sound of that in the least. "Wouldn't it be better to wait for the boats to come into view? At least we could watch for them and help in case the nymphs—in case something happens."

"And help how, with no boat of our own? Can you swim, Fellbridge?"

"I wish I could!"

He smiled. "Perhaps I shall teach you one day. But in the meanwhile, I think it behooves us to hurry to the field. If there is to be a contretemps with the Potamides over their missing tribute, I expect they'll want to hold it where it will likely have the largest audience." His step quickened; Annabel grimly clung to his arm and resolved to keep up with him if it killed her.

She had not had time to become more than a little out of breath when the sound of thudding hooves could be heard from behind them. To her surprise, rather than withdrawing to the side to allow the approaching horsemen to pass, Lord Quinceton turned and stood firm in the middle of the path.

A pair of horses so large and broad that their usual occupation must have involved drawing a plow soon cantered into view, their gait majestic if no faster than a trot would have been in a lesser beast. One of their riders, a husky Eton sixth-former, shouted "Whoa, then," when he saw them standing in the path, and drew rein.

"I say," his red-haired companion began, as his lumbering steed finally halted just a few feet away. "It's really rather bad form to be blocking the path in such a fashion."

"My apologies for troubling you, but I should be greatly obliged if you would lend me your horse," Lord Quinceton replied calmly.

"What?" The boy goggled at him.

"Your horse. It is vital that I get to the field without delay. Quite possibly a matter of life and death."

Annabel gasped.

The red-haired boy sneered. "Oh, really? And why, precisely, should I believe that? What do you think this is, Montem—only you're demanding people's cattle instead of their money?"

"No. I always thought Montem was a silly custom."

But the husky boy prodded his friend. "The lady seems to think it's serious," he said, gesturing at

Annabel. "If I may ask, sir, who are you, and what guarantee can you give us that you won't, er, steal our horses? They're not ours, you see, and perhaps we were a trifle out-of-hand to have borrowed them without the farmer saying in so many words that we could—"

Lord Quinceton reached into a pocket, then handed his card up to the boy. "And I have no intention of making off with your horse. You shall ride with me and reclaim it at the field as soon as we both arrive there."

The boy looked at the card and whistled. "Beg pardon, my lord. If it's as you say—you can take Diablo here, and I'll go with Gerrold. There's no saddle, I'm afraid." He slid off the horse—it was a long way down—adjusted the blanket, and handed over the reins. "Here, I'll give you a leg up."

"A plow horse named Diablo. Why am I not surprised?" Lord Quinceton said, making use of the boy's offered hands as a step and heaving himself astride the enormous animal. Diablo turned its head and surveyed them with an air of gentle surprise. "What's his friend's name?"

"Lucifer. The farmer has a sense of humor." The boy grinned.

"See here, Watts!" The red-haired boy's complexion was fast rivaling his locks in hue. "You can't just hand over one of our—"

"Stow it, Gerrold. If it would help, sir, we can ride ahead and clear the path for you—although how I'll get up on Lucifer without a mounting block is an interesting ques—"

"Excuse me." Annabel stepped forward.

"Er, ma'am?" The husky boy started, as if he'd

forgotten she was there.

"Lord Quinceton, do you actually intend to leave me here while you ride off to rescue *my* son?" Annabel demanded.

Lord Quinceton looked down at her, one eyebrow raised. "Can't stand to miss the action, Fellbridge?"

"Why, you—you—"

"Mr. Watts, would you be so kind as to assist Lady Fellbridge? Between us we can probably hoist her up onto this block of marble you call a horse."

Annabel suddenly remembered that a bronze muslin walking dress and half-boots were not appropriate riding attire, but it was too late to change her mind: young Watts, blushing violently, mumbled, "If you'll forgive me, ma'am," and caught her round the waist. She gamely jumped to add her own momentum to his lifting and felt Lord Quinceton's hands catch her up under the arms from behind at the same time—and suddenly she was seated sideways on Diablo's broad back. The small crowd of spectators who had come up behind them and gathered on the path to watch their doings cheered.

"You'll have to hold on to me, Fellbridge," Lord Quinceton said, glancing back at her over his shoulder. "I don't intend to go at a sedate walk."

Annabel thought of the horse's lumbering canter. Why had she thought this would be a good idea? It was too late to rethink her actions, however, so she slid her arms awkwardly around his middle. "What is the thing that boy said?" she asked. "Mountain, I think?"

"Montem. It's a quaint Eton custom that would get anyone else hanged for highway robbery. The boys have *carte blanche* on Montem Day—it's only done once every three years, now—to stop carriages on the Bath road and demand a fee for continued passage."

Good heavens! "Why, whatever for?"

"For the benefit of the Senior Colleger moving on to Cambridge, to help with expenses."

"What an odd custom."

She felt him shrug. "Eton has a lot of those. It started out as some sort of initiation rite for new boys, I believe. Lord knows why it changed."

"Hi, are we off?" Watts had managed to scramble up behind Gerrold on Lucifer, neither of whom seemed sanguine about the idea. "Tally ho and all that!"

Lucifer shook his head as if exasperated and commenced an amble, then broke into a thunderous trot at the boys' urging. "We'll clear the path, sir," Watts called back to them. "See you soon!"

Diablo, seeing his companion dashing off— relatively speaking—into parts unknown, followed suit, and Annabel's tentative hold on Lord Quinceton quickly tightened lest she be tossed ignominiously from her precarious sideways perch.

For some minutes she did nothing but hang on. But as she eventually grew used to their movement down the narrow river path, she was able to consider her position in relation to Lord Quinceton. It was an odd sensation to have her arms around him; she had embraced no other man to whom she was not closely related but Freddy. The difference between them was a revelation: Freddy had been more than a little podgy around the middle—a great deal more, in fact—while Lord Quinceton was all strength, with no softness or superfluous flesh. Yet there was a suppleness to him as well that was fascinating—she could feel it as he moved in response to the horse's gait. The result of all the time he reportedly spent fencing at Angelo's, perhaps? Why had no one told her that embracing a man could be such a delicious experience, physically speaking?

She rested her cheek against his back and nestled closer for several more minutes, the better to feel him...then jerked her head upright again in mortification. What was she doing? Would he think she was *hugging* him, rather than just hanging on for dear life?

"Are you still in one piece, Fellbridge?"

"I'm quite well, thank you."

"Do be careful. It would be most inconvenient to have you fall off."

She snorted. "I would be devastated to inconvenience you, my lord."

"Would you? I shall have to remember that." There was a smile in his voice.

"It would serve you right if I squeezed so firmly that you couldn't breathe!"

"A challenge! Do your worst, madam."

"Very well, I will!" She pressed more firmly against his back, stretched her arms as far as they would go around him, and squeezed with all her might.

He laughed. "Is that the best you can do? Behold, I still breathe."

"It's not a fair contest! I can't get a proper grip on you, sitting sideways in this fashion."

"Hmm, true. Very well; when we have restored Diablo to his erstwhile guardians, you shall try again to squeeze the breath from me from whatever vantage point you please."

Annabel started to answer, but a recollection of what such a contest might involve sent a flood of color into her face. "You are quite ridiculous, sir. That is not necessary."

"Coward," he said amiably. "The offer stands. Ah, I believe we're nearly there."

Chapter Three

"Here we are!" Watts called back to them a moment later, unconsciously echoing Lord Quinceton.

"Here" was another green field overlooking the river, a-bask in the golden sun of late afternoon. Unlike the Brocas, this field had sprouted little clusters of folding chairs and tables where picnics had been set up by bored-looking footmen; a few early spectators had already broken out the champagne and sandwiches. On the far side of the grassy expanse, a crowd of boys clustered around something that she couldn't quite see. And as for the river, which Annabel had been facing away from on their ride on Diablo...it still flowed placidly by, empty of boats. But there was a sense of stirring below its surface, as if the current were running more swiftly than usual.

Watts and Gerrold had already dismounted, and Watts came hurrying to them. "Help you down, ma'am?" he asked.

With his assistance, Annabel slid off Diablo's

broad back. For a moment she missed the security of the sensation of Lord Quinceton's body against hers —but that was foolishness. And anyway, she should be thinking of Will and the river nymphs, not Lord Quinceton's body.

"All right, Fellbridge?" Lord Quinceton asked her, sliding off the horse in turn.

"Very well, thank you." Well, mostly; whilst she had survived the ride unscathed, her dress had not. Diablo had evidently not had a bath in the recent past. Oh dear, Winters would scold!

He nodded, handed the reins to Watts with a curt "thank you," and strode toward the river.

"Ma'am, if I may..." Watts began shyly. "Er, what was the matter of life and death?"

"I expect you'll know shortly," Annabel said. The river was growing darker even as they spoke, although no boats were yet in sight.

Watts followed her glance, and his eyes widened. "Good Lord! What's up with that? Say, Gerrold! Gerrold! Look!" He hurried toward his friend, towing Diablo behind him like an equine barge.

Annabel began to follow Lord Quinceton to the river's edge, but a chance glance at the crowd of boys across the field halted her: a momentary thinning revealed a glimpse of a table and a flaming torch.

"Martin?" she breathed. It had to be—but what had the boy been up to now? Was this the—the what-ever-it-was that he had planned in honor of the king's birthday? Somehow, he'd never told her precisely what it was he intended...

With one more glance at Lord Quinceton and the still boat-free river, she began to make her way to the crowd of boys. With any luck she could find out what Martin was up to before she needed to be on hand to help Will—if she could.

As she approached the crowd, she caught more glimpses of the planks atop the trestles that Martin had loaded into her carriage. The makeshift tables were covered with something; now and again she saw a basket, a platter, a bowl—

The table was groaning with food. Dodging and weaving between happily munching boys, Annabel saw platters of sandwiches of all descriptions, from dainty watercress to hearty spiced ham; piles of Scotch eggs in their golden breadcrumb coats; turn-overs and pasties in profusion; every conceivable kind of biscuit—and cakes, dozens of cakes, including some iced a delicate pink that looked very familiar...as did the platter on which they sat—

And behind the table stood Martin, flanked by two of his friends. The three of them were accepting coins from the crowd and making change with expert speed. Good heavens, they were *selling* all this food... some of which had come from the picnic hampers she and Mama had brought. But where had the rest of it come from? And just why was Martin selling it?

"Martin Chalfont!" she called, in a voice she knew her son would hear...and understand.

The crowd of boys froze and fell silent. Evidently they understood that tone as well.

Martin's eyes grew very large—and then his face melted into a parent-cajoling smile that she was far too familiar with. She finished pushing through the crowd and came to a halt in front of him.

"I do believe an explanation is in order," she said—which she thought showed almost Olympian restraint.

Martin didn't blink. Freddy, who had been a dreadful card player, would have been proud. "Why, Mama! What a—a surprise! I didn't expect to see you so soon."

"Clearly not." She surveyed the table. "I think that you and I must have a talk."

"Er, can't it wait? I'm monstrous busy—"

"*Now*," Annabel said, stepping around the table and firmly grasping her son by the elbow.

"See to the table, men!" Martin called over his shoulder as she propelled him some distance from the crowd. When they were mostly out of hearing distance, she fixed him with a stern look.

"Now, Martin, what is going on here? Is this why you were so anxious for your grandmother and me to bring large picnics? So you could sell it to the other boys?"

Martin fixed his guileless blue eyes on hers. "Not...entirely. And it wasn't just you and Gran—I swear!"

"I had guessed that, looking at that table."

"All our friends agreed to help. We've got at least a dozen hampers!" He looked up at her, clearly expecting praise.

He didn't get it. "Has it not occurred to you that the providers of those hampers might be just a little put out when they find their picnics have been sold to a horde of hungry boys? Martin, you've stolen their food from them—and worse, are selling their belongings for profit—"

"Not for *profit*, Mama!" he interjected, all outraged dignity.

"No? Then what is it for?"

He looked down at his feet. "For Gus."

"For…Gus?" Had she heard him correctly? "But why?"

Martin straightened his shoulders and left off looking at his feet. There was no cajolery in his expression now. "Gus told us about what he did with your Almack's vouchers when he came home with us and how bad he felt that he'd got you in trouble with the other ladies. He said he couldn't keep that money he'd made because it was wrongfully acquired—" He broke off and asked, "Did he *really* make seven hundred guineas?"

"Yes, he did."

"By Jove!" He gave an admiring whistle. "Our Gus did that?"

"Martin, what did Gus do with the money?" Annabel demanded.

"Oh, he sent it to the Exploration Society or someplace like that." He shrugged. "He said that giving it to a worthy cause was the best thing he could do to make up for what he did."

Tears started in Annabel's eyes. Oh, the gallant child!

But Martin hadn't finished. "We knew he was back in the suds as far as paying his fees here. So we decided to do something to help him, and got this brilliant idea. *I* thought of it," he added modestly. "It's a sort of Montem—it's a special Eton thing—"

"I know what Montem is."

"You do?" Martin regarded her equal amounts of respect and dismay. "But you're a—a *mother*. You're not supposed to know that sort of thing!"

"You'd be surprised, dear." She didn't think it necessary to add that she'd just come by the knowledge a half-hour ago. "Go on."

"Well, we thought we'd have our own Montem to raise money for Gus. Sort of," he added, after a moment's thought. "It's not exactly the same—"

A shout from the direction of the river, followed by several more exclamations and cries of distress, reminded Annabel that the child before her was not the only one of her sons in trouble that afternoon. Her throat tightened. Where was Lord Quinceton? And where was Will? Had the boats begun to arrive ...along with angry river nymphs? She turned to scan the riverbank, but it was crowded with arriving spectators, all staring intently at the river. What was happening down there?

"What was that?" Martin followed her gaze. "Are the boats here? Are they having a bumping-race? Brilliant!" He started for the river.

Annabel caught him by the back of his jacket. "I don't know what is happening, but you're staying here. I'm not done with you—or rather, your grandfather won't be, when he finds his picnic has been eaten from under him."

For the first time, Martin looked apprehensive. "Er, I could set aside a plate or two..."

"That might help," Annabel said over her shoulder. She gave him a little push toward his table and turned back to the river. Bother it, she should have known Martin was up to something back at the Brocas—but how could she be angry with him for wanting to help his friend? Him and Will—oh, why had she not insisted Will leave his boat when that first wave had nearly swamped it?

She hadn't gone more than a few steps before she heard someone call, "Annabel! There you are!" Maria Sefton was picking her way across the field toward her.

"Maria!" She'd forgotten that the Seftons were here today. Oh, thank goodness there was another Lady Patroness on hand! Perhaps Maria spoke whatever language the nymphs did and could plead with them not to hurt the boys in the boats.

Maria grasped her arm as they met. "I do wish fields didn't have to be so tussocky. It's quite impossible to walk across one without turning an ankle. Annabel, I'm afraid we have a rather unpleasant mess to deal with—"

"The river nymphs—I know."

Maria looked surprised. "You do?"

"Well, it's what Lord Quinceton thinks is going on. He suspects they've not received their tribute this spring and are showing their anger."

"Ah." Maria nodded. "I should have remembered he would know about them. What I wish to know is *why* they haven't received it, if that is indeed what is wrong. We shall certainly have to bring this up at tomorrow's meeting. Where is Quin, anyway?"

"By the river, last I saw him." Annabel took Maria's arm and started to steer her toward the riverbank. She spotted Lord Quinceton amid a crowd close to the water's edge, with young Messrs. Watts and Gerrold beside him, looking excited.

"I wondered what had become of you," he said as Annabel finished dodging and weaving through the crowd and reached his side. "Lady Sefton," he added, nodding to Maria.

"My other son required my attention. It seems he's commandeered half the picnics in the field and is selling them off to hungry schoolboys. No wonder he wanted to be certain that I brought plenty of his favorite iced cakes." She was amazed at how even her voice was.

"Enterprising fellow." He smiled, but his gaze never left the river.

Annabel took in the roiling surface of the quick-flowing water and shivered. "I heard a shout a few minutes ago...?"

"Just a brief water-spout. For our entertainment, I suspect. Don't worry, the boats aren't here yet, although I suspect they soon will be."

"Can't we do something before that?" Two enormous waves impossibly approached each other from opposite directions and collided as if they were adversarial mountains; Annabel winced at the spray that spumed twenty feet in the air.

"Until the authors of this commotion choose to present themselves, I can't think of anything."

"Do you know what's causing this, sir?" Watts said. "I've never seen the river—er—behave in this manner."

"No, you wouldn't have," Lord Quinceton said absently. "Ah—is that—?"

The rest of his words were drowned in a collective rumble from the crowd around them as the first of the boats came gliding into view—although gliding was perhaps not the most apt description of its action. The surface of the Thames looked positively oceanic now, and the bow of the boat pitched up and down as the boys tried to maintain the rhythm of their strokes in the face of the waves. A second boat followed them closely, then a third and a fourth, and more.

As their boats approached the field, the rowers in each stopped rowing, lifted their oars from the water, and raised them till they were vertical, perpendicular to the water—or at least as vertical as they could manage under the circumstances.

"Good God," Watts gasped. "They're not going to attempt the salute, are they?"

"They'll be over the side in no time. We'll be fishing bodies out of the river till Election Day!" Gerrold answered with ghoulish glee.

"What salute?" Annabel demanded.

"It's what they do at the end of the procession—all the boys raise their oars and stand up in their boats to salute the king," Watts explained. "But not today—surely not when the river's in such a state—"

The boys in the first boat began, as one, to stand. It would have been an impressive sight—the straight young forms, the small forest of oars—but a malevolently-aimed wave did just as Gerrold predicted and upset their boat. Boys and oars were launched into the angry waters amid a great, oddly greenish fountain of spray.

Annabel cried out. She was not alone; the spectators lining the banks were in an uproar, but their shouts were not louder than the boys' own cries of distress.

"Come on, Gerrold!" Watts shouted, stripping off his jacket and kicking off his shoes before diving for the river. At least a dozen older boys did the same, while others waded in more slowly to form human chains reaching out to the middle of the river. Then another boat went over, and another—and to her horror, Annabel realized that the third boat contained her son.

"Will!" she cried.

"Where?" Lord Quinceton asked sharply.

All she could do was mutely point toward the river; all the breath seemed to have been sucked from her chest.

Watts and Gerrold and the boys who could swim had almost reached the floundering occupants of the first boat, half of whom had managed to catch hold of the hull of their overturned craft. But now other figures were visible in the water with them—figures almost but not quite human in shape, with long arms and disproportionately short legs ending in flat, elongated feet that could be seen as they scythed through the water. And most inhuman in color; their skin was a greenish light brown, and their trailing hair very definitely green. Annabel watched, horrified, as they converged on the next arriving boat and neatly tipped it over. Others of the creatures were swimming toward the boys clinging to their boats, their long, dark eyes narrowed with angry intent.

"Well, that more or less answers our questions." Maria's voice was hollow.

Annabel leaned closer to her. "What can we do?" she whispered urgently. "That is—you and I?"

Maria shook her head. "I don't know. I'm of no help here; I've no idea what language they speak. Is there anything you could do with your shadows?"

Annabel thought furiously. Covering this stretch of the river with shadow wouldn't accomplish anything more than to make it difficult to see what was happening and inspire panic. Nor would it hamper the angry nymphs at all—they would simply stay under water. She could make ropes of shadow to help the rescuers reach the boys, but unless she kept hold of each one, they would quickly dissolve in the golden sunlight slanting down on the river.

"No," she said, and heard her voice catch on a sob. "There's nothing we can do."

The nymphs had almost reached the first boat. One of them rose up in the water and shouted, "If we don't get our due, then we'll have to take you! A good dinner you'll make us all!" A boy shrieked and almost lost his grip on the overturned hull; something appeared to be tugging on his legs beneath the roiling surface of the water.

Annabel's knees all at once no longer seemed capable of supporting her weight. Will! Oh God, her poor darling boy!

But a hand, warm and firm, grasped her arm, keeping her from collapsing. "Bear up, Fellbridge!" Lord Quinceton said. "The boys aren't being hurt— the nymphs are just trying to frighten them. See? None have gone under."

"They're succeeding remarkably well at frightening me!" she managed to mutter, and willed herself to remain standing until her legs capitulated and agreed to behave themselves. Was that Will there, near that boat? So much obscured her view—floundering boys, dropped oars, and the angry gray-green of the water itself. "If they are hungry, we could have invited them to our picnic—except Martin has likely sold off all the iced cakes and sandwiches—"

Lord Quinceton's hand on her arm tightened. "That's it!"

"What?"

He released her arm and grabbed her hand. "Come on. It's worth a try."

"What is?" she demanded, then squeaked in surprise as he started to hurry away, still gripping her hand.

"Where are you going?" Maria called after them.

"To do something about this," Lord Quinceton replied over his shoulder as he threaded a path through the crowd. "Where is your son and his table?" he said more quietly to Annabel.

"Over there, at the far side of the field. Near the trees." Annabel was getting a stitch in her side, her hat felt in imminent danger of flying off her head, and Maria's hated tussocks seemed to be catching at her toes. "What—are you going—to do?" she puffed.

"Precisely what you said. Invite the nymphs to our picnic."

It was on the tip of her tongue to accuse him of lunacy, but she refrained. "Do you really—think that will work?"

"It will be a sign of respect. Right now I suspect it's mostly the Potamides' pride that's been hurt. If we can soothe that now, it will give us time to rescue the boys and negotiate their proper tribute—and find out why they haven't already received it," he added grimly.

Just before Annabel's wind completely gave out, they arrived at Martin's table. The crowd around it had thinned somewhat; many boys had been drawn away by the commotion on the water, but a dozen or so still milled around. They drew back as she and Lord Quinceton strode into their midst.

"Listen here, dry bobs!" Lord Quinceton shouted. Annabel wondered how he had any breath left to do so. "Where's Martin Chalfont!"

"Here, sir." Behind the table, which still held a bounteous number of cakes, tarts, and sandwiches,

Martin drew himself straight. But Annabel could see the apprehension in his eyes as he looked at Lord Quinceton, who suddenly appeared very tall and authoritative indeed.

"We need this food down at the river. There's a problem there, and this might solve it. You—all of you"—he waved a hand at the nearest boys—"grab a plate and follow me."

"Hey!" Martin ran around the side of the table, waving his arms. "You can't do that! We're raising money for Gus! They'll kick him out if he can't pay his fees!"

"Would you rather raise money for Gus or save your brother's life?" Lord Quinceton asked. "Don't worry about Master Blackburn. He has already been provided for. Now help us carry this down to the water."

"My brother?" Martin gulped and looked scared. "What's wrong with Will?"

"Nothing for now, but I can't promise it will remain that way unless we hurry." He swept them all with a stern look. "I'm relying on your assistance. Now go!"

He'd hit just the right note; Martin's fear turned to determination. "Come on then, men!" He grabbed a platter.

Annabel picked up a plate of sandwiches. "Master Blackburn has been *what*?" she said to Lord Quinceton. How did he know anything about Gus?

He didn't reply but seized a platter of her iced cakes and turned toward the river. She and Martin and the rest of the boys fell into place behind him.

"Is Will hurt?" Martin asked in a small voice.

"No, of *course* not," Annabel said, as firmly as

she could.

"But your friend said—"

"Will is not hurt," she repeated. "But he is in trouble, as are all the other boys who were on boats."

"What will the food do to help them?"

Annabel hesitated. "It's...difficult to explain. Just do what Lord Quinceton says when we get to the river. Promise?"

He nodded vigorously, but a small sigh escaped him. "And we were going on dreadfully well, too. I'll bet we would have sold everything by the time we needed to go back to the Brocas for the fireworks."

At the river's edge, pandemonium reigned. A group of sodden boys, rescued by the swimmers, huddled on the bank; alas, Will was not among their number. Rescuers still braved the seething river and the nymphs, dragging boys to shore, but the waters were almost too turbulent for them to risk further forays. The spectators shouted and waved, boys ran about doing the same, and the various horses (and a cow or two) borrowed for the occasion milled skittishly about the field, forgotten by their riders in the excitement.

Lord Quinceton was standing by the water's edge, his feet bare, being helped out of his coat by a sodden Watts. A pair of wide-eyed younger boys looked on, holding his hat and the platter of cakes.

"There you are, Fellbridge," he said conversationally as she came up to him. "Would you be so good as to stand guard over my boots for a quarter-hour?"

"Your *what*?" Annabel handed her plate of sandwiches to Martin. "Good heavens, you aren't planning to *swim* out to the nymphs, are you?"

"I rather hope it doesn't come to that, but I shall have to wade out some ways, I expect, if I'm going to be able to speak with them. I'm afraid I must impose upon you to take charge of my hat and coat as well."

"Are you quite certain about this, sir?" Watts asked, trying not to drip on her as he handed Annabel the coat. "I can swim out there again if you need me to."

"Thank you, but I'm quite certain." Lord Quinceton untied his cravat, gave it to Annabel, and began to unbutton his waistcoat.

"But what are you going to *do*?"

"Not a great deal. My intention is to walk out no farther than I need to in order to speak with the nymphs and offer them something to eat."

"Something to eat?" Watts looked astonished.

Lord Quinceton smiled. "They have a tremendous appetite for sweets. I hope that a few plates of cakes and biscuits will distract them from harassing the boys and allow us to get them all safely ashore."

"Will you rescue my brother, sir?" Martin was pale, gazing out at the shrieking boys clinging to their boats.

Lord Quinceton shrugged out of his waistcoat and handed it to Annabel. "I will do my best to make sure *all* the boys are safe," he said seriously. "But if the opportunity arises, I shall certainly do whatever is in my power for your brother."

Martin nodded.

Annabel took the waistcoat. His clothes were warm in her arms, and she resisted the urge to hug them to her chest for reassurance. "Be careful, Quin," she said quietly.

He glanced at her from where he stood ankle-deep in the water, a slight smile quirking the corners of his mouth. "I will." Then he took the plate of Martin's favorite iced cakes—Martin watched them go with a regretful little sigh—and walked slowly into the Thames.

Chapter Four

Annabel scarcely dared breathe as Lord Quinceton waded deeper into the turbulent water, pausing now and then to steady his footing.

"If he slips, ma'am, I'll be out there in a trice," Watts assured her.

She forced her grip on Lord Quinceton's clothing in her arms to relax. "I don't expect that he will."

"No, I don't either." Watts hesitated, then blurted, "Does he really believe that giving those creatures *cakes* will stop them?"

"He wouldn't be doing this if he didn't." The water was to his chest, and he was now carrying the platter of Mrs. Dailey's cakes over his head. She was relieved to see him halt and steady himself before opening his mouth.

"Potamides of the Thames, I bear you greetings!" he shouted.

For a moment, nothing changed: the boys' shrieks still mixed with the howls and laughter of the nymphs swimming wildly about them while the thrashing snake that was the river continued to roil in its channel.

Suddenly a head—no, two heads, broke the surface a few yards from Lord Quinceton. They regarded him in silence, circling him as if examining a sculpture in an exhibition. He bore their scrutiny calmly. Then one of them rose up in the water—how was she able to do that?—and gave forth a string of strange, liquid-sounding syllables in a voice that somehow managed to be heard over the general cacophony. The other nymphs fell silent, and even the boys' cries grew quieter.

The nymph who'd silenced the rest with her call circled Lord Quinceton again. "I have seen you before," she said, halting in front of him. Even from shore Annabel could see that, whilst her face had two eyes, a nose of sorts, and a mouth, it was not human. "Many years ago."

Lord Quinceton somehow managed to bow while still holding the tray over his head. "My grandfather had the honor of serving as His late Majesty's envoy to your court. I accompanied him once to a meeting."

"Good Lord," Gerrold said, a little too loudly. "Is she their queen?"

"Ssh!" Annabel hissed. Lord Quinceton had managed, at least temporarily, to engage the nymphs and bring a halt to the dangerous turmoil in the river. He did not need distractions.

"Ah, that was your grandfather?" The nymph nodded slowly, then grinned. Her teeth were very white—and very pointed. "I do remember you. You were just an elver then."

He smiled back. "I compliment your memory, madam. I was indeed very small."

"And very delicious-looking. We wanted to keep you, as I recall." Her grin vanished abruptly. "Would you care to tell me why we should not keep these?" She lifted a webbed hand and gestured at the boys in the river. "Why have we not received our customary gifts? Is your grandfather ill?"

"My revered grandfather is many years gone, alas. I don't know why you haven't yet received a visit from the King's present representative, but I intend to find out. In the meanwhile, I hope you will condescend to accept a smaller gift as an earnest of our good will." He held out the tray.

The nymph frowned. "I don't see why we should, when we already have *them* to eat."

"You do, madam. But I venture to say that you might find these even more palatable—and that it is not behavior worthy of a queen to eat children in their mothers' sight." He indicated Annabel standing on the bank. She tried to look both deferential and anxious.

The nymph's eyes widened. "What? *All* these are her sons?"

Lord Quinceton opened his mouth, then closed it again and shot Annabel an amused look over his shoulder. "Indeed they are, madam."

"*What?*" Annabel almost dropped his clothes in the river. "They're not all mi—"

"Ssh," Watts hissed.

"Well." The nymph was clearly impressed. She nodded to Annabel. "You are a good mother. I didn't know humans bore such litters."

She reached out and took a cake from the

platter that Lord Quinceton offered her, sniffed at it suspiciously, then took a bite. "Oh," she said, and crammed the rest of it in her mouth. She gestured to her hitherto silent companion to take the platter, grabbing another cake as it passed her. "Do you have more of these?" she asked through a mouthful.

"More of those, and others as well," Lord Quinceton said. "If you will wait a moment, madam, I will have them brought out."

He turned and waded his way back to shore. "Get whoever is brave enough and start bringing those platters out," he said to Watts as he took the plate of sandwiches from Martin. "But send the rest to keep bringing in the boys."

"Yes, sir." Watts darted away.

"I can't *believe* you told her these were all my children!" Annabel said through gritted teeth.

He grinned. "I can't help it if she misunderstood me. Besides, your, er, fecundity impressed the old girl enough to make her stop and try the cakes, rather than nibbling a first former. Please, stand back," he called in a louder voice. The spectators on the bank had started to crowd toward them. "This isn't over yet. Please allow the boys with plates through."

In a very few minutes, Watts had gathered a handful of older boys to wade out with the plates of dainties brought by Martin's "men" and offer them to the nymphs who now drew close. They snatched happily at the macaroons, the glazed fruit, the chicken sandwiches, the cheese-cakes and lemon tarts, exclaiming to each other in their strange, gurgling language, while behind them other boys systematically ferried their stranded schoolmates into shore. When Martin's supplies ran out, other picnic baskets were ransacked by willing onlookers to keep the nymphs happily munching until all the boys had been brought in to safety. Lord Quinceton stood in waist-deep water, directing traffic to and from shore, until the nymph's leader swam toward him. He joined her in deeper water.

"Your gift was a good one," she said, licking icing off her webbed fingers. Annabel thought she might have polished off the entire plate of cakes by herself; wouldn't her cook, Mrs. Dailey, be flattered to hear that the queen of the Thames river nymphs admired her baking? Not that she was going to tell her about this afternoon's events—the poor woman would probably have a spasm.

"I am delighted that it found favor with you, madam," Lord Quinceton said, nodding his head.

"Not that we don't expect our regular tribute," the nymph queen added. "I think I want another plate of these when your man comes to parley with us."

"You shall have them."

"Good." She fixed him with her dark, pupil-less eyes. "But it is not good that this happened. We will permit it to pass because of you. But I will expect to receive your man soon. And he will not be late next year, or things will not go well for humans on the Thames." There was a cold implacability in her voice that gave Annabel the chills.

"I understand, madam—and give you my word that I will discover why this has happened and remedy it."

The nymph regarded him a moment longer, then nodded. "I will accept your word." She looked behind her, then made a gesture accompanied by a string of words. Several nymphs disappeared beneath the river's surface; a few moments later, the overturned boats that had drifted downstream could be seen making their way back up the river, along with bundles of oars. Watts' friends who'd helped bring the plates to the nymphs went out to receive the returned boats and bring them in to the bank.

"Thank you for that, madam," Lord Quinceton said. "The boats are precious to the boys."

"Are they?" She shrugged. "I just didn't want them clogging up my river." She gave a short cry, and the rest of the nymphs vanished under the water. "I will expect my tribute soon," she said to Lord Quinceton. Then she too was gone.

Martin had barely moved from Annabel's side, apart from relaying plates of food. Now he fetched a deep sigh. "Those ladies took everyone's serving platters and plates," he said.

Annabel laughed shakily and gave him a one-armed hug. "They're welcome to them, so long as your brother is safe." Where was Will? Surely all the boys had been accounted for, or—

"Well, Fellbridge?" Lord Quinceton had waded in from the river.

Annabel blinked at him standing before her, his dripping shirt plastered to him, the wet linen revealing his firmly muscled arms and torso with damp, loving exactitude. Oh, *my*. A rush of hot color flood her cheeks. "Er—Lord Quinceton—"

"Would you care to try squeezing the breath from me now? I do believe we had a wager to settle on that subject." He held his arms out to her, his eyes belying the innocent tone in his voice.

"I beg your pardon," she snapped. "It was not a wager!"

"Wasn't it? My mistake," he said meekly.

"Mama!"

The well-loved voice made her forget everything but the fact that her son was safe. She looked wildly about her. "Will! I'm here!"

A moment later, Will had wormed his way through the chattering spectators around her and hurtled toward her, nearly knocking her over.

"Oh, darling!" She bent to embrace him, not caring that he was both sodden and trailing streamers of river-weed caught in his buttons.

"William, if you do not keep this about you, I am convinced you will catch your death in those wet clothes." Mama hurried up behind him and draped a lap rug from Annabel's carriage over his shoulders.

"*An ounce of prevention is worth a pound of cure*, my boy." Papa brought up the rear. "I say," he said cheerfully to Lord Quinceton. "I'd heard of the Thames nymphs, of course, but never more than half-believed they were real. Just thought the King's Maintenancer was another royal sinecure to be handed out."

Mama ignored him. "You too," she said, thrusting another lap rug at Lord Quinceton. "It would be a shame if the only man with the bottom to do anything about this disgraceful situation should succumb to an inflammation of the lungs."

"Yes, ma'am. Thank you, ma'am." Lord Quinceton meekly took the rug from her. Annabel felt an odd mixture of relief and regret as he draped it about his shoulders. "If Fellbridge can be convinced to part with my clothing, I promise I shall make myself respectable again as soon as I'm a little drier."

Annabel suddenly remembered that his coat, cravat, and waistcoat were still draped over her arm. She started to form a sharp retort, then met his eyes—and saw, above the teasing smile, that they held an expression of understanding...although understanding of what, she couldn't say. She mutely handed him his clothes, and to cover her confusion, embraced Will again.

"That was some quick thinking on your part, sir." Papa was still talking to Lord Quinceton. "Who knew they'd fancy a cake or two? Good thing you came prepared."

Mama coughed gently. Annabel opened her mouth to reply, but Martin spoke up. "He didn't bring all that food, sir. We did. Well," he added, after a moment's thought. "Us and the Sheltons and the Bowleses and the Beckets and—and a lot of others."

"The Beckets...?" Papa's face turned red. "Are you saying that you just fed those nymphs their picnics?"

Martin nodded. "And yours, too," he added.

He began to splutter. "Why, you larcenous young imp—"

"Don't be silly, George. It was either that or allow those creatures to eat your grandson," Mama said briskly. "Did you really want that?"

Annabel shuddered and hugged both Will and Martin.

"I saved back a little bit of our picnic," Martin said in a small voice.

"And besides, there's still the champagne," Mama added.

Papa brightened. "Is there? Then I suppose we

won't starve." He took Mama's arm and began to lead her back toward the field.

"Man does not live by wine alone," Lord Quinceton murmured in such a sanctimonious tone that Annabel was startled into a giggle.

Martin looked confused. "I thought it was, 'Man does not live by *bread* alone?'"

"It is," Will said. "Come on." He tugged his brother's arm, and they set out after their grandparents. "Did you save back any of Mrs. Dailey's cakes for us? I'm starving."

"He'll be over this in a trice, you know," Lord Quinceton commented as the boys broke into a run. "Do you wish to follow? I would offer you my arm but fear it is still wet."

Annabel looked at his proffered arm, which was indeed wet...and took it anyway. "I must thank you for having the wits to save my son, sir," she said, a little stiffly to cover her emotion. "Not to mention the rest of the boys."

"They weren't *my* wits. You were the one who made the suggestion to invite the nymphs to picnic with us; I merely recognized its utility."

"Then I thank you for that."

"No need for further thanks, Fellbridge." There was a smile in his voice. "You've already done so, and handsomely."

"I have?" Annabel frowned. "How? I don't—"

"Quinceton!"

A small man, dressed more in country squire than town fashion, was striding toward them, hat in hand. As they approached, he paused and bowed. "Sir Edward Simms, at your service, sir. We have met once or twice at White's."

Lord Quinceton made a politely non-committal reply, but the man was too intent on his mission to notice. "I had to thank you for what you did this afternoon, sir, facing down those hags. My son was in one of the boats and doesn't swim a lick. You were as cool as a cucumber out there, by God! Didn't so much as blink an eyelash!" He took Lord Quinceton's hand and wrung it. "My boy's alive and well, thanks to you. Wait till they hear about this at White's! You'll be stood your weight in toasts, I'll warrant—"

"No, I will most emphatically not," Lord Quinceton said, quietly but very clearly.

"What?" Sir Edward dropped his hand and began to bristle.

"If you feel the need to thank me, you may do so by *not* talking about what happened today, at White's or anywhere."

The man looked astonished. "But—why?"

"What happened here has...ramifications that are not readily apparent. Ramifications of concern to His Majesty's government. Today's events will be a matter of discussion at very high levels indeed; gossip about it will not be welcomed, nor will it help anyone involved." He fixed Sir Edward with a stern look. "So while I accept your thanks, I hope that any further discussion of the event on your part—and everyone else who witnessed it—comes to an end here and now."

Sir Edward gulped and nodded. "I—I understand, my lord. Not another word." He bowed again, awkwardly, and hurried away.

Lord Quinceton sighed. "I was afraid that would happen."

"You can scarcely blame him, can you? How

often does one see a river full of rampaging river nymphs threatening to eat the students of Eton?"

He smiled reluctantly. "Not very often, I'll grant you that. But this should not become the chief topic of conversation in London's clubs and ballrooms this coming week. It is far too delicate a matter."

She nodded. However, it would certainly be a topic of conversation in one London venue tomorrow: she and Maria would be informing the Lady Patronesses of the day's events.

He sighed again. "I can see I shall have to spend the rest of the afternoon talking to all the Sir Edwards here."

"I expect my father would help you. He loves to have an excuse to talk to people."

"Spoken like a dutiful daughter." He smiled at her sideways. "I am glad to see that you can speak lightly about the Potamides."

"I couldn't have a half-hour ago." Annabel couldn't repress a shudder.

"But you can now. You're a woman of eminently good sense as well as good looks...but I already knew that."

Annabel blushed.

"I have been thinking, daughter," Papa began, pouring himself another glass of champagne.

"Oh dear," Mama said under her breath.

"What have you been thinking, sir?" Annabel held out her glass for him to refill. She suspected she would need it.

They had found the table and chairs her footman John had put out for them, with cushions and her third-best linens and china, and nibbled through the food Martin had left, washing it down with liberal amounts of champagne. Annabel was grateful for that; whilst she could joke about the river nymphs, the thought of them still left a chill inside her that the champagne had gone only a little way toward banishing. Watts and Gerrold had joined them for a while, behaving like boys invited to their first grown-up party.

Lord Quinceton had indeed cajoled Papa into wandering about the picnicking groups, cautioning them not to discuss the river nymphs back in town. Lord Sefton had helped, and the other members of the House of Lords present had added their voices to theirs. With any luck, the story would not become the latest *on-dit*.

And now the three boys—for Gus had joined them—were running about the field shouting and carrying on with their friends. The sight of that did even more than the champagne to warm her.

Papa was evidently watching them too. "Those grandsons of mine. Look at them, running around as if they were heathen savages!" He gestured with his glass, slopping a little champagne onto the grass. "Back when I was a boy, we never did such a thing."

"Indeed not!" Mama said. "I believe you and your brothers ran about like *Christian* savages."

He looked down his nose at her. "As you were not there, madam, I do not understand how you can say such a thing."

"Your mother told me." She gave him her sweetest smile. "And Grandmother Shellingham would *never* lie. Besides, all work and no play makes Jack a dull boy."

Papa harrumphed. "Be that as it may…Annabel, those boys need a firm masculine hand to rein them in. Appropriating everyone's picnics without so much as a by-your-leave and selling them off! I don't care if it was for a good cause," he said as she opened her mouth to protest. "They should not have done it. It's high time you married again and gave those boys a father."

"Papa!" She had been *very* right to fortify herself with more champagne.

"Oh, George." Mama closed her eyes and winced as if she had the headache.

"I quite agree with you, sir," Lord Quinceton said.

"What!?" Annabel almost dropped her glass.

He gave her the blandest of looks. "I was merely agreeing that your sons would indeed benefit from frequent exposure to the good example of a wise, responsible older male."

Mama made a small, peculiar choking sound.

"Precisely!" Papa beamed at him.

"Oh?" Annabel narrowed her eyes at him. "And just which 'wise, responsible older male' would you suggest should be frequently exposed to my sons?"

"Why, their grandfather, of course. Who better to set a good example for the coming generation? Upon consideration, sir, you perhaps ought to consider setting aside the champagne. I'm not persuaded it sets the example to your grandsons that you'd wish."

Papa, who'd been draining his glass, coughed and sputtered. Mama pounded him on the back, not bothering to conceal her smile. "Pray inform me, sir," she said to Lord Quinceton, "whether you take more pleasure from quizzing my husband or my daughter."

He returned her smile. "At any other time, I would be pleased to oblige you, ma'am, but fear the answer would just get me into more trouble."

"Very likely," Annabel said darkly, but something in the twinkle in Lord Quinceton's eyes would not allow her to maintain her frown. She looked away, an unwilling smile tugging at the corners of her mouth.

Papa finally caught his breath and looked up at the darkening sky. "It's probably time we got back to the Brocas. They'll be starting the fireworks soon." The boys who had rowed, including Will, were already gathering at the river's edge near their boats, joking and jostling as if the day's earlier events had not happened.

"I am *not* walking this time," Mama said firmly.

"Of course not. We shall drive, of course." Annabel rose and gestured to John to begin to pack away their picnic, then waved to Martin. "It's time to go, if you would care for a ride to the Brocas," she called.

"Except there won't be any room for you, dear, if Martin and his friend come with us in the landau," Mama said as they began to stroll in the direction of the carriages. "So you shall have to go with Lord Quinceton."

"Just what I was thinking, ma'am," he agreed.

When had the pair of them become so thick? Annabel was about to ask why *she* didn't accompany him when Mama spoke again.

"Annabel, my love, your dress is quite ruined, you know," she said, surveying Annabel critically.

Annabel looked down at herself. If not sodden, her front was still damp and wrinkled from hugging the very wet Will—was that a stray bit of river-weed?—and her hem was definitely soaked from passing trays of cakes to Lord Quinceton and the others. She did not even want to know how much dust and dirt decorated the back of her skirt, courtesy of the fiery-footed Diablo. "Yes, it is," she said with a sigh. "Winters will be very cross with me."

"Can you blame her? That dress is beyond redemption, and I'll wager the poor thing probably never gets any of your cast-offs to sell because you two are so diligent about making your dresses over."

Annabel cringed. Did Mama have to say such things in front of Lord Quinceton? He knew she had to scrimp—everyone knew it—but to make an ann-ouncement of it was the outside of enough.

"Well, never mind," Mama continued. "I shall take you shopping for a new one tomorrow; your father will be occupied with showing off his new carriage."

"You don't have to do that—"

"Nonsense. I shall be at loose ends whilst he peacocks about Hyde Park with his friends." She ignored Papa's indignant protest. "Oh, but you have your Almack's meeting in the morning, don't you? Afterward, then. My mantua-maker will be delighted to see us."

"I have often thought, ma'am, that pink is a most advantageous color for your daughter," Lord Quinceton offered.

Mama stopped walking and examined Annabel

consideringly. "Yes, I do believe you are correct."

He paused as well. "Nothing too pale."

"Oh, no. Pale pink is far too insipid. Something darker, perhaps with an apricot tinge."

"Exactly as you say, Lady Shellingham."

"Or cinnamon. A cinnamon pink might look well."

"I think either would do admirably."

Annabel looked at the pair of them standing side by side and staring at her, nodding slowly and in such mutual understanding that she could not decide whether to laugh or shriek. "Are you two quite finished?"

"Annabel!" Mama pretended to look hurt. "We're only trying to *help*."

"Finished? Never, Fellbridge." Lord Quinceton offered her his arm to lead her to his curricle.

Chapter Five

Tuesday afternoon after the Fourth of June was cloudy, but no rain threatened Annabel and her mother as they strolled in Hyde Park, talking desultorily and smiling and waving whenever Papa went by in his new barouche. He'd had a different companion for each circuit; Mama applauded his efficiency in managing to show off to the maximum number of friends and acquaintances in the smallest amount of time.

"I knew he would begin to get impatient to return to his roses, no matter how excited he was about his carriage," she commented. "That's why I was anxious to get our shopping completed."

"Completed? We don't have five more milliners and three more glove shops to visit?"

"Don't be cheeky, dear," Mama said imperturbably. "I probably shan't have the opportunity to return to town until October, so I had to stock up. And there was that small matter of your dress."

Or rather, dress*es*. Upon her return from her

Almack's meeting yesterday, Annabel had found Mama closeted with Winters, the two of them resembling a pair of generals planning a protracted military campaign. Before she could do more than quickly use the water closet, Mama had whisked her off, clutching a list she and Winters had evidently made and which she wouldn't allow Annabel to see.

By late afternoon Annabel had been fitted for a new walking dress to replace the one she'd ruined the day before—as well as a carriage dress and two evening dresses. Three of the four were in shades of pink, as was the lace- and ribbon-trimmed satin dressing gown which Mama insisted upon buying her.

"Mama, I don't *need* all these," she whispered as Mama's mantua-maker, Mrs. Carpenter, happily wrote up the order.

"Yes, you do. Poor Winters will be chuffed to have something new to dress you in—you don't want to deny her that pleasure, do you?" Mama opened her eyes very wide.

Annabel sighed. "Mama, you're being manipulative. It's not fair."

"It's for a good cause, dear. Trust me."

If she were to be honest, Annabel could not help being a little pleased at Mama's gift—well, perhaps more than a little if honesty truly were to be respected. Who would not be at the thought of four lovely new dresses, plus two hats, two pairs of slippers dyed to match the evening gowns, and six new pairs of silk stockings? Precisely *why* Mama had insisted on all the pink was not a question she wanted to delve into too closely.

Mama consulted the watch pinned to her

bodice, then glanced behind them. "Hmm," she said.

"What is it? Did you have an appointment somewhere?"

"No, of course not. I was just thinking what a useful name Carpenter is for a mantua-maker. Only think—when French things are in fashion, she can become Madame Charpentier with very little trouble. Since the war is going so badly, I suppose that's why she's plain Mrs. Carpenter for now. Still, I think it's very clever of her."

"Marrying a man named Carpenter had nothing to do with it, I suppose." Mama could say the most marvelously ridiculous things sometimes. "However, I rather doubt there is a Mr. Carpenter unless his present abode is the churchyard. She's far too good a businesswoman to allow a husband to hover in the background. I will allow that perhaps her father was named Carpenter."

Mama's brows delicately knit themselves. "I hadn't considered that."

Annabel was about to reply, but a carriage slowing to match their pace distracted her. She looked up to see Lord Quinceton sweeping his hat off in salute. Unusually, a groom rode beside him.

"Good afternoon, Lady Shellingham. I passed your husband a few minutes ago, wearing an expression of the most becoming modesty as he drove his new barouche with Lord Wrayne beside him." He nodded to Annabel, eyebrows raised inquiringly. "Fellbridge, I see you are quite recovered, at least outwardly."

Mama stopped walking, forcing him to halt as well. "Why, Lord Quinceton, what a *surprise* to see you here!"

The unfurling of a small, suspicious thought made Annabel say, "Is it?"

Mama ignored her. "I am very glad to see you, sir. I was just noticing that I'm really quite fatigued and would prefer to return to our hotel, but I don't want to cut short Annabel's enjoyment of the day. I would be much obliged if you would take her up and permit your groom to wait with me until Lord Shellingham chances by again."

The suspicion transformed into a certainty. Good Lord, Mama had *planned* this. But how? She would have had to send Lord Quinceton a note arranging the meeting, and—

"Nothing would afford me greater pleasure, ma'am." He nodded to his groom.

"Mama, you are quite beyond anything," Annabel said. The groom leapt down and went to the horses' heads; Lord Quinceton leaned over and held out his hand to help her into the vacated seat. "And so are you, sir!" she added severely when she was seated beside him.

He tucked the lap robe over her. "I'll take that as a compliment."

"We'll see you at Grillon's at seven for dinner, dear," Mama said as he gathered up the reins again. "Have a lovely drive!"

Lord Quinceton was silent for a few moments as they eased into the flow of promenading carriages. "Your mother is a remarkable woman," he finally said.

"My mother should be *hanged*." Annabel was still seething.

He laughed. "Oh, come now, Fellbridge. Is it really all that bad? Just say the word, and I shall set you down at once." When she did not reply he added, "If it makes you feel any better, I dared not disregard her directions about meeting you this afternoon. She threatened to be *disappointed* in me."

That drew an unwilling smile from her. "It's just...embarrassing."

"It shouldn't be. She's so charming about it that I certainly don't mind. She has much more finesse than my mother when she tries her hand at the same game."

How did she not know his mother? "I don't believe I've ever met Lady Quinceton."

"That's because she's no longer Lady Quinceton. She married Lord Ballymena a few years after my father's death and moved to Ireland. She comes to England only rarely."

Was it only Annabel's imagination that she thought she heard him add, "Thank God!" under his breath? Before she could decide he said, "I fell in with your mother's plans so readily because I had hoped to have an opportunity to speak with you."

"On what topic?"

"The expected one, I suppose—what happened at Eton." He slowed his team a little and looked at her earnestly. "More specifically, the Potamides and the King's Maintenancer."

"What about them?"

"Just this: are you planning to 'investigate' them?"

"Goodness, no! Why should I want to do that?"

He frowned. "That won't fadge, ma'am. I know you too well. After what your son went through, I would expect you'd be preparing to—pardon my language—investigate the devil out of them."

"Well, I'm not." Oh, they certainly would be investigated—but not by her.

At yesterday's Lady Patronesses' meeting, Maria had acquainted everyone with the previous day's events at Eton, with Annabel supplying details. There had been smiles at Lord Quinceton's unusual but effective method of dealing with the immediate crisis as well as several expressions of surprise: Annabel was glad to see she wasn't the only one who hadn't known about the Potamides' existence.

No one had been amused, however, by the news that the king's appointed representative, Lord Rossing, was not performing his Maintenancing duties.

"Needless to say, this could become a serious problem," Maria said. "Not just on the Thames but on other rivers as well."

"I don't quite know what to say, since I hadn't even heard of the Potamides before this," Sally said. She sounded peeved about the fact. "Which I suppose should not be too surprising since it's a Crown matter. But that very thing puts it beyond our purview, does it not? And if Lord Quinceton is aware of the problem, won't he be able to report it?"

"I should care to know to *whom* he will report it," Dorothea said. "Certainly not to this Lord Rossing, whom I do not know and do not wish to know."

"Maria and Georgiana knew about the Potamides already. What do they think?" Clementina asked.

Georgiana and Maria exchanged glances. Then Georgiana said, "I agree that this is not our business and we should not try to involve ourselves—in any *official* way."

Sally nodded. "But unofficially, perhaps? Information is always useful to us."

"Information about Lord Rossing?" Frances was in attendance that morning. Annabel had not yet had the opportunity to ask how her aunt did; at any event, the lack of mourning implied that the lady lingered yet. "Oh, I think he might be an acquaintance of my brother's, but I am not sure. I had no idea about these Poma—no, Po*ta*mides. Shall I see what I can discover about him?"

Sally looked relieved. "Yes, please, Frances. And thank you for telling us about this, ladies. Annabel, I'm very glad that your son was not hurt."

"So am I," Annabel agreed fervently.

After the meeting Frances had gone straight to her. "Annabel! What a dreadful thing that must have been at Eton yesterday! Your poor son! Oh, I do wish I had been there to see Quin vanquish those horrid creatures!"

"He didn't vanquish them—he fed them." Did Frances have to be so *obvious* about her infatuation with him? "How is your great-aunt, by the way? Is she on the mend?"

"My—oh, yes, my aunt." Frances shook her head. "No change, really. Thankfully, her physician doesn't think we should give up hope of a recovery just yet. But you must tell me all about yesterday— what did Quin do? What did he say? He's so clever! And *brave*!"

The brave and clever Lord Quinceton sighed, recalling Annabel to the moment. "I promise I haven't the least interest in investigating Lord Rossing or anything to do with him," she said firmly.

"I am relieved to hear you say that. This is not a

matter that you should be concerning yourself with. In *any* way."

"Yes, I—I had come to that conclusion."

He looked at her. "Why does that answer fail to fill me with confidence?"

"Don't be horrid. I don't want to even hear the words 'river nymph' again for as long as I live. And anyway, I fully intend to have some fun in the next few days. I am going to Epsom for the races to-morrow."

"Oh?" He sounded surprised. "I did not know you were a racing enthusiast."

"I'm not. But several friends are going—it seems there's a wonder horse everyone's talking about who's supposed to be running, and I thought, 'why not?'"

That wasn't quite true. She was indeed going to Epsom, but not purely for fun. Mr. Almack had reported a possible matter of investigation at the annual race meet, and Georgiana and Maria had been assigned to investigate, with Annabel to assist as needed.

"Then perhaps I will see you there. I usually stop in for a day or so." He hesitated. "May I ask you a question without fear of giving offence?"

"You may certainly *ask*, sir."

"Whether I get an answer is another issue?" He smiled. "Fair enough. I hope you aren't thinking of trying to, er, raise some capital at Epsom?"

"What, bet on races?" Annabel laughed. "No, not at all. I wouldn't have the first idea of how to choose a horse to bet on."

"Your husband didn't either, but he never allowed that to stop him."

Freddy *had* always gone to Epsom, hadn't he? She'd assumed it was because it was what gentlemen did—and this race meet was very fashionable. That he was gambling heavily as well as carousing with his friends hadn't really occurred to her. "No," she said quietly. "I won't be placing bets."

They drove in silence for a moment. Then she said, "May I ask *you* a question without fear of giving offense?"

"Ask away, Fellbridge. I am notoriously difficult to offend."

"I am glad to hear that. At Eton—no, it's nothing to do with the Potamides or the King's Maintenancer," she said quickly as his brows drew together.

"What, then?"

She took a breath. "What was your meaning yesterday when you said that Gus Blackburn had been taken care of?"

"Oh, that." He laughed softly.

"Yes, that." His laugh nettled her. "The boy is in a sad position and may not be able to continue at Eton—"

"He'll be able to stay at Eton as long as he likes. I had a talk with the new Head—Keate, is it?—in May, and we were able to come to an agreement."

An *agreement*? "Are you saying that *you're* paying his tuition?"

"Er, yes, I am. Room and board and his other classes as well, as I recall. I left it up to Keate to arrange the details and send them to my steward."

It took her a moment to recover from her astonishment. "But—that is, you don't know him, do you? No, of course not. You didn't even recognize him on Sunday when he came to speak with me."

"No, I hadn't yet laid eyes on the boy," he agreed.

There was an amused note in his voice that Annabel knew—and mistrusted. But she couldn't withdraw now. "Then why are you paying for his schooling?"

He shrugged. "Because it seemed to matter to you."

She just managed not to gasp. He was paying Gus's fees—for her sake? A gulf of meaning suddenly yawned at her feet; did she dare look into it?

"Yes, it does matter to me. Thank you," she finally said. Her voice sounded stiff even in her own ears. "When I am in better frame, I trust you will allow me to reimburse you for your trouble."

"You? Never. If Master Blackburn wishes to do so at some later date, I will accept it if he wishes, but don't intend to ask for it. In the meanwhile, I am arranging a method of compensation with him that I expect will be satisfactory to both of us."

"But—"

"But if you should care to thank me, Fellbridge, there's one way you can."

"How?"

He smiled again, but there was no mockery or teasing in it this time. "At one point on Sunday, you addressed me in less formal terms than you usually do."

"I...don't know what you're talking about."

"Just before I went into the river, you called me Quin. Not 'Lord Quinceton' as is your wont."

She swallowed. "Did I?"

"Yes, you did. I confess to having felt some

elation, as it implied that you were perhaps thinking of me in friendlier terms than you did a month or two ago."

Her face grew hot. Any moment now, the feather from her hat sweeping against her cheek would burst into flame. "I—uh...that is—"

He ignored her. "At the time, I took it as thanks for getting your son out of trouble. But I would not be averse to hearing you use it more often." He paused, then added, very gently, "Please?"

I hope you enjoyed the fifth installment of The Ladies of Almack's! There's more—much more!—to come. If you'd like to keep up with the news from King Street, sign up for my newsletter for new release announcements, extras, and more about the ladies: https://marissadoylenewsletter.link/

Also, if you enjoyed reading *Turmoil on the Thames*, please consider telling your friends who might also enjoy it or posting a review on the site where you purchased it or on your favorite social media site such as Goodreads or LibraryThing.

Author's Notes

N.B.: Any resemblance between a certain event in Chapter 4 to a well-known aquatic moment in a popular and well-loved Jane Austen television mini-series is of course purely coincidental.

A little background on Eton College

Eton College was founded by King Henry VI in 1440 as a charity school for deserving poor boys, to prepare them to enter King's College at Cambridge. While its continued existence seemed in doubt in the years after its founding, it eventually became one of the best known and most prestigious of boys' board-ing schools. Of course, any institution that has been around for centuries acquires its own culture and history. We know about the Fourth of June (still part of the social calendar, by the way), but here's the skinny on a few other bits of Eton history and custom mentioned in this story:

- *Eton slang - dry bobs:* When a place has

been around as long as Eton has, it not surprisingly collects a vast amount of folklore, traditions, and slang. One of those slang terms is "dry bobs", which Quin uses when addressing Martin and his co-conspirators. It means boys who prefer cricket (played on dry land, obviously) to rowing. If Martin was a dry bob, his twin Will, out on the river, was a "wet bob."

- *Montem:* Eton Montem (or Ad Montem) was another tradition observed from the 16th century to the 19th (it was abolished in 1847.) Originally it seems to have been a sort of initiation rite for new boys, conducted at the Montem Mound, or Salt Hill, a couple of miles from the college. It eventually evolved (or devolved) into a good-natured sort of highway robbery, when carriages and horsemen on the nearby Bath road would be stopped on Montem day (sometime in May or June, depending on the ecclesiastical calendar) by groups of boys demanding a payment in order to be allowed to go on; the money thus raised was for the Senior Colleger's anticipated expenses at university. By the 1770s it was only held once every three years but was attended by luminaries including George IV and, later, Queen Victoria and Prince Albert. The birth and growth of the railway system spelled its death sentence: so many rowdy crowds came out from London for it in 1841 and 1844 that Eton's headmaster abolished it before the 1847 celebration.

- *Lodgings for boys Oppidans/Collegers:* Until recent times (again relatively speaking, considering how old Eton is), a large proportion of boys attending Eton lived in boarding houses in town outside of the school, often run by respectable widows or by Eton teachers as a side gig, which provided room and board—hence Annabel's concern that their house "dame" (in quotes, because dames could be male or female) was not feeding her sons sufficiently. Boys who lived in these boarding houses were known as *Oppidans*, from the Latin word for "town." *Collegers* were boys who lived on campus; they were scholarship students as per the original foundation of the school who were guaranteed admission to King's College, Cambridge, on completing their education at Eton. By later in the 19th century, this system had broken down in favor of school-run "houses" for all students.

Making one's curtsey to the queen

When a young lady of means was considered to be of marriageable age—the number varied but was generally at least seventeen—she "came out" to society in order to meet possible appropriate husbands. This meant parties and dinners and balls and (if she were lucky and well-born) vouchers to Almack's. And (again) if she was well-born and well-connected, she might be presented to the queen at court. Being presented was not strictly a requirement for being "out", but one could not be invited to parties given by the king and queen (or, shortly, the Prince Regent) if one had not been presented. So you can imagine that young persons entering society (yes, young men were presented as well) did not want to run the risk of being excluded if they had any social pretensions at all.

The Duke of Cumberland incident

George III's fifth son, Ernest, Duke of Cumberland, was one of the least popular of the king's unpopular sons. Unlike most of his brothers who were on the plump side, Ernest took after his mother and was rail-thin; a saber cut down one side of his face, received when he fought the French in Holland at the Battle of Tournai, gave him a rather sinister appearance despite his handsome features. And unlike all his brothers, he was an avowed Tory and never dabbled in Whiggery or any liberal causes, being particularly opposed to Catholic Emancipation. He had an unpleasant reputation from his Army days as being a savage disciplinarian, and rumors about his personal life were rife.

But those rumors were nothing compared to the gossip that ricocheted around London after the wee hours of May 31, 1810.

According to the duke, he went to bed around one a.m. in his apartments at St. James Palace after attending a concert earlier in the evening. He stated that he was awakened by two blows to his head, then quickly received four other blows and a saber cut to his thigh as he tried to flee to the room of one of his valets, Neale, calling out that he had been murdered. Though a small lamp burned in his room, he said he saw no one. The valet dashed to his master's defense, waving a poker about, until he tripped over a sword—the duke's own, covered with a considerable amount of blood. While Neale tended to his master, the duke requested that his other valet, Joseph Sellis, a native of Corsica, be summoned as well. When the servants went to Sellis's room, they found the door was locked. After various backing and forthing involving doors that should have been locked but weren't, Sellis's room was finally gained—and Sellis himself found with his throat slit by a razor. There was no sign of a struggle.

Ew.

So what had actually happened?

The jury called to hear the incident's inquest found, on weighing the extensive testimony and physical evidence, that Sellis had attacked his master and then committed suicide. Based on the accounts given by all the servants, that was probably what happened, though we'll never know what inspired the attack.

But public opinion whispered otherwise—remember how disliked the duke was? It was rumored that the duke had seduced Sellis's wife, and murdered Sellis when the valet threatened to go public with his knowledge, then arranged matters to look as though he had been attacked instead. Other rumors postulated an affair between the duke and Sellis, and that the duke had murdered him when he threatened blackmail, while others favored the theory that Sellis had discovered an affair between the duke and his other valet, and was murdered by the duke in order to keep the affair secret. Some who accepted that Sellis had indeed attempted to murder his master suggested that he had done so in revenge for the duke's seduction of his wife. Others guessed that he was tired of the duke's constant stream of anti-Catholic jokes and mockery (Sellis was Catholic) and had simply had *enough*.

The duke survived, though it took months for him to recover (his brain could actually be seen through one of the wounds in his head, and his thumb had nearly been severed by the saber.) His reputation, however, never recovered, and he would go on to be accused of even worse things, such as being the father of his own sister's illegitimate child and of scheming to bring about the death of his niece Victoria, who until she had children was all that stood between the duke and the crown.

Makes the royal scandals of today look pretty tame, doesn't it?

The Duke of York and his mistress

The king's second son, Frederick, Duke of York, was also (like his younger brother the Duke of Cumberland), a soldier...in fact, he was named commander-in-chief of the British Army in 1798. Though he wasn't perhaps the most inspired field commander, he was a more-than-able administrator, and his reforms of the army's structure and management were likely just as responsible as the Duke of Wellington's strategic genius for Britain's ultimate victory over Napoleon.

But in 1809-1810, that was all in the future...and no one would have believed the duke was any good as an administrator either, for he was neck-deep in scandal.

Like most of his brothers, the duke was a ladies' man. Though fond of his wife, Frederica of Prussia, he generally had a mistress in his keeping, and in 1803 that mistress was Mary Anne Clarke, a popular courtesan (and an ancestress of Daphne du Maurier.)

Mary Anne's tastes were expensive; though the duke had set her up in her own house with an allowance of £100 per month, she was spending at five times that rate. To supplement her income, she hit on the scheme of using her position as the duke's *belle amie* to sell army commissions, promotions, and transfers to the highest bidders, undercutting the government, which was also in the same business (yes, at the time, that was how things worked): she'd take the money and see that the names were added to the lists to be approved by the duke.

Word eventually got out, and a formal committee was set up by Parliament to look into the matter. The duke sent Mary Anne packing and resigned his position as commander-in-chief; he was reinstated a while later after the commission found that while he was aware of Mary Anne's activities, he himself had not benefited financially from them. Mary Anne managed to negotiate a good pension from the royal family after threatening to publish the duke's love letters to her, and after the war eventually moved to France, where she lived comfortably until her death in 1852.

Ladies' maids and cast-off dresses

While most servants did not make very much in salary, many positions had traditional perquisites attached to them that could prove quite lucrative. Butlers, for example, could claim candle ends and empty bottles to sell; cooks could sell dripping saved from the cooking of meat; while this sounds strange to modern ears, a comfortable sum could be accumulated from these activities.

Personal servants—ladies' maids and valets—probably had the best perks: it was generally accepted that they could lay claim to their employers' cast-off clothes, either to sell to second-hand clothing dealers, to send home to family and friends, or to modify for themselves. Annabel's maid, Winters, likely doesn't get much of her mistress's cast-offs, as Lady Shellingham observes.

The King's Maintenancer of the Tamesian Potamides

This office of course does not exist (at least, I don't think it does.) But there are any number of royal offices with similar obscure names and purposes left over from the Middle Ages, my favorite being the Queen's (or King's) Swan Marker and Swan Uppers, whose job it is to perform an annual count of the swans on the Thames, which (nominally) belong to the Crown.

AN EVENT
AT EPSOM

Chapter One

Mid-June 1810
En route to Epsom, Surrey

"I have always wondered why they call them 'downs,'" Maria Sefton said, gazing at the rolling green countryside outside the carriage window. "Don't they go up as much as down? Indeed," she said, warming to her subject, "since they must go up in order to go down, why are they not called 'ups'? It seems dreadfully arbitrary."

Across from her, Annabel smiled. It was an exceedingly Maria-ish thing to say. "I don't know, but 'Epsom Downs' sounds much better than 'Epsom Ups,'" she replied.

"That's true." Maria's brow wrinkled. "I shall ask Derby about it when I see him. If anyone would know, it is he."

"Except I believe there are downs elsewhere and not only in Surrey," Annabel couldn't resist adding.

"Oh, dear. That does complicate the question."

"Does Lord Derby know we're coming?" Georgiana Bathurst, seated next to Maria, asked. She'd spoken barely a word since they'd left London and had spent the intervening hours wearing a slight frown as she gazed fixedly at nothing. Annabel had feared she was carriage-sick, but they'd not needed to pause for her to cast up her accounts in the hedge-row. The only other conclusion to be drawn was that something was troubling her.

"Of course he is expecting me. I don't think he knows you're coming," Maria replied. "This investigation was Mr. Almack's idea, not Derby's. However, I am certain he would be monstrous glad of our help if it turns out that there is indeed something not-quite-right going on here."

They were on their way to Epsom, site of two of the most hotly-contested (and lucrative) horse-races in England—the Derby and the Oaks Stakes—which had also become one of the more popular events of the season. Mr. Almack's death had not blunted his keen interest in the Sport of Kings, and a curious story had come to him that made a man—er, ghost— of his experience sit up and take notice.

"Speaking of peculiar, there's something verra odd going on in racing circles," he'd announced at Monday's Lady Patronesses meeting after they had discussed the incident with the Potamides at Eton. "Something that I think you ladies might want to look at."

"Odd in what way?" Sally had asked, taking a fresh leaf of paper and dipping her pen.

The tale Mr. Almack had recounted had indeed been an odd one. Earlier that spring a new filly had appeared on the local race circuit around New-market and had won almost every race she ran. Her owner, a Sir Oswald Broxley, was known amongst the gentlemen of the turf as a not-very-successful amateur breeder and trainer. With this horse, however, his luck finally seemed to have turned the corner. When asked, Sir Oswald was not forth-coming about Maharahnee's origins; he would only smile smugly and say that she'd been bred and born on his family's estate.

Dorothea had snorted. "I do not see what is so mysterious about this as to be of interest to us."

"I'm getting to that part," Mr. Almack replied, a little testily. "What is of interest is that she's a verra intelligent horse; as far as anyone can see her jockey is more or less along for the ride whilst she chooses her own path. She also doesna seem to need to rest; she'll run one day and be at a race twenty miles away the next day, ready to go."

They'd all been silent, absorbing that. Sir Oswald was not known to possess a wagon capable of carrying horses, so how could this Maharahnee win a race one afternoon, then walk twenty miles to the next one in less than a day and be ready once again to race?

Sally had finally spoken. "Either this Sir Oswald has managed to tame a kelpie—"

"*Can* one tame a kelpie?" Frances interrupted, wide-eyed.

"Nae, it canna be. It's a filly, and most all kelpies are male." Mr. Almack sounded amused. "'Twould be difficult to hide that."

"Oh. Yes, it would." Frances blushed. "I beg your pardon, Sally. Pray go on."

Sally nodded and went on, "—or some poor horse has been put under a compulsion spell. I expect it must be that." She turned to Mr. Almack's empty—or rather, apparently empty—chair. "I presume the horse's owner is making a tidy profit in winnings?"

"Aye, he is. And from all accounts, he needs it— the man's known to have the worst luck—or judgment—in three counties." Mr. Almack's tone made it clear which he thought was the case. "The Oaks Stakes—it's a race for three-year-old fillies, ye ken—comes up at the end of this week at Epsom, and if there's somethin' not natural about one of the competitors, I think we should look into it."

"I expect we should." Sally looked down the table. "Maria, this would seem to be a matter you would best be able to get to the bottom of. Will you take it on?"

"It would not be any trouble at all, as Sefton and I had already planned to go to Epsom on Wednesday to stay with Lord Derby," Maria said. "If Georgiana isn't otherwise occupied, perhaps she would come as well. Georgiana?"

"Yes, I suppose, if my rheumatism does not confine me to bed." Georgiana sighed. "And so long as it isn't a kelpie."

And so Maria and Georgiana were undertaking the investigation, with Annabel to assist as needed with gathering information. A footman had been dispatched at once to secure accommodation for them at an inn in the vicinity. Annabel had doubted he would—rooms would be almost impossible to find in Epsom at this late hour. Fortunately for them he was an engaging fellow, and the fund Mr. Almack had left for the Lady Patronesses' expenses a deep one; comfortable rooms had been found for Annabel and Georgiana at the Horse and Oak, conveniently close to the racecourse. Maria of course would be a guest at Lord Derby's house.

Annabel watched the green hills ebb and swell through the dust raised by the carriages in front of them—the closer they got to Epsom, the more crowded the roads had grown—and could not help wishing that she could have spent these days alone. On Monday this had seemed as if it would be an amusing investigation to help with.

But that had been Monday. Now it was Wednesday—and her life had turned upside down in the intervening day.

Not a great deal had actually *happened* on Tuesday, aside from the prodigious amount of shopping she'd done with Mama, which had cast her maid Winters into transports of joy. The part of Tuesday that had plunged her into such confusion had been, outwardly, a small one: the brief exchange she'd had with the Marquis of Quinceton whilst they drove in Hyde Park that afternoon.

Such a little thing on the face of it, those few words. Except that they had forced her to confront the fact that she *did* regard him differently than she had three months before—that she now found him more than a little attractive, more than a little...loveworthy.

When he had asked her—shyly, almost (fancy the haughty Marquis of Quinceton being shy!)—to call him Quin, she'd darted a glance at his face. There was a warmth in his eyes that made her look away again before he could see her discomposure. And his softly voiced, "Please?" had nearly undone her; she'd whispered, "Yes, Quin," so quietly that there should have been no way he had heard her above the jangle of harness and the clop of his horses' hooves.

But he'd heard her.

And now—what?

Oh, the immediate "what" was simple: to investigate this miracle horse for the Lady Patronesses. It was a shame, however, that she would have to help conduct the investigation with a brain that had apparently regressed to that of a green girl in her debut season engaging in her first flirtation.

If only there had been time to confide in Mama; she'd clearly grasped the situation with Quin at Eton. Heavens, she'd shamelessly arranged their meeting in Hyde Park yesterday. But there had been no chance to talk, as Papa had invited friends to join them for dinner last night at the hotel, and then he and Mama had left early this morning to return to Belsever Magna. She would have to wrestle with this alone.

Very well, then. Wrestle she would.

Life as a widow—even if not a wealthy one—was in many ways most agreeable. Emily thought she should enjoy herself more and take a lover, and indeed the idea was tempting after her less-than-satisfying marriage to Freddy. But while other women seemed to be able to do so even when they weren't widowed, she couldn't contemplate the idea with Emily's pretty insouciance. She did not long for dalliance, but for love.

And if she found a man she could wholeheartedly love, well...men had an unfortunate habit of expecting to control the women in their lives, as she well knew. Was she prepared to give up her life of relative freedom and subject herself once more to the tyranny of a man, deliciously tempting as that might be if the tyrant were someone as attractive as Quin?

In which case, a few days away from London was probably a good thing after all. She would have time and distance to mull over her feelings about Quin—unless he had been serious when he'd suggested that he might look in at the races. Then again, finding her amongst the thirty or forty thousand other race-goers would not be an easy task. So she could assume she'd have a quiet few days to contemplate—

"I suppose our first task will be to find this Maharahnee as quickly as possible, so that Georgiana and I can talk to her before the race on Saturday," Maria said, breaking into her thoughts. "You two can try to discover where she is stabled, assuming she's gained enough of a reputation. Your being at a local inn is very helpful."

"That makes sense." Annabel gave herself a mental shake. She and Georgiana could ask innocent questions, and if required, she herself would do some more covert information gathering—eavesdropping, to be blunt—safely concealed in a shadow. But if all this investigation required was finding out where the horse was kept and Maria having a heart-to-heart talk with it, she would probably not have much to do. In fact... "I wish Emily were here. We could simply turn her loose on this Sir Oswald and find out exactly what is going on."

"Annabel, you know we require solid evidence of wrong-doing. Emily's skills are useful to shape the direction of investigations, but we never rely exclusively on what she reads," Maria said, a little reprovingly. "And anyway, Dorothea wanted her to help investigate that odd business with the ghost and the new gas lamps in Pall Mall."

"*Those* things." Georgiana shook her head. "There's something off about that."

"Gas lamps?" Annabel asked. "I'm not convinced about them either, but I can see how useful they might be for street lighting."

"That is not what I meant. Have you not noticed how busy we are this year? When in past years have we had more than one investigation happening at any time or had them so close together as we have this year?"

Annabel blinked. "I don't know. This is only my second year as a Lady Patroness. Is this year busier than usual?"

"I hadn't paid much attention," Maria said slowly. "But I do believe you are correct, Georgiana—this is probably the busiest it's been since the nineties."

The nineties, when war with France had first kindled, then blazed. Annabel glanced at the faces of the other women and guessed their thoughts were flowing on similar lines. "You don't think that the French—" she began.

"That the French might be responsible for how busy we've been of late?" Maria said. "I don't know. I don't at all see how the situations involving Mr. Marjoribanks or the Ronderleys could have anything to do with the war. The Sirens are perhaps questionable; Aunt Molpe may not have told us everything about how they came to be in England, but I rather doubt it."

"But the Potamides—and the gas lamp incidents Dorothea and Emily are investigating...?" Georgiana said.

"Frances will be making discreet inquiries into the Potamides," Annabel said. "If there's any possibility that Lord Rossing might not—not be loyal, surely she'll find out *something*."

"Yes, and I shall be interested to hear what she finds out," Georgiana replied.

After that, they all fell silent while the carriage moved slowly with the stream of traffic flowing toward Epsom. Annabel couldn't suppress a faint shiver; joking about sending Angelique Ronderley to Paris to sabotage Napoleon's pictures in the *Musée Napoléon* was one thing. But contemplating that an Englishman such as Lord Rossing might be doing the Emperor's bidding here in his own country—and engaging in activities that might have sent her son and his Eton classmates to a watery grave in the Thames...she shivered again. Thank heavens Frances was looking into it.

After dropping Maria at The Oaks, the Earl of Derby's house, they continued on to their inn. The Horse and Oak was not a large hostelry, but it had been recently painted and boasted a handsomely carved and painted sign, and the girl who came out to bow them into the inn's common room while an ostler took charge of Georgiana's carriage wore a spotless white apron.

"This way, if yer ladyships please," she said, bobbing a curtsy then backing into the inn, as if they were royalty.

The common room itself was equally spotless, from the shining andirons in the hearth to the mathematical straightness of the cushions in the settles. "This looks promising," Annabel murmured to Georgiana.

"Thank you, mum—the missus will be right glad you noticed," the girl said, showing them a gap-toothed grin. "We was up at four, sweepin' and polishin'. I don't know when we've had so many nobs stayin' all at once—I swear she'll bust her buttons afore the week's out—"

A large, fair-haired woman in a fearsomely starched lace cap bustled in. "That'll do, Liz!" she scolded. "Run along and see what's keepin' Tom wi' the ladies' baggage, then fetch in a tray to the green parlour."

"Yes'm." Liz bobbed another curtsy before scuttling out the door.

The woman set the tray of clean tankards she'd been carrying on a table and fixed them with a penetrating look from her small blue eyes. "You're Lady Bathurst," she said to Georgiana.

"I am," Georgiana said, looking taken aback.

The woman nodded. "Thought so. Not a bad likeness. And *you're* Lady Fellbridge."

"Er, yes," Annabel replied. Not a bad likeness to *what*? "We were expected, I believe."

"Mm-hmm." The woman examined her a moment longer. "They didn't do a very good job on you," she finally announced.

"I beg your pardon?"

"*La Belle Assemblée.*" Her pronunciation of "Assemblée" made even Georgiana's lips twitch. "My daughter is maid to Sir Francis Buxton's wife up in Lunnon, and Lady Buxton passes along her copies of *La Belle Assemblée* when she's done wi' them herself. My Martha brings 'em to me when she visits, on account she knows I've a fondness for the pictures of the society ladies they put in sometimes." She pointed to the wall farthest from the fireplace where a row of engravings had been tacked to a beam. "If some fancy gentlemen can collect butterflies and birds, I can do this. Least I don't try to kill you and have you stuffed."

Annabel recognized the engravings from the magazine's *Biographical Sketches of Illustrious Ladies* feature and winced. She had merited an appearance in it last year as a new Lady Patroness; Will and Martin had been mightily amused by the accompanying engraving of her. "No, I'm glad you don't have to do that, Mrs.—er—?"

"Oh, lud, listen to me going on about my pictures." She curtsied again. "Mrs. Bunwich, your ladyships, and welcome. Did our Liz greet you proper? Her head's goin' to be proper turned, all the high folk we have with us this week. Well, not that I object to having your sort here—gives us a bit of tone for the rest o' the year, it does. Do y'know, I don't have anyone less than a baron stayin' here this week?" She leaned forward and said in a stage whisper, "I've even got a marquis here—and he's not any old marquis, but a dook's heir!" Her very cap seemed to bristle with pride.

Oh dear. Hopefully no untitled persons had been ousted from their beds to accommodate her and Georgiana. "How exciting for you."

"It is—but here, I shouldn't keep you ladies out here. Step this way to the private parlour—*one* of our private rooms, I should say. We have three." Mrs. Bunwich herded them past a set of stairs to a green-curtained room set with chairs and a small table. "Now where's Liz? That girl has the brain of a grass-hopper—"

"Here we go!" Liz backed her way into the room, bearing an enormous tray. "Butter on the bread was churned this morning, and the jam's our own blackberry—picked before Michaelmas, so the devil didn't drag his tail 'cross 'em," she announced as she set out a pitcher of lemonade and plates of sandwiches and cakes. "And yer things'll be brought up directly. I just gave yer maids a cup o' tea in the kitchen. Give 'em a minute to drink it, and I'll show 'em where yer rooms are," she called over her shoulder as she vanished again with her tray.

Mrs. Bunwich handed her and Georgiana glasses of lemonade. "She's a good girl, Liz is, but she does tend to rattle on. Sandwich?" She offered them one of the platters, then took a sandwich herself. "I must say, I was a bit took aback when your footman told me it would be two ladies looking for rooms. It's usually the gentlemen what want to come for the racing. Not that I don't know you're a widow, ma'am," she added, nodding to Annabel. "Fond of the races, are you?"

"I—er, don't know. That is—" Annabel said, thinking fast. "It happens that a—an acquaintance of Lady Bathurst has a horse that's doing frightfully well this year, and since I'd never been to Epsom, she invited me to come along to see her race. What was the horse's name again, Georgiana?"

Georgiana raised an eyebrow but didn't drop the line Annabel had tossed her, thank goodness. "Maharahnee. She belongs to Sir Oswald Broxley—but he's more my husband's acquaintance than mine. Have you heard of her, Mrs. Bunwich?"

The landlady gave a most ungenteel snort. "Heard of her? Who hasn't? The betting on her's been through the roof, I hear. That Sir Oswald will need a cart to bring home his winnings if his horse runs as she's expected to."

"My goodness." Annabel made herself look suitably impressed. "Where might we see this paragon?"

Mrs. Bunwich's brow wrinkled. "I hear Sir Oswald's putting up at the Red Boar—they only have the one private parlour, by the way—but I don't know where he's keeping his horse. There's tempo'ry stables set up near the race-course, but I don't think you'll be wantin' to go down there without a gentleman to go wi' you. It's not a place for ladies to go to alone, if you catch my drift."

Annabel caught Georgiana's glance and grimaced ever so slightly. Drat, they should have thought of that; a racecourse probably *wasn't* the place for them to be alone. Odd that Mr. Almack hadn't said anything about bringing an escort—but how could they, while doing Lady Patroness work? Yes, most of their actual work would be done in secret, most likely by night—but first they needed to discover where Maharahnee was, which would require actually wandering about the Down. It was too bad that Quin wasn't here; she would be able to count on him to help without asking too many difficult questions.

That was one of the things she liked about him—

"Annabel!"

Georgiana and Mrs. Bunwich stopped talking. Annabel turned in her chair and beheld Lord Glenrick, staring at her from the doorway of the parlour

Chapter Two

"Annabel, my dear!" Glenrick crossed the distance to her in two strides and took possession of both her hands, drawing her to her feet before she'd had a chance to utter a word. For a moment she thought he might embrace her, directly before Georgiana and Mrs. Bunwich. But he contented himself with raising her hands to his lips in quick succession, devouring her with his eyes as he did.

"L-lord Glenrick—what a lovely surprise," she stammered. "I did not expect to see you here."

For a brief instant he looked reproachful, and she realized she'd not called him Alec as he'd request-ed—was it only a week ago? How much had changed in seven days—

"Nor I you," he said, his expression smoothing over as he gazed at her. "I've never been so delighted to be surprised. It has been too long since we met. Much too long." He squeezed her hands fervently.

Annabel gently detached them from his grasp.

"But you have been occupied with family matters. Your great-aunt—she is better?"

"Poor Aunt Elspeth pulled through. This time." He sighed. "Perhaps I should not say so, but it might have been better if she had not. Her condition remains precarious, but Frances and I thought it safe to return to London for now."

Annabel blinked. His Aunt Elspeth? Hadn't Frances said it was their Aunt Mary who was on death's doorstep? But before she could say anything, Mrs. Bunwich had leapt from her seat with a broad smile.

"You know each other!" She clapped her hands in glee. "Well, of course you do—don't everyone in Lunnon with a handle to their name know each other? But you ain't just acquaintances, I can see. Fancy that you both should end up at my inn, all coincidental." Her sharp eyes softened as she looked at Annabel. "It's as if it was meant to be—you stayin' here instead o' that bad-tempered Sir William and his sons. I knew it as soon as I saw you."

Annabel winced under her smile. So their coming *had* lead to evictions.

"My sentiments exactly, Mrs. Bunwich," Lord Glenrick said. "I too knew, as soon as I saw Lady Fellbridge, that it was meant to be." He smiled at Annabel.

Mrs. Bunwich looked as if she were on the verge of swooning. *"Oh,"* she sighed.

Georgiana gave a faint sniff. Annabel started; she'd forgotten Georgiana was here and had to fight a strong urge to drive Lord Glenrick from the room with the fireplace poker. How embarrassing this was!

And how embarrassing that she was embarrassed. Shouldn't she find Lord Glenrick's behavior thrillingly romantic? Instead, all she wanted to do was sink through Mrs. Bunwich's scrubbed oak floorboards. How was she supposed to respond to such a statement?

Fortunately, she didn't have to, as Lord Glenrick was still speaking. "You must be my guest for dinner this evening, Annabel. That is, if I might prevail upon good Mrs. Bunwich to produce one of her delicious meals..." He quirked an eyebrow at that lady.

Mrs. Bunwich practically inflated. "I should say you could—*and* have it here in this parlour."

"You are most kind," Annabel said quickly. "But as I am here with Lady Bathurst..."

"Good afternoon, Lord Glenrick," Georgiana gave him a small, thin-lipped smile.

To his credit, he appeared highly abashed. "Lady Bathurst! My apologies." He bowed. "I fear that my delight at Lady Fellbridge's presence overcame my manners—and my eyesight. You must *both* be my guests for dinner."

Annabel hesitated. "Georgiana?" It was most kind of him, but she and Georgiana had planned to dine early and pretend to retire soon after, so that Georgiana could survey the city of tents that clustered near the racecourse for Maharahnee's "stable."

"We should be very happy to join you, sir," Georgiana nodded her acceptance. "If I may ask that we do so earlier than later. It is a long trip here, as you well know, and we are tired."

He looked rueful. "I'm being selfish. Of course you are tired after that drive. I shan't keep you late, I promise. Nor should I keep you from your refreshments. Mrs. Bunwich, a word, if you please..."

He and the landlady withdrew to the doorway to discuss the dinner. Under cover of their conversation Annabel murmured to Georgiana, "Oh, thank you! I was too disconcerted to think of a way to do that. I had no idea he would be here."

Georgiana took a sip of tea. "Lord Glenrick appears to be most particular in his attentions to you," she observed.

Annabel looked at her quickly, trying to detect a hint of judgment. Then she gave herself a mental shake: Lord Glenrick had made plain his interest in her by the involuntary warmth of his greeting. Georgiana was simply stating the obvious. She *had* to stop expecting the worst from Georgiana if they were going to work together on this investigation. "Yes, he has been," she replied, as neutrally as Georgiana had spoken.

They were both silent, listening to Lord Glenrick order a most elegant meal. Annabel remembered her mother's comments on the state of his finances; was he at Epsom to attempt to fatten a lean purse, as Quin had warned her against doing?

Quin. If *he* had been the one to stroll into the room, what would her reaction have been?

Lord Glenrick and Mrs. Bunwich returned, both evidently very pleased with each other. "Ladies, I have ordered dinner for six o'clock. I trust that will be an agreeable hour?" Lord Glenrick asked, his eyes on Annabel.

"Indeed, yes. You are most kind."

He bowed. "I look forward to this evening with the greatest pleasure." He gazed at Annabel a moment longer, then left.

"Ooh!" Mrs. Bunwich fanned herself with her hand as she fell into her chair. "He was looking at you as if he hoped you'd be on the bill of fare, Lady Fellbridge."

"Oh, no." Annabel felt herself blush furiously.

"Oh, yes he was. Mark my word, if he don't go down on one knee by the end of the week, I'll eat my kerchief."

Georgiana made a small noise that sounded suspiciously similar to a laugh and took another sip of tea.

Mrs. Bunwich got a dreamy look on her face. "And just think, it might happen right here in my inn!" The dreaminess shifted into calculation. "Won't *that* impress folks when they hear 'bout it!"

Annabel began to feel a little desperate. "No, indeed, Mrs. Bunwich, I have no intention of re-marrying at this time—"

"Not even a future dook?" Mrs. Bunwich managed to look both scandalized and skeptical at the same time. "Dooks don't grow on trees, m'lady. There'll be no time to be missish when he ups and pops the question if you don't mind my saying so. Oh, lud, I'd better get started on his lordship's dinner!" She jumped up and hurried from the room.

Dinner with Lord Glenrick was not as difficult as Annabel feared it might be. He was dressed with the utmost elegance in dark blue satin knee breeches and a black coat, with a silver pin in the shape of a thistle set with glittering jet and surmounted by a golden bee fastening his cravat. He made certain that his seat was as close to hers as possible, but Georgiana's presence seemed to restrain him; she received only a few meaning looks and one lingering hand pressure, for which she was grateful.

To her further gratitude, the dinner proved helpful as far as the investigation went, for Lord Glenrick turned out to be an acquaintance of Sir Oswald Broxley and familiar with his extraordinary filly.

"Broxley's luck with his horses turned not a moment too soon," he told her and Georgiana over the savory of stewed celery and cheese toast that Mrs. Bunwich served to end their meal. "He was within a whisker of losing his stud farm when Maharahnee started winning races for him. The only reason he hadn't lost Broxley Park was an entail."

"I feel for his wife and family!" Annabel's sympathies lay entirely with that poor woman.

"The man's unmarried—there's an older sister and a much younger brother from his father's second marriage. He cares far more for his horses than he does for them—or at least, he cares more for what his horses can do for him."

"And yet I understand this Maharahnee goes from race meet to race meet without rest in between," Georgiana said. "Exhausting your horses does not seem a prudent action when one is hoping to repair one's fortunes by that animal."

Lord Glenrick lifted his hands. "It doesn't to me either, and if he's exhausting her in such a way, he's a fool. He's possessed of a devilish bad—your pardon!—an excessively bad temper. He's fortunate to have a good man looking after his stud, an old retainer inherited from his father. I don't think Jem Salter would allow Maharahnee to be mistreated. And they say she's always seemed in high, frisky form before the races. I've only seen her run once, myself."

"How intriguing! I should love to see this Maharahnee." Annabel hoped she'd put the right amount of wistfulness in her voice. How fortunate he knew all about this! It would solve the problem of how they were going to find Maharahnee without wandering about on Epsom Down unaccompanied by a gentleman.

Glenrick smiled at her. "It's a fine evening for a stroll. Perhaps we could find her if we looked."

"Oh, could we? I confess I am prodigiously interested in seeing her." Annabel returned his smile.

"I will leave you to enjoy your stroll, if I may," Georgiana said, rising. "I think it time I retired. Thank you for your hospitality, Lord Glenrick."

"Oh, no, Georgiana!" Annabel rose too. "I expect it will not be too long a walk. Do you not wish to see the famous Maharahnee?"

Georgiana hesitated, casting a quick look at her then at Lord Glenrick. "Not tonight, I think. You shall show me her tomorrow, when Maria comes."

Lord Glenrick had immediately risen when Georgiana had. "I understand perfectly, Lady Bathurst. Long carriage rides *are* exhausting. But I promise you that Mrs. Bunwich's beds are as excellent as her dinners." He cocked an eyebrow at that lady, who had just bustled in to clear the table.

"Oh, my lord, you are a one." Mrs. Bunwich was practically preening.

Annabel tried to catch Georgiana's eye. It wasn't vital that she come too—Annabel was certain she'd be able to find Maharahnee's stable again later on. But she was not persuaded that she wanted to be alone with Lord Glenrick, despite it still being well before sunset and the race grounds teeming with other race-goers out enjoying the evening. He would almost certainly steer their conversation down paths she likely did not, at this point, wish to follow.

"Georgiana?" she asked quietly, under cover of Lord Glenrick's banter with the landlady and with as speaking a look as she could muster. "I—"

"Annabel?" Lord Glenrick had finished reducing Mrs. Bunwich to a fawning puddle.

"I don't care to leave you alone here," Annabel said, a little desperately.

"I assure you, I don't mind in the least." Georgiana rose. "Have a pleasant walk."

Oh, bother! But she could not beg Georgiana to accompany her. So she went upstairs to retrieve her shawl and bonnet then rejoined Lord Glenrick waiting by the door. He held out his arm; she took it because to not do so would be rude, and he tucked it firmly over his so that she was drawn close to his side as they stepped into the yard.

The Horse and Oak was situated on a lane that ran along the rise at the edge of Epsom Down itself, south of the village of Epsom. Annabel saw at once that their evening stroll would not be a short walk; the majority of the stabling tents appeared to be at least a quarter-mile away or more. It was probably for the best that Georgiana had not come with them, then; walking there and back twice in one evening would not have benefited her sciatica.

But she could not help wishing for her presence now as Lord Glenrick drew her still closer to his side.

"I never suspected, when I rose this morning, that the day would close in such a fashion," he said quietly. "When I beheld you in Mrs. Bunwich's most superior parlour, it set my heart racing like—"

"Like Maharahnee?" Annabel suggested.

As she'd hoped, he laughed. She took the opportunity to insert a little more space between them.

He promptly closed it again. "Precisely like Maharahnee. Indeed, my next impulse was to gallop across the room and clasp you in my arms, Bunwiches and Bathursts notwithstanding." His voice lowered. "I spoke truly, my dear—I've missed you deeply, especially after that golden afternoon at Hampton Court. I've relived certain moments of that day over and over in my mind this last week."

Annabel bowed her head. She had been doing the same thing these last two days—only it hadn't been memories of time spent with Lord Glenrick that she'd pored over like a miser with his gold. A sodden, mischievous Quin, standing knee-deep in the Thames, inviting her to hug him; the warmth of his back against her cheek as the farm horse Diablo carried them down the footpath; the catch in his voice when he'd said *please* on their drive in the park—

Good heavens, this would *not* do!

Two weeks ago, Lord Glenrick's words might have thrilled her to her core. Today they merely left her melancholy. She could not return his feelings because hers—much to her surprise—were seemingly already engaged. Somehow, between his teasing and his steadfast presence when she needed him, Quin had managed to insert himself into her life—and into her heart.

Well, the question she'd asked herself about Quin on the drive here had been answered; it had merely taken another man's attentions to clarify her own feelings. Poor Lord Glenrick! If only she could find someone else for him... Did she know of any especially charming and wealthy (keeping Mama's comments on the state of his finances in mind) heiresses to whom she could introduce him? Perhaps the Colchester girl who had come out this year—a little on the gauche side but she would outgrow that—and there was her £30,000 dowry to consider—

"You are quiet, *ma belle*," he said, his voice caressing.

The endearment—and his tone—made her uncomfortable. "I was woolgathering," she said brightly. "My goodness, is this Bartholomew Fair or a race meeting?"

They had come to the edge of the temporary canvas village. Tents large and small, threadbare and ragged or beflagged and caparisoned, were pitched side by side with booths selling pies and gingerbread, handkerchiefs and ribbons, draughts of Epsom water, and tinware. A fiddler played nearby, his cap laid on the ground to collect pennies, almost drowned out by someone else shouting the particulars about a cockfight to be held that evening. A wizened woman wearing dozens of thin bangles about her wrists called out to passers-by, offering to tell their fortunes. And persons of every quality, from beggars to aristocrats, rubbed shoulders in the spaces between the tents. Although a few women could be seen here and there, they were not many, and Annabel was grateful for Lord Glenrick's arm as they passed groups of lounging, staring men. When she and Georgiana came back tonight to visit Maharahnee, they would have to take care to stay well hidden.

"Bartholomew Fair?" Lord Glenrick chuckled. "Now that you mention it, I can see the resemblance. Epsom is close enough to London that it draws a goodly crowd to see the races, which in turn draws its own crowd to entertain *them*. Hi—you, boy!" He stopped a youth pushing a wheelbarrow filled with sacks of oats. "Where might the filly Maharahnee be stabled?"

The youth took in their clothes and Glenrick's cultured voice and evidently calculated that being respectful was the most potentially lucrative course of action. "Next row down, sir, 'bout fifty yards that way. Hard by a girt yaller 'n green tent—outlandish old thing. Jem Salter'll be on guard outside it. Can't miss *him*." He held out his hand with an ingratiating grin.

Lord Glenrick snorted and tossed him a coin and guided Annabel between a tent selling roasted apples and another fitted out as a barber shop. In the next "street" more of the tents appeared to be serving as stables. Annabel took careful note of any landmarks and distinctive features as they passed them by; getting lost was the last thing she wanted to happen.

The "girt yaller 'n green tent" was indeed large and unmissable, in broad stripes of green and yellow trimmed with scarlet and scarlet pennons flying from its corners and center pole. Judging by the sounds issuing from it, a convivial dinner party was in full spate within. Flambeaux were stuck into the ground before the tent, between which a powerful-looking young man, clad in a sober suit, stood sentinel. He regarded them keenly as they passed. And next, beyond him—

The tent beyond was neither large nor grand, being formed of stained gray canvas liberally adorned with patches. It barely looked long enough to hold a horse. Seated on a low stool before it, a man was rubbing grease into a bridle. He was as bald as an egg, had a jockey's wiry, fine-boned build, and stared up at them with narrowed black eyes, so dark as to seem pupil-less.

"What?" he barked as they paused.

Annabel was taken aback by his ferocity. What a choleric temper! But another look at him made her wonder if that was actually the case; he didn't seem angry so much as wound so tightly that the smallest irritation might cause him to fly to pieces. A pity Emily wasn't there; she would probably have been able to read him like a book.

Lord Glenrick did not appear to notice the man's tension. "This is where Sir Oswald keeps his filly, yes? The lady hoped to catch a glimpse of her."

The man's eyes narrowed even further if that were possible. "The lady'll have to wait till Maharahnee runs, same as everyone else. I ain't disturbing her just so you can gawk at her." He scowled at Annabel.

Lord Glenrick drew himself up. "My good man, I'll thank you not to be so rude—"

"Of *course* we don't wish to disturb your charge," Annabel said quickly. "We only stopped in case she was out. It must be a strain, preparing for a race—even for a dumb animal."

The man—this must be the Jem Salter the boy

with the wheelbarrow had mentioned—gave her a long look up and down and seemed to relent. "'S all right, ma'am. I kin get—you know—prickly when people start actin' as if it's their right to see her. You come back tomorrow—mebbe she'll be gettin' her exercise."

"You are very kind, er—"

"Salter, ma'am." He bobbed his head.

"Salter," she repeated. "Good evening." She nodded to him and pulled unobtrusively on Lord Glenrick's arm. She could feel Jem Salter's eyes on her back as they left.

"Peppery little fellow," Lord Glenrick said when they were out of earshot. "I didn't care for how he spoke to you."

"He was being protective of his master's property, for which he can scarcely be blamed." Annabel did her best to subtly steer them back by the way they had come, to make certain that she had memorized the route. This place was a veritable city made of flapping, fluttering canvas—and, like a city, was perilously easy to get lost in. Thank heavens for that ridiculous yellow tent being where it was!

"Still, I did not care to see my dear friend spoken to so roughly." They turned into the alley between tents that led to the first main thoroughfare. The sun was lowering, painting the canvas walls with rosy light.

"I am grateful for your concern, sir, but I am not some fragile flower who cannot survive an occasional cold wind." She glanced up at him, smiling.

As he met her glance, a change came over his face and he halted. "Annabel," he said, so low that it sounded like a growl. In the next instant he had crushed her against him, covering her mouth with his.

She gasped in surprise, which he seemed to take as encouragement; his kisses grew deeper and more impassioned...and deeply unpleasant. She turned her head and managed to worm a hand up to push at his chest. "Lord Glenrick, no! Stop!"

"Annabel," he murmured, kissing the side of her throat.

She pushed again, this time staggering back a step. "Pray, sir—!"

He tried to reach for her once more, then seemed to recollect himself and allowed his hands to fall. "Forgive me, my darling." His breath came fast and ragged; it took him a long moment to master it. "When you looked up at me with that delicious little smile, I could not stop myself."

She watched him warily. "Sir, I—"

"You have bewitched me, *ma belle*. I am completely in your spell." He took her gloved hand and pressed his lips fervently into her palm.

Oh, *really*. Annabel snatched it back. "I had no intention—"

"That matters for naught. Your mere presence drives me to madness. I want you, Annabel. I want every last, luscious inch of you. If only you had come alone—if that Bathurst female were not here with you, I know what I would wish to do." He took a step closer, eyes intent on her face.

She turned away from him. *Yes, that's all very well,* replied a voice in her head that sounded remarkably similar to her grandmother's. *But notice there's no mention of loving or honoring or cherishing you.*

But even more than that, she did not *want* him to kiss her—or do anything else to her, for that matter. His...*attack* had been the antithesis of delicious, as far as she was concerned. Thank heavens Georgiana was indeed here with her; in fact, she almost wished now that they *were* sharing a room.

She straightened her shoulders and turned back to look at him. "My lord, I—I fear that I do not share your feelings. Furthermore, I cannot think this is the time and place to discuss such...matters." It was a miracle that no one had chosen to come down this particular alley a moment ago!

He had the grace to look abashed. "You are right. I humbly beg your pardon, my darling. This was not the time or place." He offered her his arm. "Shall we return to the inn?"

"Yes, please." Annabel took his arm, not without trepidation, and they continued on. She was careful this time to not let him draw her too close to his side again...but surely that had not been the cause of his behavior. Nor, on reflection, did she think had she done anything to encourage his advances, even when considering her actions through the filter of her inner Grandmother Shellingham.

But she must make it clear *now* that while she enjoyed his company for a stroll or a ride in the park, she did not welcome it in her bedchamber. And there was no time like the present. "Lord Glen—" she began.

But he had spoken as well. "I find it difficult to credit that it is already June. Before we know it, the season will be over. Do you go to Brighton in August?"

Annabel closed her mouth on her interrupted words. Should she forge ahead, or allow him to smooth over the matter with polite conversation? She hesitated, weighing the alternatives...and the moment passed.

"I...usually I bring my sons to visit my parents in August," she finally said. "I've never been to Brighton; my husband often went for a few weeks' stay while I was in Somerset."

"Oh, you must come this year. Surely a week or two would not be out of the question, would it? Frances always enjoys our visits there; she would be delighted if you were present as well."

His mention of Frances was reassuring; she'd half-expected him to suggest a private *rendezvous*—inasmuch as anything in Brighton in August could be private, packed as it was with the Prince of Wales and his friends and hangers-on. But still... "Thank you. I—I am doubtful that it could be managed, but I shall give it some thought."

The rest of their walk back to the inn through the slowly deepening dusk was quiet, offering no good conversational openings for making clear her feelings—or lack of them—to Lord Glenrick. Very well, if it could not happen tonight, tomorrow or the next day would have to suffice. She hoped he would accept a rebuff philosophically, so that they could remain friends. One never knew; some men could be touchy about having their advances rejected.

Especially if that rejection coincided with another man's advances *not* being rejected.

Not that Quin was precisely making advances to her; it was more as if...as if he was encouraging her to make advances to *him* now that she thought about it. If matters between them continued in this way, then Lord Glenrick might well come to regard Quin as a rival.

Or would he? The interactions that she'd observed between the two men were odd. Quin had once warned her against Lord Glenrick without explaining why she should be wary of him. Yet she'd seen the pair of them together at the Summer Exhibition, and Quin had accepted Lord Glenrick's invitations to the opera and to Hampton Court—or had those been Frances's invitations?

It was all dreadfully perplexing.

But even if Quin were not here, she would not be falling into Lord Glenrick's arms simply because he wanted her to. That, at least, was *not* perplexing.

Some hours later, Annabel was again walking the tent alleys of Epsom Down—this time wrapped in shadow and with a cloaked Georgiana by her side. Sneaking out of the inn—even with Georgiana—had been the least of her difficulties. The greatest had been her maid, Winters.

When she'd gone up to her room after returning from her walk with Lord Glenrick, Winters was waiting for her, as was proper. Annabel allowed her to take her hat and shawl to put away but refused, nonchalantly but firmly, when Winters offered to help her prepare for bed. "Thank you, but I find I am wide awake. Perhaps I'll sit by the fire in one of the parlours downstairs and read for a bit. You don't need to wait up for me."

Winters bent to put the folded shawl into Annabel's portmanteau. When she straightened, there was a faint line between her eyebrows. Annabel raised her own. "What is it, Winters?"

"What is what, my lady?"

"Something's troubling you."

"Oh, no—"

"You're wearing the face you usually save for informing me that my glove box now contains at least five mateless gloves and that I must either stop losing them or permit you to purchase more. Since my mother was kind enough to replenish my glove supply, that can't be it. What have I done?"

Winters' pursed lips twitched into an unwilling smile. "It's not really my place to say—"

"That won't fadge. I know you too well; if you thought it wasn't your place, we would not be having this conversation."

Winters' internal struggle lasted a moment longer. Then she sighed. "I beg your pardon in advance, my lady. I know it's none of my affair. But—" She stopped, biting her lip.

Annabel left unsaid the cajoling words she'd been about to utter. Winters was truly unhappy. "Please tell me," she said simply.

"It's—if you wish to read, may I not bring you another candle so that you can remain here instead? It's—not fitting that you should be down in the parlour alone."

Ah, so that was the problem. "Thank you, but Mrs. Bunwich assured me that she's closed the inn to anyone not actually staying here. I won't be jostled by the locals. In fact, the parlours were empty when I came in a moment ago."

"It isn't the locals I'm worried about." Poor Winters looked desperately uncomfortable. "I daresay you'll think I'm putting my nose in where it don't belong, my lady, but Mrs. Bunwich's Liz was telling me after you went out that Lord Glenrick was asking her earlier which room you were in and whether you were sharing it with Lady Bathurst or me or had it to yourself. 'I thought 'er ladyship 'ud want to be knowing that, so she can leave th' door off the latch if she wishes,'" she mimicked. "She actually *winked* when she said that!"

Oh, dear. Winters' scandalized expression might have made her laugh if she hadn't been so annoyed. Drat Lord Glenrick! What did the man think he was about? The last thing she wanted to stir up was gossip joining their names—and with the inn's other guests all being members of the *ton*, that was not too far-fetched a possibility. "Thank you for warning me. I can imagine it was uncomfortable for you."

Winters looked relieved. "Do you wish me to stay here with you tonight, my lady? I could fix up a pallet from a few blankets."

Make that *double* drat on Lord Glenrick. How would she be able to slip out with Georgiana to pay a call on Maharahnee if Winters were hovering over her like a Spanish duenna guarding her charge? "N...no, thank you, Winters. I trust he will be enough of a gentleman not to do anything so crass as to invade my room."

Winters turned painfully red and looked away. "Yes, my lady."

"And I have no intention of inviting him to do so, either." She hesitated. Something in Winters' averted face wouldn't allow her not to say something. "But I—er, do have an engagement this evening outside the inn that I must keep."

"An engagem—" Winters looked up, startled, and then quickly away. "Yes, my lady."

"I promise you, I will not be out alone—and I won't be with Lord Glenrick."

Winters still would not look at her. "No, my lady. Will you be wanting me to wait for you?"

Annabel sighed. Winters was only a few years older than herself but sometimes felt rather like her mother's lieutenant, deputed to keep an eye on her. "If you wish to, Winters. But I don't know how long I'll be."

Winters drew herself up. "I'd prefer to wait, my lady."

So at least she had not had to sneak out of her room. She'd waited for Georgiana's knock and cast a shadow over them before they tiptoed down the stairs and out the inn's door.

Despite the actual creation of a shadow being easier in nighttime—there was plenty of raw material to work with, after all—it was more difficult to maintain it well. Night was not all black; just as day did, it had its own variations and textures of shadow. She had learned from experience that turning herself into a figure of inky blackness could make her stand out on, say, a moonlit night. Indeed, one balmy spring evening at Belsever Magna, as a girl, she'd sneaked outside to play with shadows and had given the Vicar of St. Matilda's an apoplexy; the poor man was on his way home after dining with her parents and had been convinced that the dark, featureless figure coming toward him on the drive was a demon straight from the pits of hell. It had been excessively difficult not to dissolve into giggles in church the following Sunday when he gave a heartfelt sermon on maintaining one's vigilance against the powers of darkness.

There was little light in the sky this evening as it was only a few nights past the new moon. But their journey was made more complex by sudden encounters with drunken race-goers bearing torches and lanterns, stumbling their way between parties.

"It is astonishing what excuses men will find to engage in foolish behavior. All this for horses running about in a field," Georgiana murmured as they stepped aside to avoid yet another group of inebriated men crossing their path.

"I know," Annabel murmured back. She probably could have spoken in normal conversational tones and not have drawn a bit of notice.

In the darkness, broken by the occasional torch or lantern, the tent city looked completely different from how it had only hours before. Annabel missed the turn for the alley she and Lord Glenrick had gone down earlier but found the thoroughfare; when she spotted the big yellow-and-green-striped tent with its red pennons still flying and the two tall torches burning brightly before it, she breathed a sigh of relief. It sounded as if the party inside it was still in full spate, which would provide some cover for Georgiana to talk to Maharahnee.

No Jem Salter stood guard outside Maharahnee's tent, but that only increased the chance that he might be inside it. If only Clementina were with them; her ears would have easily discerned whether he was or not. Instead, Georgiana would have to investigate on her own.

On the trip to Epsom, it had been decided among them that Georgiana would take the form of a goat to make the first attempt to talk to Maharahnee. Many horses seemed to find the company of goats calming, and in that form she would surely appear less threatening than another horse or a person. But she would first take the shape of a mouse and slip inside the tent to confirm that Jem Salter wasn't there.

They moved into the narrow gap between the two tents, where the shadows were deeper. Georgiana grimaced as she unfastened her cloak and handed it to Annabel. She wore a plain black robe beneath it, long-sleeved and high in the neck; she possessed an entire wardrobe of plain gowns in varying shades of white, tan, brown, and grey to aid in her assumption of different animal forms. "I do not look forward to—" She pressed her lips together.

Annabel could guess the rest of what she had been about to say. "We could wait until Maria is here tomorrow," she murmured. "I expect she could find a way to talk to Maharahnee."

Georgiana shook her head—and then she wasn't there. Only a small black mouse stood in her place, staring up at Annabel.

"Good luck," Annabel said quietly. "I'll be here."

The mouse scurried toward the tent and nosed along it before disappearing under its edge. Annabel prepared to wait. For a few minutes, all she heard were the sounds of conviviality from the yellow and green tent—men talking loudly and laughing, the clink of a wine bottle on the rim of a glass—ah! There beneath the other noises had been the soft bleat of a goat. So Jem Salter was not inside, and Georgiana had found her way in to Maharahnee. With any luck she would be able to find out what was going on and they would be able to go back to London tomorrow. A little distance from Lord Glenrick would be helpful at present, and perhaps Quin—

The bleating sounded again; this time a horse's restless stomp and a sharp snort answered it. Another bleat was followed by an angry whinny—and then Georgiana was there, looking about her wildly until Annabel took her arm and drew her shadow around them both. "Georgiana! Are you hurt?"

It took another few moments for Georgiana to catch her breath. "This is—there is something wrong here," she finally gasped out.

"What happened?"

Georgiana took a few more shuddering breaths. "I don't—truly know. After I made certain that—that Mr. Salter was not there, I took on a goat's shape." She swallowed. "Of course, Maharahnee was startled. But when I tried to speak to her, she became terrified. I left her before she took it into her head to bolt through the tent wall."

"Did she—" Annabel searched for the correct word and gave up. "Did she *say* anything?"

"Nothing." Georgiana frowned. "Or perhaps I ought to say, almost nothing. I think her terror said a great deal—if only we could understand its source." She straightened her back and gave a small hiss of pain.

"Here." Annabel had been about to hand her her cloak, but instead reached around to settle it over her shoulders. "Would you...that is, it's not a short walk back to the inn. If it would help to take a small form,

I could carry you—"

"I will be able to walk," Georgiana said curtly, and drew the cloak more closely around her.

Annabel stifled a sigh as she pulled a shadow over them for the walk back. She'd only been trying to *help*.

Chapter Three

“**M**aharahnee was *afraid* of Georgiana?” Maria turned to stare at Annabel. “Are you certain of that?”

They were driving down one of the “boulevards” in the tent city near the Epsom race-course, weaving through the busy morning bustle of horses and people in the curricle in which Lord Sefton had driven down from London. Maria drove it with a careless ease that rather surprised Annabel—and just now, as Maria stared at her for far too long, alarmed her.

“Shouldn’t you be watching where we’re going?” she asked nervously, gesturing at the reins held slackly between Maria’s gloved fingers.

“Oh.” Maria faced forward again and made a soft whoofling sound. The horse nodded his head and continued his pace. “I don’t in fact drive,” she said to Annabel. “I simply tell Hermes where we want to go. It’s much easier than messing about with reins and whips and all that nonsense. He’s perfectly capable of trotting smartly up and down the lanes looking at everything while we talk. It's as if the carriage drives itself, really. *Very* useful."

"Er..." Annabel began. If Maria was unconcerned about permitting a horse to decide where—and how fast—they went, it was probably better to forget where she was and concentrate on their discussion. "Ah—yes, Georgiana was quite certain of Maharahnee's reaction. I was there and heard nothing that makes me doubt her assessment of the matter."

"How excessively odd." Maria gazed broodily at Hermes' hindquarters. "And Georgiana is there with her now?"

"Yes." Georgiana, in the shape of a barn swallow, had gone to perch unobtrusively on Maharahnee's tent; after last night's strange encounter, they had agreed it would be the best way to observe what was happening there. Annabel had offered to take the first watch that morning, but Georgiana had insisted on going despite the fact that she was clearly in discomfort.

"I expect I should not try to speak with her, then," Maria said. "At least, not yet. If a goat frightened the poor creature so much, a human addressing her in her own speech will likely send her into a panic." She frowned. "But why *did* a goat upset her so? Most horses I've spoken with *adore* goats. They think they're the most darling things."

"We wondered the same thing. And I agree that your speaking with her might not be the best course to follow. That is why we've decided simply to watch her for now."

"I wish I could be of some help with that. It is a great deal of work for you two to be doing on your own. And you're only supposed to be assisting on this investigation, you poor thing. I must say, nonetheless, that I'm monstrous glad you're here." Maria patted her hand. "Let us have a look at this Maharahnee. Might we drive past her tent or whatever it is she's in?"

"Well…" Annabel looked about in consternation. "I'm not certain I can tell how to get there from here…only that it's next to an enormous yellow tent with hideous green stripes."

"That will do to begin with." Maria leaned forward and made a series of snorts and squeals and other peculiar noises, pitched just loud enough to reach their horse's ears. He listened, then jerked his head up and down.

Maria sat back in her seat. "There. Hermes will find it for us—but I suppose it best if we watch as well. My word, this place gets busier every year. The first time Sefton attended, there were scarcely a thousand watchers and nothing resembling this." She waved her hand at the rows of tents. "It's a good thing Georgiana took a bird's shape. You need wings to be able to make your way around here."

"Indeed." Annabel took a breath. "I am…concerned about Georgiana. Her shape-changing seems to be…ah…troubling her a great deal recently."

"I know." Maria sighed. "You younger ones can't understand—why should you?—that growing old has its share of aches and pains for all of us, but triply so for Georgiana, who can change her form from one creature's to another's. Doing so uses parts of her anatomy that aren't typically used in her natural shape, which aggravates the expected discomforts imposed by her age. Do you recall what she said in the carriage yesterday? She was correct that we are seeing a much higher number of investigations this year, and that has put an unwonted strain on her. I must tell Sally on our return not to send her out on any investigations for at least a few weeks." She sighed again. "What with Clementina's being in an interesting condition, that leaves us sadly under-manned—or womaned."

A few moments later, Hermes whinnied. Maria whinnied briefly in reply, and his trot slowed to a walk. "We're almost there, he says," she told Annabel. "Can you see it?"

Annabel leaned forward. "Er...there! On the left. Do you see the striped monstrosity? It's the next one beyond it."

Maria followed her discreetly pointing finger. "I see it. Good heavens, my parents had a marquee like that for *al fresco* fêtes in the gardens. Theirs was not so outsized—or ugly, now that I think of it. I don't suppose we had better stop, but we can circle round again. Hermes?" she called, and made another peculiar equine sound. The horse's walk slowed further.

As they drew abreast of the striped tent—quiet this morning, with no sounds of jollification coming from under its be-pennoned roof—Annabel saw that the same strongly built, soberly suited man she'd seen the night before was seated in a straight chair in front of the tent, idly watching the passers-by. He met her gaze as she and Maria passed, and she was certain that she saw a flicker of recognition in his otherwise impassive expression. Who was he, and why was he keeping watch in this fashion?

"Not much to see, is there?" Maria murmured, and Annabel dragged her attention back to

Maharahnee's tent, which wore a derelict air with its flaps down and no tightly coiled Jem Salter sitting before it. But Maria had spoken too soon. Just as they passed the smaller, shabbier tent, the flap of patched canvas covering the entrance was pushed roughly aside and a man of about forty years—or thirty-five hard-lived ones—strode out, scowling and muttering under his breath. He was dressed fashionably but carelessly, with a faded foulard neckerchief for a cravat and well-made boots that had not seen polish for some time. He paused long enough to glare at everyone and everything in his immediate vicinity, half-raising the riding crop he clutched in one hand, and then stalked away, still muttering.

"My goodness." Maria frowned at his retreating back. "I do believe that was Sir Oswald Broxley himself. From what I was able to learn last night from Derby, he's a thoroughly unpleasant creature."

"He certainly looks it." Between her bad-tempered owner and peppery trainer, poor Maharahnee must have a difficult existence. "I hope Georgiana has learned something this morning."

"So do I." Maria said something snorting and whoofling to Hermes, then sat back. "I asked him to go to the end of the row and turn round to drive by again. Then we'll go back to your inn and wait for Georgiana."

By the time they made it to the end of the tents and had ambled back again, a crowd had gathered in front of Maharahnee's tent. Oblivious of the fact that she was supposed to be driving, Maria stood up to see what had drawn them, steadying herself with a hand on Annabel's shoulder. "There's a man currying a horse in front—oh, I do think that must be

Maharahnee!" she exclaimed, shading her eyes with her other hand. Annabel tried not to wonder what she'd done with the reins. "I'll tell Hermes to pull over so that we can have a look." She sat down again, to Annabel's relief.

Hermes obligingly brought them to the edge of the growing crowd. From her seat in the curricle, Annabel had an excellent view over everyone's heads: there indeed was Jem Salter, still fierce-looking but moving calmly as he curried his charge. And as for Maharahnee herself—

"She's so...*dainty*," she said in an undertone to Maria. Maharahnee's glossy brown coat with one endearing white sock on her back left leg and small head with delicate nostrils reminded her of her favorite hack, Primrose, in Papa's stables at Belsever Magna. Was this how a prize-winning racehorse should appear? A voice murmured in the back of her mind: *if Quin were here, he would probably know.*

"Yes, she is," Maria replied. "I shall be interested to ask Hermes what he thinks of her."

The horse stood quietly, without fidgeting or shifting, and allowed Jem Salter to groom her. But she seemed to regard the people jostling to get a look at her with a tense, distrustful air that called to mind the distraught creature Georgiana had confronted last night. Annabel felt a pang of pity for her.

"Shall we go back to the inn?" she asked. "Poor Maharahnee does not need us gawking at her as well, and Georgiana will undoubtedly be back soon. I hope she was able to hear whatever conversation Sir Oswald had with Mr. Salter."

Maria gazed at Maharahnee a moment longer. "The poor thing looks ready to jump out of her skin.

Perhaps that explains her reaction to Georgiana, but..." She gave a soft snort, and Hermes stepped back into the flow of carriages and horsemen traveling down the roadway.

As they passed the striped tent once again, Annabel stole a glance at its seated guardian. This time, he met her look with a polite nod. So he did recognize her...but why should he have any interest in her? She started to turn to look back at him, then stopped herself. She couldn't allow this minor mystery to distract her from the larger one of Maharahnee.

As soon as they were free of the crowd, Maria addressed a series of snorts and whinnies to Hermes. "I asked what he thinks of our friend back there," she said to Annabel, by way of explanation.

Hermes' response, compared to Maria's question, was almost comically terse—a sort of half-whicker, which resolved into a brief snort. Maria looked confused and spoke to him again, and once again his response was brief.

"Well?" Annabel asked.

"I don't know." Maria was frowning. "He must not have understood what I was asking him."

"What did you say?"

"I asked him what he thought of the horse we were looking at while we stopped at the edge of the crowd a moment ago."

"And?"

"And—" Her shoulders hunched. "It makes no sense. He said, *What horse?*"

Georgiana's maid, Nettles, was waiting in the Horse and Oak's entrance hall when Annabel and Maria came in from their drive. Unlike her employer, she was plump and cheery-looking, but her face as she accosted them was anything but cheerful.

"Her ladyship's just back and having a lie-down because she's completely done in." She fixed Maria with a reproachful look. "Your ladyship knows how it is with her. I hope you weren't planning to make her go out again today."

"Nettles, you know I'd never make her do anything. But when she feels it's her duty to do something, there's no stopping her. Why, Lady Fellbridge tried to convince her to stay abed and leave her to go in her place just this morning, but you know how she is."

Nettles shook her head and sighed but relented enough to give Annabel an approving nod. "I do know, m'lady. It's only that taking the shape of anything with wings particularly troubles her lumbago."

Annabel barely managed not to splutter in surprise. Georgiana's maid knew what she was?

"Then we shall endeavor to see that she doesn't again while we're here," Maria said. "You have my word."

"Thank you, m'lady." The maid dropped a curtsy. "Speaking of words, she wishes to have one with you now that you're back."

"We'll go up directly. And we shan't keep her long," Maria promised.

Once they had climbed the stairs and were out of earshot of the anxious maid, Annabel could no longer restrain herself. "Georgiana's maid knows what she is?"

"Hmm? Oh, yes—she's been Georgiana's maid forever, you know. I imagine that trying to hide an ability such as hers would have been a dreadful chore. Nettles's utterly devoted, and I understand she's monstrous clever with making gowns for Georgiana to match various creatures—it makes changing ever so much easier, Georgiana says. Here we are." She rapped briskly on a door and opened it when a weak voice bade them enter.

Georgiana regarded them from a prodigious pile of pillows on the bed. "You saw Nettles?" she croaked. "Oh, my voice. Birds do that to me." She waved a hand before her throat irritably.

Maria took the chair by the bed. "We promised her we wouldn't tire you out. I presume you learned something? We happened to drive by Maharahnee's tent when someone I'm certain was Sir Oswald came thundering out."

Georgiana sniffed. "Thundering is a good word. He is a thoroughly horrid man! It is not to be wondered that poor Maharahnee's so nervous, the way he growls and glares at her."

"What was he growling about?" Annabel asked.

"No, start at the beginning." For all her seeming vagueness, Maria could be remarkably incisive when leading an investigation.

"Almost nothing occurred until he came in. Then he and Jem Salter had a bit of a set-to about a number of things. Sir Oswald wants Maharahnee out on display as much as possible, to draw crowds and encourage betting. He also wants Jem Salter out and about picking up gossip and any information he can get on competing horses. Jem Salter said—quite reasonably, I thought—that he could not be two places at once—showing Maharahnee *and* skulking around the pubs—which set Sir Oswald into a rage."

"Naturally," Maria said.

"Naturally," Georgiana echoed. "What wasn't natural was the rest of what was said. Jem Salter told Sir Oswald that she was extremely upset that morning when he came in."

"She? That is, Maharahnee?"

"I am only reporting what was said."

"Of course," Maria soothed. "Pray go on."

"I am trying to. He then said that she had used her code. The sentence was uttered with no small degree of emphasis."

"Her *code*? Are you certain that's what he said?"

"My hearing is perfectly acute in bird shape," Georgiana said haughtily. "That is the precise word he used. Sir Oswald said that it would be too difficult under the circumstances—yes, those were his words, too—but Jem Salter said she'd been insistent. And Maharahnee at that very moment gave a loud whinny."

"As if she understood what was being discussed," Annabel said. This was getting stranger and stranger.

"Indeed."

"How interesting. Anything else?"

"Sir Oswald continued to protest, but when Maharahnee grew more upset, Jem Salter told Sir Oswald that unless he honored their agreement, he wouldn't ride in the race."

That made it sound as if Jem Salter had some degree of say in their joint affairs...but Maharahnee was the more interesting player in the scene Georgiana had described. Annabel met Maria's glance. "You don't suppose that Maharahnee is... sentient?"

"I am beginning to wonder," Maria said. "What did Sir Oswald say to Jen Salter's ultimatum?"

"He agreed that they would meet tonight at three to discuss the matter." Georgiana sank further into her pillows, as if the very mention of a three-o'clock-in-the-morning meeting exhausted her... which it probably did, under the circumstances.

"Three?" Maria sighed. "I don't mind staying at a ball till three, but...very well. At least we can rest until then."

Annabel and Maria were in place fifteen minutes before three, making their shadow-wrapped way through a damp, chilly night-time fog that had risen from the hollows below the downs. Annabel was convinced that the top of her head would fall off after one of her yawns, but the chill kept her alert. They had found a conveniently located tear in the side of the tent, at eye-level, which was covered by a patch with frayed stitches. Annabel could not help wondering at the ease of it all. Might someone else be keeping an eye on Maharahnee and her owner's doings?

She was about to whisper as much to Maria—it was a pity that the ongoing party in the green-and-yellow-striped tent behind them was apparently in a lull, or she would not have had to whisper—when voices from within Maharahnee's tent sent her to peer through the slit in the canvas. Unfortunately, Maria's reaction was the same, so that they knocked heads smartly. Maria winced, but fortunately did not cry aloud. After a moment of maneuvering, they found a comfortable position that allowed them both to peer one-eyed through the tear.

Jem Salter was lighting a second lantern from the one that hung from a nail on one of the tent's poles. The added light illuminated Sir Oswald Broxley's face, which wore what must be a habitual scowl. "Well?" he said harshly.

"Give her a minute, will you?" Jem Salter handed him the lantern he'd lit and lifted something from a wicker hamper in the corner of the tent. It appeared to be a large linen sheet with ribbons tacked to its corners. He turned to the third occupant of the tent, a skittish-looking Maharahnee who was restlessly shifting her feet, and tied the sheet around her neck by the ribbons so that it hung before her, apron-like.

"There you go, miss," he said gently, unfastening her halter and removing it.

"Ah," Maria breathed, and grasped Annabel's arm.

Annabel was grateful for the bite of Maria's fingernails into her skin, for it kept her from gasping out loud when Maharahnee was suddenly no longer there. In her place stood a small, brown-haired woman somewhere in her thirties, clutching the sheet to her. She stood blinking for a moment as if to catch her breath. "Thank you, Jem," she said in a low, throaty voice, then coughed. "Thank you," she repeated, less hoarsely.

"I left a damned promising card game to be here." Sir Oswald was tapping the riding crop he habitually seemed to carry on one booted toe. "Whatever you have to say, dear sister, it had better be worth my while."

Sister! Annabel looked quickly between the red-faced man and the pale but straight-backed woman. Yes, the resemblance was there—but what was going on? Why was Sir Oswald's sister—a shape-shifter!—posing as a racehorse for him?

"You drink this before you try to talk any more, Miss Charlotte." Jem Salter handed the woman a leathern tankard. "You don't want to strain your throat."

Charlotte took the tankard with a nod and drank its contents while Sir Oswald stood and fumed. When she'd finished drinking, she lowered the tankard and fixed him with a fearful, wide-eyed stare. "We must stop this masquerade at once!"

"Now, miss—" Jem Salter began soothingly, reaching to pat her shoulder as if she were still a horse.

"We must stop *nothing*," Sir Oswald said from between gritted teeth. "What is this bilge you're talking?"

"It is *not* bilge!" Charlotte stamped her foot. "We have been discovered!" She turned away from him, her shoulders hunched. "I should never have allowed you to convince me to come here. Were it not for Florian—"

"What's going on, Miss Charlotte?" Jem Salter glared at Sir Oswald, who had made an exasperated noise.

"Last night—I don't know when—a mouse ran into the tent. I paid it no mind—they often do that, looking for dropped oats—but this mouse stopped and looked up at me—and then it—she—"

"*What?*" Sir Oswald exploded.

"She turned into a goat," Charlotte whispered. "And she tried to talk to me."

Sir Oswald, who had been about to speak, closed his mouth and narrowed his eyes.

"Tried to talk to you?" Jem Salter had paled too. "What did it say?"

"She told me that she was my friend and that she wanted to help me." Charlotte shivered. "I could not answer her—I dared not! I—I panicked, and the goat changed back into a mouse and escaped the way she had come in." She clasped her hands before her. "Don't you see? Someone *knows*. Someone has figured out what we are doing. Oswald, I can no longer maintain this ruse. Please, may we go home? I'll take Florian and find a cottage somewhere for us. I have mother's bequest—we shan't be a burden on you—"

"The devil you will." Sir Oswald grabbed her wrist, twisting it as he yanked her toward him until they were practically nose to nose. "We are *not* going home. You will run on Saturday, and you will win, and win well—very well." His voice dropped to a malevolent silkiness. "You will win if you ever want to see that boy again."

Charlotte gasped. "Oswald! What do you intend?"

He smirked at her, then turned on his heel and stalked from the tent.

Charlotte stared after him, rubbing her arm where he'd twisted it, then turned to Jem Salter. "Oh, Jem! What am I to do? What will happen to us if we are caught? And where has Oswald hidden my poor little brother? This is—I cannot think—there's too much—"

"Now, Miss Charlotte." The older man patted

her shoulder again, awkwardly. "I 'spect we'll get through this—"

"Yes, until it's time to run the next race, and the one after that. Oswald has so many debts that there will be no end to this until I am too old to run, and then what? And if someone has discovered us, what will we do? Will they want money from Oswald to keep our secret as well?" She grasped his arm. "You must help me put a stop to this. Please, help me find Florian—we'll all escape from Oswald together. Or you could go and work for someone else. I know any of Oswald's acquaintances would hire you at once—Sir Thomas Bettany or Lord Runston—"

"We'll talk about that later." Annabel noticed that Jem Salter would not meet her eyes. "We'll get through this race an' go home, and then we'll talk. It's only another day or two—you're worrying yerself sick over naught. And ye'd best think 'bout changing back now—too long in yer natural shape'll make you too stiff to run. I've got a nice fresh pot of my liniment here—"

"Jem—"

"After Saturday," he said firmly. "I promise you, we'll talk after Saturday."

Maria tugged on Annabel's arm. "Enough," she mouthed when Annabel looked at her.

Annabel nodded, and they tiptoed away under cover of her shadow. Only when they were well away from the tent city and close to the Horse and Oak did either of them speak.

"It's as I suspected," Maria finally murmured. "She's a shape-shifter. That explains so many things—the running of races at far-apart location, and Hermes' odd reaction to her."

"He's forcing his own sister to pose as one of his racehorses!" Annabel was incensed. "And has done something dreadful to their own brother."

"I did some judicious asking about this afternoon among Lord Derby's guests," Maria said. "It seems that Sir Oswald's father remarried after the death of his first wife—that would be the mother of Sir Oswald and Charlotte Broxley. There's a younger brother from that second marriage." She hesitated. "It seems the boy's a bit of an invalid. He was blinded after an attack of the measles."

"Good God!" Sir Oswald was even more of a villain than he appeared, then. "We must do something to help them."

"And to prevent Miss Broxley from racing on Saturday. That would be wrong for many reasons." Maria stopped; they were at the inn's front door, which they'd wedged open when they left. Maria was going to spend the rest of the night with Georgiana— or early morning, for the eastern sky was already brightening. "We shall have breakfast as planned at nine with Georgiana so that the three of us can discuss what we learned tonight. Get what sleep you can; I suspect this will be a monstrously busy day."

A few hours later, Annabel shut the door to Georgiana's chamber and leaned against the wall next to it in order to give a jaw-cracking yawn before making her way back to her room. She'd managed to snatch about three hours of sleep last night—or this morning, rather—before Winters came in to dress her—an unfortunately highly observant Winters who took one look at her and asked, "Did you not sleep well, my lady?"

"What? Oh, no, I slept very well, thank you." Annabel tried to smile brightly at her maid. It was evidently unconvincing; Winters pursed her lips and did not reply. Annabel was seized by a sudden conviction that Winters must have looked in on her for some reason and found her bed empty. Did she think that her mistress had been visiting someone else's bed?

But Winters said nothing further as she helped Annabel dress and did her hair. Annabel was grateful to be able to escape to Georgiana's chamber after her maid's chilly silence.

Not that she and Maria and Georgiana had had much to discuss. After relating the conversation she and Maria had eavesdropped on to Georgiana over a pot of Mrs. Bunwich's excellent coffee and a plate of rolls, they decided that one of them must find the earliest opportunity to speak with Maharahnee/Miss Broxley and offer their help. Since she wasn't, strictly speaking, a horse, any of them (not only Maria) should be able to speak to her and be understood.

But Maria had engagements that day with her host, Lord Derby, and Georgiana would remain in her room that day, according to Nettles; therefore, it was up to Annabel to find an opportunity to speak to Miss Broxley. Winters had probably already finished setting her room to rights and gone down to the kitchens for her own breakfast, so Annabel could go back there to fetch her hat and gloves and spencer and make her way down to stand watch at Maharahnee's tent. With any luck she'd have a chance to relay their message of help—which would no doubt lead to another three-in-the-morning meeting, alas!—and be back here by noon for a nap. A blissful, at least two-hour nap, with her stays loosened and her hair unpinned—

She rounded the corner—her and Georgiana's chambers were at different ends of the L-shaped inn—and was arrested by the sight of a male figure standing in the doorway of her room, his back to her and one arm resting high on the doorframe. Below his arm she could see Winters, her demeanor wary but polite.

"Gone already? And here I had hoped to coax your mistress into breakfast before going for a drive with me," the man was saying.

Lord Glenrick! The last thing she had time for today was parrying his advances. Oh, why did everything have to be so complicated?

Without hesitation, she scooped a handful of shadow from a fold of her skirt and cast it over her. She would wait at the corner of the passage until Lord Glenrick had gone downstairs and then retrieve her hat and gloves, telling Winters that she would be spending the day with Maria. Complication solved.

"Please tell Lady Fellbridge that I had hoped to see her today," Lord Glenrick was saying. "Perhaps she would do me the honor of dining with me this evening in the parlour downstairs. You will tell her that I was looking for her?"

Winters must have replied in the affirmative, for he said "good girl" and produced a coin from his pocket before turning and going to the staircase. Annabel listened as he descended them, then commenced counting to three hundred to ensure he did not return and to allow at least a brief pause between his departure and her arrival to her chamber. As for dining with him—heaven knew where she would be at that time. She would have Winters politely decline for her if Lord Glenrick returned while she was on duty at Maharahnee's tent.

She whisked off her shadow and walked down the hall in as natural a manner as possible, and breezily opened the door. The offhand greeting she had planned to say to Winters died on her lips as she crossed the threshold.

Winters was not bustling around the room in her usual diligent fashion. Instead, she was seated on the edge of Annabel's bed, her hands clutching each other in her lap and her face as pale as if she'd caught sight of the proverbial ghost. She stared up at Annabel with an almost fearful look on her usually placid, round face.

"Why, Winters! What is it?" Annabel dropped to her knees before her and took one of her hands. "Are you ill?"

Winters opened her mouth, but no sound emerged. With a visible effort, she finally managed to speak. "I...saw you. You were there, and then...you weren't."

Oh. Annabel sat back on her heels. Oh *dear.*

"I saw you—behind Lord Glenrick when he was here a few moments ago. You...you were down the hall," Winters was saying. "You had just come around the—the corner in the passage and you stopped, and then...then you raised your hand and—" She looked at Annabel plaintively. "Did I really see what I think I saw?"

Annabel thoughts whirled. Whilst she had always been as careful as possible, she had on occasion been caught in the midst of concealing or un-concealing herself. On each of these occasions, the person who had seen her had been easy to convince—no, been *eager* to be convinced—that their eyes had played tricks on them and that she certainly had not appeared before them from nowhere. Most people did not want to know that there was much more to the world than what they saw and knew every day. So she could, very easily, pat Winters' hand and say no, *of course* she hadn't seen Annabel disappear into thin air—it was all a trick of the dazzling morning light—and that perhaps she was overtired and needed a good cup of tea and a bit of a lie-down...

But this was Winters, whom she'd known most of her life and whose judgment she trusted and good opinion she valued. Did she want to alter that by lying to her?

Or should she continue to trust Winters by telling her the truth? Georgiana had confided in Nettles; she could not think that Winters wasn't worthy of the same consideration.

She sat down on the bed next to Winters. "I...that is..." She took a breath and met Winters' gaze. "Yes, you did."

Winters' eyes widened. She opened her mouth, but no sound came forth.

"It's something I've always been able to do, ever since I was small. I don't know why I can, but watch." She rose, swept a handful of shadow from under the edge of the bed, and draped it over her head.

Winters recoiled. "Dear God in heaven!"

Annabel quickly brushed it off. Had she miscalculated in her decision to tell Winters? "Don't be alarmed! I'm still here—and I promise you, this...thing I can do is not anything God would disapprove of, even if I do wonder why he saw fit to bestow it on me. It is nothing bad or evil...it simply *is*. Well, perhaps I have been a little bad, when I was small. I used to use it to escape from my old nurse—you must remember her from when you were employed at Belsever Magna! Now that I think about it, even then I think her eyesight was poor enough that I didn't need my shadows to fool her."

Winters laughed shakily. "No, likely not."

Annabel drew more shadow from under the bed and draped it over a pair of her slippers on the floor. "But I don't use it to hide myself or anything else for idle reasons."

Winters contemplated the seemingly empty place where her slippers lay hidden. "If I may ask—was there a—a particular reason you wished to avoid Lord Glenrick?"

"Yes, as it happens." Here was the tricky part. "We did not come to Epsom merely for amusement. I am here to assist in the conduct of an investigation."

"A—an investigation? What—that is, I expect it's none of my business, ma'am." But the interest in her expression said otherwise.

"On the contrary, I would greatly value your help. As I said, I am here to assist—others."

Winters digested this. "Such as—Lady Sefton? And Lady Bathurst? What could they possibly—" She stopped abruptly, reddening.

Annabel couldn't suppress a grin. "They might surprise you. I'm not the only one with an unusual gift."

"They too...? Do they do things such as you do

with—" She gestured toward Annabel's hidden slippers.

"Not quite. They have their own talents. Some of us have taken it upon ourselves"—no need to bring the Lady Patronesses and Almack's into it yet; poor Winters had had enough shocks for today— "to...ah...take care of situations that involve the unusual." She paused—would Winters be able to believe her? "Right now, we're investigating someone running a horse in races who also happens to be his sister."

Winters' eyes grew round. "His *sister*?"

"Yes." It did sound odd when phrased that way, didn't it? "She has the ability to take the shape of a horse—a very fast and clever one. They've been winning races left and right, but we've discovered that she's not a willing participant in the scheme, and we're trying to find a way to help her. I must go this morning to observe her—yes, hidden—and to find a way to speak with her. That is why I hid from Lord Glenrick just now. I would never have been able to get away if he had seen me."

She sat and again took Winters' hand. "I hope you comprehend that I have told you all this because I trust your discretion completely. Not only for my sake, but for the sake of the work the—er, my friends and I do. Stopping a cheat may not seem to be much, but we are doing what we can to make the world—or at least our small part of it—a better place."

Winters returned the pressure of her hand with a firm squeeze. "I...well, I can't say that I understand, my lady, because I don't understand *that*." She gestured toward Annabel's invisible slippers. "But about doing what you can—that I understand. It's not often a female can do anything much. The men want to keep that sort of thing to themselves."

"That's an astute observation," Annabel said. If she were for some reason to tell Lord Glenrick what she was doing in Epsom, he would undoubtedly tell her not to trouble herself over the matter, that he would resolve it (most probably by going directly to Sir Oswald.) Quin, on the other hand...oh, if only he were here instead of Lord Glenrick! She would ask him to draw Sir Oswald and Jem Salter aside to talk horses and be in to talk to Maharahnee in a trice... She shook her head.

"There's something else, Winters," she said. "Lady Bathurst's Nettles knows all about her mistress's—er, work and is a great help to her. If you were inclined, you could be of similar help to me...but I know that might be asking too much of you. If all of this is more than you—that is, if you would prefer to find employment with a more conventional employer, I promise that I will gladly give you the highest recommendation. But I ask that you'll keep my secret—or try to forget this ever happened—"

"No, my lady." The fierceness in Winters' voice surprised Annabel. "I don't want to leave you and work for anyone else. If you can do good for the world, I can help you—and be doing some good, too."

Annabel held up their still-clasped hands, then mimed an exaggerated handshake. Winters laughed, and they regarded each other with satisfaction.

Chapter Four

By that afternoon, Annabel judged that Winters had already earned her place as an investigative aide-de-camp: she chose a sturdy pair of half-boots for Annabel to wear, along with a cool, comfortable gown and spencer and a hat that would not obstruct her vision in any way. She also obtained a small stoneware bottle of lemonade for Annabel to bring to her watch at Maharahnee's tent.

Annabel needed the comfortable attire: nearly five hours had gone by without her getting a single chance to talk to the horse. Jem Salter had stuck to his charge as if he were a solicitous burr, tethering her outside to curry her coat and discuss the finer points of her conformation with the curious crowds who came to see her. Annabel remained in the shade to the tent's side; now, at half-past three, she was in the shadow cast by the green-and-yellow-striped tent, just around the corner from the front of Sir Oswald's tent so that she could listen in on conversations. The somberly clad young man she'd seen before was once again seated before the striped tent, obviously observing the crowds jostling around Maharahnee with considerable amusement. Annabel envied him his chair.

Well, eventually Jem Salter would have to go in search of his supper, although he had produced a lunch of bread and cheese that Annabel had also envied; still, with any luck he would prefer to dine early and she would have her chance. What was Miss Broxley thinking about as she stood there listening to the roughly and not-so-roughly dressed men discussing her haunches and her wind and asking Jem for a look at her teeth?

She looked again at the watch pinned at her waist. Forty minutes past three, and the crowd at the front of the tent was finally showing signs of thinning. If only Jem Salter would decide that he, too, could—

"Hoy! Salter!"

Annabel craned to peek further around the corner of the tent. Sir Oswald Broxley was striding toward it—a Sir Oswald she'd not seen before. This one had a spring in his step and was smiling broadly as he swung his riding crop jauntily by its strap. She edged closer and prayed she wouldn't trip or sneeze.

"Maharahnee has had enough excitement for one day." Sir Oswald had reached the tent and was cheerfully but firmly shooing away the remaining gawkers. "Excuse us, won't you? But be certain to place your bets for her—you'll be missing out if you don't." He jerked his head at Jem Salter. "Bring her inside, then come out here. We need to talk," he added, mouthing the last sentence.

Hmm. Annabel's joy—at last, a chance to talk to Miss Broxley!—faded. Sir Oswald evidently had something to say to Jem Salter that he did not want his sister to hear. Should she stay to listen to that, or seize the opportunity to speak to Miss Broxley while she was unguarded?

She started to creep back toward the tent, but something about the unwholesome glee in Sir Oswald's manner stayed her steps. Best to hear what he had to say; with any luck, he and Jem Salter would leave to dine together, and she could talk to Miss Broxley then. She watched Jem Salter lead Maharahnee back into the tent, speaking softly to her as he did, and waited until he came back out.

"What is it, then?" he said, a little truculently, to Sir Oswald.

"Quietly, you dolt." Sir Oswald took his arm and drew him further from the tent. The man in front of the striped tent watched them with interest. Annabel slipped closer.

"Listen, Salter. Whatever else happens, we have to win that race," Sir Oswald was saying.

"Tell me somethin' I don't know."

"Cut out the insolence, man, and listen. If you still want a job at my stables when this is over, she had better win."

"Well, I like that!" Jem Salter jerked his arm from Sir Oswald's grasp. "I've about had it with your jaw, you bracket-faced rascal. Findin' another job'll be a relief, and no mistake. Least I wouldn't be tryin' to cheat my races."

Sir Oswald scowled. "Just make certain she wins, damn you, because we stand to make a hell of a lot more than the purse alone if she does."

"How?"

A little of his former elation lit his voice. "Because I'm a deucedly clever fellow, that's why. I just made a deal with Lord Turffley that he'll buy Maharahnee for ten thousand guineas if she wins the Oaks Stakes."

Annabel barely smothered a gasp. Jem Salter didn't; his face was turning an alarming shade of purple. "What? You can't sell your own sister!"

"Quietly! I'm not actually selling her, you idiot. Turffley wins Maharahnee and takes her back to his stables. A week or two later—no, make it three so that it doesn't look suspicious—someone leaves the stable door open and Maharahnee runs away...and changes back into Charlotte and comes home. No one will be the wiser, and we'll be ten thousand guineas richer." He leaned closer to Jem Salter. "So that's why she has to win Saturday or else. Ten thousand will go a long way toward clearing my debts. Do whatever you have to—use the spurs or beat her till she bleeds. *We have to win!*"

That time, Annabel could not restrain her gasp. Sir Oswald's head whipped around. "Who's there?" he snarled.

Annabel took a cautious step backward—but not before Sir Oswald whirled, laying about him with his riding crop. He caught her on the arm; she cried out as she lost her balance and fell to her knees. The shock made her release her covering shadow.

Sir Oswald's eyes bulged as he looked down at her. "What the devil! Where did you come from, sneaking around here?"

Annabel tried to edge away from him, but her anger bubbled over. "You—you blackguard! Spurs?

For *shame*!"

He loomed over her, raising the crop again. "You spying little bitch! I'll show you what—"

"No, you won't," an unfamiliar voice said. From her vantage point on the dusty ground, she saw a hand close on Sir Oswald's upraised arm. The hand was attached to the arm of the young man from the green-and-yellow-striped tent.

"Get off me!" Sir Oswald tried to swing at him with his other arm, but another figure caught that one.

"Release him, Somers. Listen to me, Broxley. I don't care for bully boys—you don't deserve to be called a man—who raise their hands against women," the Marquis of Quinceton said.

Quin? Annabel gaped up at him.

"And I don't care for interfering chawbacons who stick their noses into other people's business," Sir Oswald growled. He drew his arm back to strike Quin, but before he could, Quin's fist shot out and landed squarely on his jaw. He staggered back and fell.

Quin probably didn't see him fall; he'd already turned to Annabel. "Are you hurt?" he asked, reaching both hands to help her up.

Quin. He was *here*, precisely when she needed him—as he always was. She took his hands and allowed him to pull her to her feet. "What are you doing here?"

"Why, Fellbridge! I distinctly remember telling you that I might take a look-in at Epsom."

The smile in his eyes, contrasting with his otherwise serious expression, did nothing to calm her rapidly beating heart. "But here? Now?"

"Ah. Yes, well." He glanced at the young man from the green-and-yellow-striped tent who had stopped Sir Oswald's attack. "We, ah, fortuitously happened to be in a most convenient location. Permit me to introduce my valet, Somers."

Annabel looked from him to the young man and back again, and the events of the last two days resolved themselves in a new light. "Your valet—good heavens! You are saying that striped monstrosity belongs to *you*!"

His lips twitched. "You cut me to the quick, madam! It's not a monstrosity—it's an heirloom. My grandparents hosted many a garden party from it on the south lawn at Sayre Hill that are still talked about today." He glanced down, and she realized that they were still holding hands. She pulled hers away self-consciously.

"Are you hurt?" Quin asked again, more quietly.

Hurt? She blinked; yes, she had fallen, hadn't she? And her arm...the place where Sir Oswald had caught her with his crop throbbed sharply. She shivered, remembering the way he'd glared down at her. "I—"

"I believe a chair might be indicated," he said. "Permit me to take you to one." He held out his arm.

"Thank you." But before they left for his tent—*his* tent!—she glanced back. Jem Salter had hauled a dazed-looking Sir Oswald to his feet and was leading him away. Neither of them looked at her.

The interior of the monstrosity was capacious, but the afternoon light shining through the green-and-yellow-striped canvas cast a slightly jaundiced light on everything within it. The center held a round table with half a dozen chairs and a pair of divans, the setting, no doubt, of the jollification she had heard the other nights. Behind a partly drawn curtain at the back of the tent she saw a neatly made campaign bed and quickly averted her eyes. *Prude!* called a voice in her head that sound remarkably like Emily's.

Somers pulled out one of the chairs as Quin led her to it. She sat and suddenly remembered how sore her feet were.

Quin was watching her; she felt his regard as if it were a tangible thing. "Some Malmsey, I think, Somers," he said.

"At once, sir." Somers went to the folding table that served as a sideboard.

"You don't have to—" Annabel began.

"Yes, he does. Trust me, Fellbridge, you need it."

He was correct, of course. She knew that with the first sip. The wine began at once to dissolve the cold knot in her midsection. She took another sip, and another.

Quin sat in the chair next to her, still watching her. She sighed. "I suppose you wish to know what that was all about."

He nodded to Somers, who bowed and left the tent. "I do admit to some curiosity," he replied.

"If I tell you, will you explain to me how you 'fortuitously happened' to pitch your monstrosity directly next to Sir Oswald's?"

"There's no great mystery there, but yes, I will."

"No mystery?" She regarded him skeptically over the rim of her glass.

"None at all. I'm here because you mentioned an interest in Sir Oswald Broxley's horse. Therefore, this seemed to be the most...logical location in which to establish myself if I wished to see you."

Her cheeks grew warm. "Why didn't you simply come to my inn, if you wanted to see me?"

"I would have tomorrow if I hadn't seen you by then. You're at the Horse and Oak," he added when she opened her mouth. "Your man Hanscomb kindly informed me of your direction. But I wished to be here for now in case I could offer you some trifling assistance."

She coughed slightly to overcome the lump in her throat. "You were needed. As you can see. I— thank you for that."

"Tosh," he said cheerfully. "Broxley is a bad 'un —always has been. I expect he's up to something with this new horse of his—the scoundrel has debts as bad as Prinny's, practically."

Annabel hesitated. He would undoubtedly think she was mad if she told him about Miss Broxley —or think she was bamming him shamelessly. Or perhaps not—this was the man who, less than a week ago, had faced down the river nymphs of the Thames with her.

For her.

She took a deep breath. "Yes, he is bad. His horse, Maharahnee—is actually his sister."

Quin had been about to sip from his own glass; instead, he set it down and looked at her, eyebrows raised. "His *sister*?

"Yes."

For a moment he stared fixedly at his glass, twirling it by the stem. "You...er, know this for a certainty?" he finally asked.

"Yes. She—ah—is able to take the shape of a horse when she wishes."

He exhaled and shook his head. "You do get yourself into the damnedest situations, Fellbridge. What else?"

"She is not doing this willingly; he's holding something to do with their younger half-brother over her head. We—er, I have been trying to find an opportunity to inform her that help is at hand if she wants it. And besides, the race would not be a fair one. That is not...honorable."

"Well, it could be argued that if Miss Broxley is truly taking a horse's form, then no rules are being broken—but I agree, it isn't honorable. And if she's being forced, then... You said 'we'. Who else is in on this?"

Drat. She had hoped he wouldn't notice her slip. "Lady Bathurst and Lady Sefton." She put down her glass. "Speaking of whom, I ought to go back to the inn. They will be waiting for me. Thank you for the wine—and for the chair."

He rose at once. "You will permit me to escort you." It wasn't a question. "Sir Oswald did not seem in any shape to molest you further, but his man was."

"I don't think Jem Salter will leave Maha-rahnee. He's very protective of her."

"It's good to hear someone is. Fellbridge?" He held out a hand. Annabel did not argue, but took it and let him help her to her feet. The steadiness of his hand was comforting, somehow.

Outside the monstrosity, Somers was in his acc-ustomed seat but rose to greet them. "No sign of our friend next door," he said quietly.

"Somers has been keeping an eye on Broxley," Quin said to Annabel. "And one out for you as well."

So that was why she had noticed him watching

her. "Thank you, Somers."

"My pleasure, your ladyship." He bowed and resumed his watch.

"It is curious that Somers knew to watch for me," Annabel commented as they began to make their way back to the inn. "I don't believe we have previously met."

"Oh, I showed him your likeness," Quin said offhandedly. "He has a good eye."

Annabel blinked, unable to frame a reply. He had her likeness? But how?

The walk back to the inn was a quiet one. At first, Annabel kept going over and over again in her mind that dreadful moment when Sir Oswald had come at her with his riding crop. The horrid man! They had to do *something* to help Miss Broxley escape him.

What was the nature of the hold he had over his sister? If it indeed had something to do with their younger half-brother, that made him appear even more despicable. Maria and Georgiana would surely want to try another night-time visit to Sir Oswald's tent to offer their help to Miss Broxley, but would they be able to now? If they did, would she be able to stay awake that long?

But somehow, what had seemed to be an impossible situation before now felt much less difficult ...simply because Quin was here. Not that she would ask for his help—but knowing he was here made a difference. She stole a glance at his profile, and found that he was looking down at her.

"Better, Fellbridge?" he asked.

Perhaps it was the glass of Malmsey, drunk on an empty stomach, that sent a burst of warmth through her. Or maybe it was something else. "Better," she answered.

He smiled slightly.

As they approached the Horse and Oak, Quin regarded it with a critical eye. "I don't believe I've ever stayed there. It looks pleasant enough."

She felt restored enough to laugh softly. "Pleasant! Do not let Mrs. Bunwich hear you say that. This inn is not merely *pleasant*—why, there is not a guest below the rank of baron staying here this week, I have been told by our estimable landlady."

As she knew he would, Quin caught the spirit of her words at once. "You must be referring to your *superior* landlady," he said. "Exactitude in speech is a virtue to be cultivated, Fellbridge."

"You are correct—I do beg your pardon." She lowered her voice. "You must come in—perhaps we can catch a glimpse of her. She's truly very kind, but I suspect this week has rather turned her head."

The hall and taproom were empty of Bunwiches, containing only a few customers conversing quietly over their tankards of ale. Bustling sounds from the direction of the kitchens indicated Mrs. Bunwich's probable location.

Quin was looking about him appraisingly. "Three parlours. Most superior indeed."

"Yes—oh, you must see Mrs. Bunwich's collection. She's quite the tuft-hunter." She drew him into the parlour where Mrs. Bunwich's array of images from *La Belle Assemblée* hung from a beam.

"A veritable rogues' gallery," he said, smiling up at the engravings of illustrious ladies.

"I beg your pardon, sir. *My* picture is among them, and I am no rogue!"

"Is it? Where?"

She pointed, then went to stand beneath it. "Here."

He followed her and looked up at the picture appraisingly. "Oh, yes. That one. I confess, I found it disappointing. Even colorized it bears almost no resemblance to the original."

She laughed. "I know. My sons were vastly amused—" Then the import of his words struck her. Colorized? He'd gone to the trouble of having an artist colorize the engraving of her?

He was still gazing meditatively up at it. "The brow and the eyes are—not good, I must say, but not offensively bad. The nose is somewhat worse, however. And the shape of your face—I have no idea what the engraver was thinking of." He looked down at her with a glint in his eyes that she could not interpret— and then reached up to draw a finger down the side of her face. "And the chin—abominable. No resemblance to yours."

Annabel was transfixed by the low intimacy of his voice as well as by his touch. "Is—is that so?"

"Yes, it is. A pity, as the original chin is a charming one, with the merest hint of a dimple—*there*." He pressed one fingertip lightly into her chin.

Everything—the engravings, Mrs. Bunwich's parlour, all of Epsom—had vanished. Annabel knew only the lurking smile in Quin's eyes, the caress of his words, the warmth of his touch. "Quin," she barely breathed.

"But what that engraver did to your mouth is positively criminal." His fingertips brushed over her lips, first the bottom, then the top. She found that it had suddenly grown difficult to breathe; entirely of their own accord, her lips parted. "These lips are nothing—*nothing*—like the image. But perhaps I am expecting too much of the engraver. I don't think anyone could truly do them justice."

They gazed at each other for the space of a few heartbeats, Quin's eyes dark and intent. Could he read what she knew her eyes were saying in return? Had he stopped speaking because he too was no longer master of his breath?

His fingers drifted down to her chin again, and he tilted his head, as if asking a question. In answer she lifted her face closer to his and closed her eyes.

The touch of his mouth on hers was expected— and yet a revelation. Her hands slid up to his shoulders because she desperately needed to hold on to something; never had a kiss—not Freddy's, not Glenrick's—made her feel as if she were floating in warm honey. She was grateful when his arms encircled her...and then gratitude turned into something much more urgent.

She was dimly aware that he was drawing her closer, that his kisses had become hungrier, deeper— but she also knew that he was holding himself back, allowing her to set their pace rather than crushing her to him. And then she stopped thinking at all and simply felt and tasted and existed in the moment in his arms.

Continued existence, however, required breathing—and some indeterminate amount of time later she broke the kiss to draw in a deep, ragged breath. She felt him do the same—and then he gently pressed her head to rest on his shoulder and brushed his lips over her forehead in something between a caress and a shower of kisses. It was heaven. But actively kissing him had been heaven too. Did heaven truly contain so many places of wonder?

"Fellbridge?" he murmured into her hair.

"Mmm?"

"I would be much obliged if, in the future, you would avoid placing yourself into the position of nearly being horsewhipped. I recall another recent occasion wherein a disgruntled person pointed a gun at you and suggest that anything similar to that situation should also be avoided."

She smiled against his shoulder. "But you have been so kind as to help avert any unpleasantness that might have occurred on both those occasions."

"True. But I am kept awake at night worrying about what might happen if, some day, I am not present when a similar event should transpire."

"I would not care to think that I am causing you to lose sleep."

"You've interfered with my tranquility for years, Fellbridge, so I ought to be used to it. But not quite in this fashion." His arms tightened around her. "I cannot bear the thought of losing you now."

She nestled closer to him; his heart still beat hard and fast, and she slid her hand down to rest over it. Oh, Quin. From now on, this sound—his strong, steady heartbeat—was the one that would give her the most joy in the world, along with her sons' happy laughter—

"Annabel!"

She started, jerking back from Quin's embrace, and turned toward the doorway.

Lord Glenrick stood there, hat in one hand, his face pale and set. Behind him, Mrs. Bunwich was barely visible fluttering from side to side, trying to see past him.

"What is going on here?" he asked. There was an edge to his voice that Annabel had never heard before.

"Lady Fellbridge met with some unpleasantness whilst out walking," Quin said. How was he able to keep his voice so cool, so steady? "I was fortunately near enough to hand to administer aid and escort her back to her lodging."

"My poor darling!" Lord Glenrick had crossed the room and taken her hands, turning her away from Quin before she could gather sufficient wits to say anything. He gazed anxiously into her face. "What happened? No, do not answer that. I would not distress you further by asking you to recount it. You are unhurt?"

"I—I am entirely well--truly." Or had been, until a moment ago. *Why* had Lord Glenrick had to walk in at that moment? And why did he feel he could refer to her as "Annabel" and "his poor darling"? She had certainly never granted him that privilege.

"You are flushed, and I am certain you have suffered a dreadful shock. Mrs. Bunwich, you must take charge of Lady Fellbridge and escort her to her room. I am persuaded you know exactly what she needs."

Mrs. Bunwich scuttled forward. "Oh, indeed I do, your lordship. Poor Lady Fellbridge! I'll have a nice cup of tea and a hot brick for your feet brought up at once." She put a beefy arm around Annabel's shoulders and began to lead her to the door.

"I really don't need cosseting," she protested, side-stepping Mrs. Bunwich's grasp and turning back to the two men. "Quin—"

"I am happy to have been of assistance, Fell-bridge." Quin was suddenly...not Quin. Or at least not the Quin whom she had kissed moments before. The warm laughter in this Quin's eyes had been replaced by a chill blankness.

"Will—will you please call here tomorrow?" she asked desperately as Mrs. Bunwich got a grip on her once again. "The matter we discussed—"

His expression thawed the smallest bit. "I am entirely at your disposal, madam."

She looked at him, pleading with her eyes. *Quin,* she mouthed.

But then Lord Glenrick hid him from her view, and Mrs. Bunwich was doing her best to wrestle her through the doorway. "There, poor chick," she crooned. "And poor Lord Glenrick. Here he was planning a lovely supper for the two of you—"

"Which I would not have been able to partake in, as I am already engaged for this evening." But Annabel gave up and allowed her to herd her up the stairs.

"Oh, dear ma'am, the back of your dress is all dirty!" Mrs. Bunwich exclaimed, following close behind her.

Annabel hurried her pace up the stairs, lest the landlady be tempted to dust off her bottom. "I—I slipped," she said firmly. "I truly am well," she added, when Mrs. Bunwich seemed about to want to bundle her into the room and bodily put her to bed. "I will gratefully accept some tea, however."

"Of course, your ladyship. You lie yourself down, and I'll be back directly with it." Mrs. Bunwich bustled away.

When she was gone, Annabel slipped into the

room and leaned against the closed door with a sigh. The last two hours had been such a whirlwind; first the horrible Sir Oswald, then Quin—

Quin. She paced to the window and back again, pressing her hands together because the welling of her emotions would not let her be still. That moment when he'd taken her in his arms... She took off her hat and gloves and spencer and made herself sit down in the chair by the win-dow. Their kiss in the parlour had been a watershed; from now on nothing would be the same. He had felt it too—she knew it. If only Lord Glenrick had not interrupted when he did! She and Quin might have had the chance to explain themselves, to talk about what they felt. And perhaps to kiss again... If someone had told her three months ago that she would kiss the Marquis of Quinceton and like it very much indeed, she would have laughed them to scorn.

A movement outside caught her attention, and she leaned forward to look outside. Maria had promised to return to the inn this afternoon or evening so that they could discuss their next step with Maharahnee—poor Miss Broxley! The situation was more urgent than ever.

However, it wasn't Maria below, but Quin and Lord Glenrick. They were walking away from the inn's front door, obviously deep in conversation—or at least, Lord Glenrick was talking and Quin listening. There was something peculiar about Quin's posture; he held his shoulders as an accomplished driver might when taking a team of barely broken horses out for the first time, so stiff and taut were they.

Some distance from the inn—far enough that she could not possibly hear them—they paused, Lord

Glenrick still speaking with great earnestness and vehemence. It went on for some moments; then Glenrick paused and seemed to be waiting for Quin to reply. After a pause, he said a few words. Lord Glenrick nodded and held out his hand.

Quin stared at it for a long moment. Then, rather than shaking it as she'd expected, he placed his own beneath it and raised it slightly, bending and pressing his lips to it as if—as if...as if he were making an act of homage or swearing fealty. But to *Lord Glenrick*? Why?

He lowered his hand and stood unmoving, looking down at the ground. Lord Glenrick clapped him on the shoulder, then turned and strode back to the inn, but he did not bear the look of a man who'd been enjoying a pleasant conversation with an acquaintance the moment before: his brows were drawn in a scowl. Quin looked up quickly, watching his retreating back.

What had just happened? The whole tableau had been...strange. And disquieting. What could they have been talking about? Why had Quin done that?

Then she stilled, for Quin's gaze had traveled up the inn's front and fixed on her in the window. Their eyes locked, and she leaned forward. Should she call out to him? She half raised her hand—

And then she gasped in surprise. He had turned on his heel without another glance at her and was stalking firmly away from the inn, back toward the racing grounds.

Early the next morning, Annabel, Maria, and Georgiana once again met for breakfast, this time in one of the inn's private parlours. Annabel was glad it was not the one in which she and Quin had been last night: she would not have been able to pay attention if it were. Despite her tiredness—yesterday had been a *long* day—she had not slept well, between reliving the moments with Quin and the one afterward from her chamber window. Quin's abrupt departure without acknowledging her had left her confused and apprehensive. Surely they would straighten it out when next they met, but still...

At least Georgiana was somewhat recovered from her shape-shifting exertions. She moved stiffly and sat ramrod-straight in her chair but was as incensed as she should have been at Annabel's relation of the previous day's events.

"So Sir Oswald will not only cheat at races, but cheat at horse trading, too," she said after Annabel had finished.

"It is imperative that we stop him. But we must speak to Maharahnee—to Miss Broxley—before we do anything else," Maria said. "And from what you say, Jem Salter does not leave her side."

"I'll wager it's because he doesn't trust Sir Oswald not to do something bad to her, even if she is his sister." Annabel shuddered. "That man is unbalanced."

"Georgiana, do you feel up to trying to speak with her again?" Maria asked.

"I suppose I could," Georgiana sighed. "But how do we get to her if she is never alone?"

A knock sounded on the door, and Mrs. Bunwich bustled in. "I've a fresh pot of coffee for your ladyships," she announced. "And there's a man waiting in the tap room to speak with you, Lady Fellbridge." Her eyes were sharp with curiosity.

"To me?" For an instant Annabel wondered if it were Quin. But Mrs. Bunwich would undoubtedly have mentioned if it were; there was no way that he would have been allowed to leave the room yesterday without her having learned his name and title. "Did he give his name?"

"Wouldn't give it. He's a banty little fellow—a jockey, I'd guess, and bald as a new-laid egg." Mrs. Bunwich sniffed as she set down the coffee pot.

Bald as an egg? Annabel glanced at her companions. That could only be one person. "Send him in, please, Mrs. Bunwich! We very much wish to speak with him."

Mrs. Bunwich sniffed again to communicate her opinion of countesses deigning to receive banty little fellows at breakfast and left. A moment later Jem Salter appeared in the doorway, holding his cap in both hands. When he saw Maria and Georgiana, he stepped back a pace. "I need to talk to *you*, Lady Fellbridge. Not none of these other ladies."

"Please come in, Salter." Annabel gave him a reassuring smile but spoke firmly. "These other ladies know as much as I do about your and—er—Maharahnee's difficult situation."

At these words Jem Salter looked inclined to bolt, but Georgiana said, "Oh, come in and stop being so silly, Salter. We want to help Miss Broxley as much as you do."

Her tart words seemed, perversely, to reassure him; he sidled in almost timidly and took the chair Georgiana directed him to, then looked at Annabel.

"In case you was wonderin' how I knew to look for you, the gent who floored Master Oswald yesterday said your name, so I asked around." He took in a deep breath. "You know about Maharahnee, don't you?"

"Yes, I...*we* do."

"Are you p'haps the, er, goat who spoke to Miss Charlotte the other night?"

"No, that wasn't me." Annabel frowned. "Ought you to be here? Is it safe to leave Miss Broxley unattended? Sir Oswald—"

Jem Salter chuckled. "Master Oswald's nursing a sore jaw *and* a sore head, I expect. He went out to another card game as soon as he could walk straight after getting that leveler. I don't count on seeing him any time before noon, if then." His expression sobered. "Look, I don't know how you ladies guessed our secret, an' jes' now I don't care. All's I care about is getting Miss Charlotte out of this place. Master Oswald's gone right mad, and I can't be part of his schemes. Using spurs on Miss Charlotte! Selling her, even if it's only for a few weeks!" He shook his head in disgust.

"It *is* appalling," Maria agreed.

"It's worse 'n that. She can't keep a horse's form for that long, not without hurtin' herself. Three days is the longest she's gone, and it took her another three days 'fore she felt herself again. I—well, I worry she won't remember how to take her own shape again if she stays as a horse that long. I can't allow Miss Charlotte to risk that."

Georgiana stirred in her chair but didn't speak.

"Good heavens, no! What do you wish us to do?" Annabel asked.

"Help get her away." He looked uncomfortable.

"I didn't intend for any of this to go this far. I been working for the Broxleys since Miss Charlotte was a baby. She was always around the stables—she was nuts for her father's horses—and she told me her secret when she was a snip of a girl. We kept it a secret, but Master Oswald found it out when they was in their teens. He's allus used it as a rod in pickle to get her to do what he wants, but it wasn't till this year, when his money dealings was so bad, that he thought of all this."

"'All this' being Miss Broxley's posing as Maharahnee," Maria said.

Jem Salter sighed. "Yes, ma'am."

"We, ah, gather that Miss Broxley is not a willing participant and that there is another brother involved?"

His eyes widened. "How'd you know about *that*? No, Miss Charlotte didn't want to have nothin' to do with this plan to win races for Master Oswald. They have a brother—their dad married again in his sixties, after Lady Broxley died—but Master Oswald never could abide his little brother. The poor mite's weakly and went blind after catching the measles. Master Oswald sent Master Florian away and told Miss Charlotte she'd never see him again unless she did this. Master Florian's her pet—the new Lady Broxley died when he was still in swaddling clothes. She was weakly, too, so Miss Charlotte's practically been his mother."

"How dreadful!" Annabel wished Quin had hit Sir Oswald even more forcefully. "But will Miss Broxley consent to flee, when her younger brother is hostage to her pretending to be Maharahnee?"

Jem Salter shifted in his chair and looked down

at his cap, rather than at them, when he finally spoke. "It...happens that I know where Master Florian's been stowed."

Maria surveyed him not a little severely. "Hmmph. You do, do you? Then that settles it. We must spirit Miss Broxley away at once, and you must take her to find her brother."

"But what about Sir Oswald?" Georgiana put it. "If Miss Broxley and Salter disappear, he will go directly after them. It will lead to an unpleasant encounter, I fear."

Annabel sat up straighter. "But what if Sir Oswald doesn't know they're gone?"

"What?" Maria's brow furrowed. "How do you propose we accomplish that—oh! Of course! Georgiana!"

"Yes, exactly," Annabel said. "But I don't think Salter should go with Miss Broxley. We'll need him here to help maintain the disguise." She thought for a moment. "I...I think I know whom we can ask to accompany Miss Broxley to retrieve her brother." Quin had said he was at her disposal, hadn't he? If only she could go with him—

"What disguise?" Jem Salter demanded. "What are you planning?"

Georgiana sighed. "If it's the only way... For how long must we maintain this charade?"

Annabel looked at Jem Salter. "How far is it to where Florian Broxley is being held?"

"'Bout an hour north of London, in a nothin' of a village called Goston—he's with the mother of one of our under-grooms." The little man's face was practically purple. "Now will someone tell me what you witches—you ladies are plotting?"

Maria beamed at him. "Mr. Salter, meet your new Maharahnee." She gestured to Georgiana.

He looked from one of them to the other in confusion. Then understanding dawned. "You—you can change into a horse too?"

"Among other things." Georgiana sighed. "When my rheumatism permits."

"Other things—so *you* was the goat who talked to Miss Charlotte the other night, then? Well, I'll be dam—beg your pardon, ma'am." Jem Salter looked thoughtful. "Rheumatics, you say? Maybe 'tis and maybe 'tisn't. Miss Charlotte is always dreadful sore after she changes. I might be able to help you with that."

"That's splendid. Now, if we're going to get Miss Broxley away and Georgiana in her place, we had better hurry and do so before Sir Oswald recovers sufficiently to make an appearance at Maharahnee's tent," Maria said briskly.

At that, Georgiana rose to return to her chamber and Nettles to find an approximately Maharahnee-colored gown to wear, and Annabel borrowed paper and ink from Mrs. Bunwich to pen a note to Quin asking him to escort Miss Broxley to her younger brother. If the two of them left this morning, they would, with luck and good roads, be in Goston by mid or late afternoon.

The words conveying the request for Quin's help flowed quickly, but when she came to the end, she was stricken by indecision. How should she close her letter in light of the new...intimacy between them—an intimacy they had not yet been able to discuss? If only she could go with him—but her first duty was to assist Georgiana and Maria. After staring at her words until the ink was half-dried on her pen, she hastily wrote, *I very much hope, sir, that you will find it convenient to call on me at home after we are both returned to London, if you feel as I do that we must have many matters to discuss—*

"Annabel!" Maria called from the inn's entrance hall.

"One moment!" She signed it *In great haste, Fellbridge*, and folded the note to give to Jem Salter. Maria would take him and Georgiana back to Maharahnee's tent in Lord Sefton's curricle (what would Jem Salter make of Maria's driving "skills"?) and ascertain that Quin would be able to accompany Miss Broxley; then Georgiana would take her place. The only part of the plan they had not worked out was the timing of when Georgiana would *stop* being Maharahnee.

Jem Salter, however, seemed unconcerned. "Lady Bathurst can turn into a fly the instant Master Oswald's back is turned, and he won't be none the wiser," he said with a shrug. "So long as she can get out easy an' we give Miss Charlotte time to get Master Florian away, that's good enough."

Annabel stood in the inn's doorway to see them off. If only she could have gone with them…but it had been decided that she should play least-in-sight, lest Sir Oswald's sore head did not keep him abed. In an hour or two she would slip down to Maharahnee's tent to keep watch over Georgiana, safely concealed. It would have been nice, however, to steal a moment or two with Quin—

"Ah, behold! The elusive beauty!"

Annabel laughed as she turned to greet Lord Glenrick, descending the last few steps of the inn's main staircase, but it was a forced laugh. There was too much else going on this morning for her to want to add fending off his advances to the list. "Good morning, Lord Glenrick."

"*Alec*, my dear." He took her hand and raised it to his lips. "You are well after your fright yesterday? I regret not to be able to dine with you last night."

Ah, there was her escape. "I—I had thought myself recovered on rising this morning, but now that I am here, I fear that may have been an ill-advised judgment. I believe I shall go upstairs and rest a little more."

"My poor Annabel! Of course you must." His voice was gentle with concern. "I am desolated to hear it; I was about to invite you to accompany me in calling on one of the bookmakers to place my pittance on our friend Maharahnee. All reports say she's expected to leave the rest of the field wallowing in her dust tomorrow."

Oh, dear. Annabel hesitated. "I...er...have heard that might not necessarily be the case," she said.

"Is that so?" He looked at her sharply.

"In fact, I would strongly suggest you bet on anyone but her." At least she could save the poor man a loss that he could probably ill afford.

"Hmm. Very interesting...and I thank you for the information, my dear. Now, do go upstairs and rest, and perhaps I will be able to tempt you into dining with me tonight?" He brushed his fingers across her cheek and added, quietly, "My darling."

She smiled weakly. "We shall see."

After the flurry of excitement that had occupied the early morning, Friday afternoon seemed interminable. Once she'd explained to Winters the plan to spirit Miss Broxley away and deceive Sir Oswald, Annabel had hurried down to Maharahnee's tent, wrapped in a shadow—difficult to find, as the day was overcast— to keep watch over Georgiana. Maria, in Lord Sefton's curricle drawn by Hermes, would wander the tent city keeping an eye on her as well.

There wasn't much to keep an eye on. As usual, Jem Salter brought "Maharahnee" out for the crowds to gaze upon. But his interactions with them this morning were subdued; instead, he spent most of his time and attention on Georgiana/Maharahnee, rubbing her down and murmuring to her. Annabel seized a moment while he was talking to a pair of languid-looking dandies about Maharahnee's gallop to sidle up to Georgiana and inform her that she was there. Then she seated herself on an upturned bucket and looked over at Quin's tent.

Or what remained of it. Quin's valet, Somers, was directing the dismantlement of the green-and-yellow-striped monstrosity by a group of noisy stableboys; a light wagon, already packed with trunks, stood nearby. Quin had obviously accepted her charge to help Miss Broxley find her brother, for which she was glad—mostly.

If only they'd had a moment—a brief moment!—to speak...but perhaps it was better that they hadn't. A moment together would have meant another good-bye; this way, she could look forward to their next meeting rather than regretting their parting. Still, she was going to miss the monstrosity; it had grown on her in a peculiar way.

Noon came and went, then one o'clock and two, with no sign of Sir Oswald. Maria trotted by several times with Hermes, peering at them anxiously. Jem Salter continued to talk quietly to Georgiana/ Maharahnee. Annabel yawned and leaned her head in her hand, elbow propped on one knee. So much for the exciting life of a Lady Patroness of Almack's. Everything about this investigation had ground into dullness, as empty as the place where Quin's tent had been.

Around four, a fine drizzle began to fall from the leaden sky. To Annabel's relief, Jem Salter shooed away the remaining gawkers and led Georgiana into the tent. "There you go, ma'am," she heard him murmur as she followed them in. "No use standing out in the wet and undoin' all the work I've done on you." He led her to the back of the tent and set a bucket before her. "Don't know that you're wantin' anything to eat now since we don't know how long you'll likely be here, but at least take some water, ma'am."

Georgiana snorted softly and bent her head to the bucket. "I hope all's well with Miss Charlotte," Jem Salter continued quietly. "With any luck, they'll be at Goston soon. That Lord Quinceton'll get her to Master Florian safe and sound. He's a right 'un."

Yes, Annabel thought. *Yes, he is.*

Jem Salter watched Georgiana drink, then puttered about the tent. He picked up a bridle with a sigh—Annabel wondered if it wasn't part of Maharahnee's racing tack—and put it away in a heavy-looking iron-bound trunk in the corner.

To keep out of his way, she sidled and inched past him in the tent's crowded interior till she was close to Georgiana's head. "Still here," she whispered in her ear, under cover of the *plop-plop-plop* of the rain dripping from the tent's roof.

Georgiana whooshed softly in reply.

It was past eight in the evening before Sir Oswald finally made his appearance. He pushed into the tent without announcement, startling them all. Annabel straightened; she had fought to keep alert all day lest she betray her presence to Jem Salter, whom they had decided did not need to know about her abilities as well.

Sir Oswald scowled at Jem Salter, who was rubbing some liniment, smelling strongly of marjoram and peppermint, into Georgiana's shoulders. "Why don't you have her out where she can be seen? The wagering—"

"All the wagerin' in England won't matter a whit if she can't run 'acos she stayed out in the rain and got stiff as a board," Jem Salter said, wiping his hands on a rag.

Sir Oswald's scowl lightened fractionally. "I suppose. I want her out at daybreak, though—you hear?" He slapped Georgiana's rump, which made Annabel wince to herself. "You've got a race to win tomorrow, old girl."

Georgiana looked over her shoulder and blew out her breath in a most human-sounding grunt of irritation.

Sir Oswald laughed. "Oh, getting resty, are we? Kindly control your temper, dear sister. Don't forget that your work isn't over yet. Not by a long shot."

Jem Salter cleared his throat. "About that, Master Oswald—"

Sir Oswald looked up. "What? Is she resisting?"

"I ain't told her. It's none of my idea. You can do it."

"You didn't?" The full scowl was back. "What do I pay you wages for?"

"For takin' care of your stables. But this ain't that. It's plain wrong. You can't make *her* cheat someone in this fashion, just because you're crookeder than the devil's elbow."

"Watch your tongue, man. I can, and I will—and *she* will, if she knows what's good for her...and her precious, useless little brother—"

Georgiana stomped one of her rear feet, barely an inch from Sir Oswald's toes. His face turned an ugly red. "Don't you dare, Char—" His expression changed as he looked down at their feet, going from anger to incredulity. "What the—"

Annabel, near Georgiana's head across from Jem Salter, crouched down to see what had caught his attention. There was his foot, encased in a scuffed leather boot, and Georgiana's right back foot, with its white sock, close by it.

Sir Oswald gaped down at them for a long moment. Then he looked up at Jem Salter, his face an alarming shade of purple. *"You,"* he spat. "What did you do with her?"

Jem Salter paled slightly but stood his ground. "I don't know what you're talking about."

"This is not Charlotte!" Sir Oswald roared. "Charlotte's white foot's on her near side, not her off. You've tried to foist some other horse off on me and done a bad job of it. Where is she? Thought you could fool me, did you?" He made a small move and was suddenly holding a pistol aimed directly at Jem Salter. *"Where is she?"*

"She's gone." Jem Salter, as pale as his master was red-faced, stood tall and straight and looked Sir Oswald directly in the eye. "I couldn't allow her to run 'n win 'n have you sell her to Turffley. It was out 'n out wrong—bad enough what we've done already, but that was too far—and it wasn't safe for Miss Charlotte to even try it. I don't care if you shoot me."

Sir Oswald gave a wordless growl and cocked the pistol's hammer. Annabel gasped. "Georgiana!"

After that, everything seemed to happen at once.

"Who said that?" Sir Oswald demanded, the gun wavering as he peered from one corner of the tent to the other.

"What was that?" Jem Salter said, looking (with better acuity but no better results) toward the corner where Annabel stood, still wrapped in shadow.

And Georgiana tensed and seemed to draw herself in—then exploded outward, kicking back with her rear legs. Her right foot—the one that should not have been white—caught Sir Oswald directly in the chest. He made a ghastly wheezing noise as the wind was knocked from his lungs—

—and then he was flying backwards, until his head smashed with a horrible *crunch!* into the iron-bound chest where Jem Salter had earlier put away some of Maharahnee's tack.

Chapter Five

Ten days later, Annabel took her seat next to Emily for the Lady Patronesses' regular Monday meeting in King Street. She had missed last Monday's meeting as she and Maria and Georgiana had had the aftermath of the Sir Oswald business to attend to; Maria would be reporting on that this morning. Annabel looked across the table to where she and Georgiana were already in their chairs and nodded to them—and then looked twice at Georgiana. Was there something different about her? A new way of styling her hair?

Emily leaned over and gave Annabel's hand a quick squeeze. "I'm glad you're back! I hear you had quite an adventure!"

"It was rather more of an adventure than I'd expected," Annabel said.

She and Maria had not left Epsom until Wednesday morning. Georgiana had remained even longer—till Saturday—because she had felt honor-bound to stay and supervise Sir Oswald's care, summoning and paying for a surgeon to attend him and taking turns with Jem Salter to sit by his bedside.

"I hope you're not feeling guilty about having stopped him from doing something dreadful with that pistol, my dear," Maria had said severely to Georgiana when she arrived at the Horse and Oak for breakfast with them the next morning and had been told of the previous evening's dramatic events. "Why, he might have shot you or Annabel."

Georgiana drew herself up as if affronted...then seemed to deflate. "Not guilty, no. The man was a brute and needed to be stopped. But I do feel responsible. I hadn't realized I was capable of kicking so powerfully."

"Perhaps Jem Salter's liniment has helped your rheumatism," Annabel said.

Georgiana got a thoughtful look on her face. "Yes, I...have wondered about that."

Sir Oswald himself, with broken ribs and collar bone and a cracked skull, remained mostly insensible, barely able to take liquids and thin gruel for sustenance. Jem Salter was staying with him until he was well enough to make the journey to his home... but what would happen after that with him and his sister, Annabel had no idea. Had Quin and Miss Broxley been able to find her brother? Had they brought him home? It was torture, not knowing...and not having had a word from Quin. She tried to comfort herself with the knowledge that he had no idea of her whereabouts. Once they were both back in London, however...*oh*, how she looked forward to seeing him.

She had, however, received many words from Lord Glenrick, beginning Saturday evening after the running of the Oaks. He had found her in the entrance hall of the Horse and Oak and nearly embraced her before the interested population of the crowded taproom.

"My dearest Annabel!" He held her hands and grinned broadly at her. "Or shall I call you my good luck token? After today, I think I must."

"You had a good race?" She had not had the time—nor the heart—to attend it; she had been too busy supporting Georgiana and Nettles in seeing to Sir Oswald. Maharahnee had of course been scratched from the field; a filly named Oriana had won it instead, much to the lamentation of the many who'd bet substantially on Maharahnee.

He raised one of her hands to kiss. "I had a most gratifyingly lucrative race, thanks to your timely hint. My good luck token indeed." His buoyant manner shifted into something more intense as he gazed down at her. "I don't know how I'll be able to permit you out of my sight now."

Annabel had looked away, flushing—from embarrassment or annoyance, she was not certain. Fortunately, Georgiana hadn't been far behind her, so that he'd been able to do no more than give her hand a meaningful squeeze and step aside—

"Are we all here?" Sally called, bringing her back to the present in King Street. "Last week's meeting could scarce be called one, since so many of us were away on investigations. Dorothea, what of the gas lamps in Pall Mall? Were you able to discover why that ghost was so attached to them?"

Dorothea was looking uncommonly somber this morning; even her curls were subdued. "We were. He won't be troubling them any longer—although I should not say troubling, as if he were a fly. Thanks to him, a great calamity has been averted."

There were murmurs from around the table. Annabel caught Emily's eye and saw that her face was somber too.

Dorothea went on. "The ghost turned out to be a former lamplighter who had tended those lamps for years when they were oil lamps. Mr. Almack assisted us by catching the ghost's attention—the creature was most distraught—and was able to have sufficient communication with him after that." She nodded to the empty chair next to Sally, and Annabel realized that Mr. Almack was in attendance this morning. "That was a great help, sir."

"'Twas nothing, countess," Mr. Almack's voice rumbled. "The thanks are due to Mr. Gubbins for remaining to take care of his lights."

"Mr. Gubbins being the ghost, I presume," Sally said. "Did he not care for his oil lamps being replaced by gas?"

"No, that was not it at all. He was quite taken with the gas lamps, in fact, and wished they had been there in his day." Dorothea took a breath. "What troubled him was the fact that the gas lamps had been tampered with."

"Tampered!"

"Indeed. Clementina was able to confirm that they were leaking, and Emily was able to use her *connections*—" her lip curled, and for a moment she looked her usual sardonic self— "to investigate the matter."

"I asked Harry to look into it," Emily said, completely unabashed at the mention of her lover. "He knew the correct people to talk to, and they sent along a man who found that someone had been at the lamps and done something nefarious to them. They might have exploded at any time."

There were shocked murmurs from around the table. Sally allowed them to fade then turned, white-faced, to Dorothea. "I assume the matter has since been corrected?"

"Yes, something was done—do not ask me what these little men do to their pieces of machinery." Dorothea made a dismissive gesture. "It must have been corrected because Mr. Gubbins has not been back, and I shall assume that he has gone off to wherever it is good lamplighters go when they hang up their ladders. But what I wish to know is *who* did this. And why."

"As would I." Sally still appeared shaken. "Was Mr. Gubbins of any assistance in that? Did he see who did this?"

"Regrettably, Mr. Gubbins was nae sufficiently aware of his surroundings to be of any service in that department," Mr. Almack said. "The puir wight only knew that all was not well with his beloved lights."

"I thought of that," Emily put in. "So I asked my Harry to get whoever fixed the lamps to give him one of the tampered pieces for me, and I gave it to Frances."

Everyone turned and looked expectantly at Frances, who looked intensely uncomfortable. "I don't know!" she burst out. "I held it and touched every piece of it, and I couldn't get anything from it!"

"Nothing?" said Clementina, eyes wide.

"Nothing." Frances seemed to be on the verge of tears. "That's never happened to me before. I've always been able to read who might have made or used what I've touched, if I've tried."

The ladies around the table regarded each other in alarm. Annabel watched Sally bite her lip and stare fixedly at the polished wood surface before her. "Thank you, Dorothea," she finally said. "I think we can agree that your specific investigation can be closed. But we are left with a larger issue—and I am not entirely certain of what to do with it. The tampering with the gas lamps was not accomplished by supernatural or magical means, so I do not know that, properly speaking, the Lady Patronesses ought to investigate it any further—"

"No, Sally!" Emily cried. "We can't simply ignore it! What if the lamps *had* blown up? People might have been hurt or killed!"

"Aye, I dinna think we can ignore it," Mr. Almack said, breaking an uneasy silence. "But I won't see you ladies endangered."

"What about Lord Palmerston's man?" Clementina asked. "Could we not ask his help? If he was able to see that the lamps had been altered so as to become dangerous, could he not be our witness to the authorities without our being obviously involved?"

Annabel remembered Georgiana's words on the journey down to Epsom. *When in past years have we had more than one investigation happening at any time, or had them so close together as we have this year?* "I agree with Clementina," she said. "If he can attest that the lamps were altered..."

Sally hesitated. "Very well. Emily, may I ask you to pursue this matter with Palmerston?"

"With the greatest pleasure," Emily said. She sat back in her chair, her usually cheerful countenance anything but. "I shall speak with him about it this very day."

"Thank you. Frances, what about you? Is there anything we can do to help you? I am alarmed by the fact that you could read nothing from the lamp piece."

Frances shook her head, her eyes swimming with tears. "I am, too, Sally. I don't know—" She gave a loud sniff. Maria handed her a handkerchief, and she buried her face in it.

"Ah. Yes, well." Sally shifted uncomfortably in her seat while Frances gave a few hiccupping little sobs. "I expect it's a passing...er, difficulty. And... ah...while I think of it, did you have anything to report concerning Lord Rossing, from the business with the Potamides?"

Frances emerged from the handkerchief, dabbing at her eyes. "No—" *sniff, sniff* "—not really. I was able to learn that his poor wife has been ill this spring. Perhaps he merely forgot to pay them their tribute?" She regarded Sally hopefully, her eyes still swimming with tears.

"Er, perhaps." Sally frowned slightly. "If you could make a few more inquiries, I want to know what you discover. Maria, would you care to report on the matter at Epsom? Was it successfully investigated?"

"Yes, it was, even if it wasn't of as great importance as the gas lamps." Maria opened her reticule and looked at Annabel and Georgiana. "You ladies will be pleased to hear that I just today received a letter from Miss Broxley—"

Annabel straightened. "Did she find her brother? Are they home?"

Maria smiled. "I shall read it aloud in a moment. But first—" She gave her report, telling the Ladies about Maharahnee's identity and Annabel's patient watches and Georgiana's swift reaction to Sir Oswald's threats. "Lord Quinceton kindly escorted Miss Broxley to find her brother, and she and the boy are safe at home."

"Oh!" Frances's face brightened. "How wonderful of him!"

Annabel glanced at her and then away with a small sigh. Frances would not take her and Quin's new closeness well; he'd been such a confirmed bachelor for so long that the poor thing had been able to nurse her romantic dreams of him for years. It was a pity Frances would be hurt, but...she almost hugged herself. The first thing she'd done on Thursday morning when she'd arrived home had been to send Quin a note asking him to call on her. Since he must be back in London by now since Miss Broxley was home, then he would undoubtedly call soon. Tomorrow? Today?

"What of this Sir Oswald?" Dorothea asked. "It is a pity that you did not kick him harder, Georgiana. The man sounds too villainous to be permitted to continue to live."

"I did not intend to kill him—only to keep him from further imprudent actions." Georgiana said stiffly. "It is unlikely that he will be able to perpetrate any further villainy. The surgeon expects he will likely be an invalid for the rest of his days."

"It's no more than he deserved," Emily said warmly. "You did precisely the just thing."

"With Annabel's timely assistance," Georgiana said. "Sir Oswald was behind me. If she had not risked discovery again to warn me that he was brandishing a pistol, matters might have ended differently."

Annabel drew in her breath at Georgiana's praise. But before she could speak, Georgiana went on, "Would it be too much to ask you to read Miss Broxley's letter, Maria?"

"No, indeed." Maria drew a pair of spectacles from her reticule and put them on. "My dear Lady Sefton—" she began.

> *I am taking the opportunity of the first few quiet moments I have had in some days to communicate to you, however inadequately, my boundless gratitude for the assistance rendered me by yourself, Lady Bathurst, and, so I am told, Lady Fellbridge during the recent matter at Epsom. I am, thanks to you, in good health—and so grateful that my brother Florian can as well claim to be in good frame, having suffered little during his unexpected sojourn from home.*

> *Of my elder brother, you know better than I his condition. I understand from Jem Salter that he is not expected to fully recover his faculties, and while I cannot help feeling that he brought such a fate upon himself, I will certainly care for him as carefully as I have my dear Florian once Jem Salter brings him home. Indeed, I am considering the idea of opening Broxhurst to take in a few other blind children in a sort of school, as I have been told that Florian does wonderfully well for someone so afflicted; it will help defray our expenses*

(which I hope shall be much lessened now that my brother will no longer be running his racing stable) and I do enjoy taking care of young persons. Lord Quinceton has kindly promised that he will put the word out for genteel families who might be in need of such an institution for their afflicted child-ren.

Again, I thank you and your friends for your generosity and concern for me and my family. I am looking forward to a life not including Maharahnee, but if ever any of you should require assistance, please know that you may call for it upon me—and her—at a moment's notice.

I remain, madam, your grateful servant,

Charlotte Broxley

"Well," Emily said after a pause. "We should not forget that. One never knows when Maharahnee might be needed if Georgiana is, ah, unavailable."

"I don't believe Miss Broxley has Georgiana's ability to take whatever form she chooses," Maria said delicately. "But we should certainly remember her offer."

"Indeed," Georgiana said. "It is most kind of her."

"And Quin promised to help her." Frances sigh-ed happily. "He is the *dearest,* cleverest creature!"

Annabel glanced at Frances again. There was a small smile lurking at the corners of her mouth. Oh, Frances...

After Sally closed the meeting, Annabel sidled over to Georgiana. "I...er, hope that you...that is, you seem well," she said awkwardly. It was not at all well-bred to say such a thing, despite the Lady Patronesses' etiquette among their members being more like that of a family than that of mere acquaintances.

Georgiana smiled again—a true smile, not the tight-lipped semi-grimace she usually made. "I am, thank you. My extended stay in Epsom was worth the inconvenience, thanks to Jem Salter. And to you."

Annabel blinked. "Me?"

"Indeed. It was a chance comment of yours that led me to discuss the matter with him. The matter of a human body adjusting to changing its form," she added, no doubt in response to Annabel's puzzlement. "He was accustomed to help Miss Broxley with certain massages and exercises and with a special liniment of his own devising. He has undertaken to teach Nettles what he knows to assist me. It has already helped me to a degree I had not thought possible. The pain is much reduced. In fact, I am leaving this morning to stay with Miss Broxley for further treatment." She held out her hand to Annabel.

"Oh." Was that the source of Georgiana's difficult personality—constant pain? Annabel shook her hand warmly. "I'm so glad you're feeling better."

"I—" Georgiana took a breath. "I believe that I have not always been...pleasant to work with." She moved her shoulders as if shrugging the memory away. "It is my hope that will change. I begin to fear that we will all of us need all our wits and abilities about us in the coming months—"

"*Dearest* Annabel!" Frances was suddenly there, slipping her arm around Annabel's waist in a sisterly embrace and drawing her a little away from

Georgiana. "I've been dying to talk to you! My goodness, what a time you had in Epsom!"

Georgiana smiled, her brows contracting so that she wore her old, slightly sour expression. "Good day, ladies." She turned away.

"Georgiana, wait—" Annabel tried to slip out of Frances's embrace. What had Georgiana started to say? Why would the coming months be so challenging?

"Oh, never mind her, the old sourpuss." Frances held on, pouting. "Alec told me all about seeing you at Epsom—he was simply thrilled that you were staying at the same inn! And in the middle of everything you had to deal with that dreadful Sir Oscar!"

"Sir Oswald. And that's why we were there, Frances." Annabel strained to see where Georgiana had gone. Had she already descended to the ground floor?

"Oh, yes, of course." Frances dismissed their investigation with an airy wave. "You can't imagine how chuffed Alec was, thanks to your tip about Maharahnee. Quite a tidy sum he made! He has charged me with inviting you to dine this week—just a simple family meal. He said Epsom was too distracting, and that we deserve to have you all to ourselves for a change."

"That...sounds lovely." Annabel managed to steer Frances down the stairs to Almack's entrance. There was no sign of Georgiana; she had evidently already left. Bother! She would have to call on her later—no, she was leaving for Cambridgeshire today—

"—says you simply *must* accompany us to Brighton as our guest. He's waiting to hear from his agent about the house he intends to hire. *Do* say you'll come, won't you?" Frances clutched her arm.

Annabel forced herself to attend to her. "That is most kind of you, Frances. But until I know what my family's plans are and when my boys will be visiting their grandparents in the country, I cannot commit to anything." *Especially* not to spending a week under the same roof as Frances's brother.

Frances's face dimmed. "Oh. Of course. But we'd so hoped..."

Annabel patted her arm. "I'm not declining your invitation, you dear goose. But I can't say 'yes' yet." Or ever, but a suitably regretful *no, thank you* could wait a week. Then, because Frances looked so woebegone, she said, "Please allow me to drive you home, and we'll have a good chat on the way. My carriage should already be here."

"Oh, I wish I could." Frances's woebegone expression turned radiant. "But I already have a ride. Thank you anyway!"

They stepped out the door, held open by Mr. Willis. Annabel nodded her thanks to him then glanced out onto King Street. There was her landau, with her coachman Thomas on the box as usual. Pulled up behind it was a curricle drawn by a pair of matched bays—a curricle she knew well. And in the seat, holding the reins in one elegantly gloved hand while a street urchin stood to attention at the bays' heads—

"Quin," she whispered, her heart racing at the sight of him. He looked pale and a little drawn; she hoped that escorting Miss Broxley and her brother to their home had not been too onerous—

"Quin!" Frances cried happily, bouncing down

the steps to the pavement. "You're exactly in time, you clever boy!"

Quin looked up. His gaze briefly met Annabel's ...and then, to her disbelief, slid away from hers as if she were a stranger. "Frances," he said, his voice warm—in contrast to the bleakness in his eyes. He nodded to the boy holding his horses and climbed down, offering his hand to help Frances up into the curricle.

"Till later, Annabel!" Frances trilled as Quin tenderly tucked a lap robe over her. "I should not be at all surprised if Alec were to call on you later. Quin, you bad thing." She tapped the crown of his hat. "Didn't you greet dear Annabel?"

Quin straightened, fixing his blank gaze somewhere about three feet to Annabel's left. "Lady Fellbridge," he said shortly, with barely a nod. Then he pulled himself up into the curricle, tossed a coin to the boy, and gave the bays the signal to go. The horses stepped with their usual smartness into the road; Frances gave Annabel a little wave then turned to Quin, smiling adoringly up at him.

Somehow, Annabel made her way to her own carriage and sat alone in the seat, gripping her reticule to keep her hands from shaking. The man with whom, barely a week ago, she'd shared a kiss that had upended her world had, just now, as good as cut her dead.

Worse still, he had called her Lady Fellbridge. *Lady* Fellbridge.

She stared after the curricle already at the corner of the street—Frances's head was tilted in a confiding manner toward Quin's—and tried to remember how to breathe.

I hope you enjoyed the sixth installment of The Ladies of Almack's! There's more—much more!—to come. If you'd like to keep up with the news from King Street, sign up for my newsletter for new release announcements, extras, and more about the ladies: https://marissadoylenewsletter.link/

Also, if you enjoyed reading *An Event at Epsom*, please consider telling your friends who might also enjoy it or posting a review on the site where you purchased it or on your favorite social media site such as Goodreads or LibraryThing.

Author's Notes

Epsom, the Derby and the Oaks Stakes

One of the big events of the London social season didn't actually take place in London at all, but twenty-ish miles south of the metropolis, in the small town of Epsom located on the rolling, grass-covered terrain of the North Downs.

Epsom was known first as a spa town—the source of the purgative Epsom Salts—beginning early in the 17th century, and the infirm (and not-so-infirm) of London and beyond tottered there throughout the next decades to drink the water from one particular spring. Horse-racing was first mentioned as taking place there early in the century—perhaps as a pastime for the healthy young members of families who accompanied older relatives visiting the spring.

During Cromwell's time racing was forbidden but was back in force when King Charles II regained his throne; Samuel Pepys noted a visit there during which he saw Nell Gwyn, the king's Cockney mistress, having a merry time, and the king himself often attended races. By the 1680s there was an official course clerk, and fifty years later, twice-yearly race meetings were taking place.

Then, in 1778, the Earl of Derby and a group of friends, including Sir Charles Bunbury, the playwright Richard Sheridan, and politician Charles James Fox, hatched the idea of a new race for three-year-old fillies over one and a half miles (most races at Epsom were in the two- to four-mile range), naming it The Oaks, after Lord Derby's nearby house. In 1780 they added a second race, for both colts and fillies, over one mile (soon expanded to one and a half); Lord Derby and Sir Charles flipped a coin for the honor of naming this new race, and Derby won the toss—and so the Derby was born. Sir Charles probably wasn't too upset—his colt Diomed became the Derby's first winner.

The races soon became popular; several shorter races over the course of the meet made for more excitement among the viewers (and thus more bets placed!), which of course had the effect of drawing more than just the racing crowd, so that eventually a sort of country fair atmosphere took over, which in turn drew *more* crowds (helped by the location's proximity to London.) A verse declaims,

> *On Epson Downs, when racing does begin*
> *Large companies from every part come in.*
> *Tag-rag and Bob-tail, Lords and Ladies meet,*

And Squires without Estates, each other greet.
Bets upon bets; this man says, 'Ten to one.'
Another pointing cries, 'Good sir, tis done.'

Our friend Prinny, the Prince Regent, was one of those spectators; in the 1790s he built the first permanent structure at Epsom, the Prince's Stand (a larger grandstand would finally be built in the 1830s). By the Regency, the Derby was an established "event" of the season, and an audience of thirty to forty thousand was the norm.

La Belle Assemblée

One of the premier magazines of the greater Regency era, *La Belle Assemblée or, Bell's Court and Fashionable Magazine Addressed Particularly to the Ladies* was published from 1806 through 1837 (when it was absorbed into another ladies' magazine.) Established by John Bell (1745-1831), it covered a wide range of topics and published serialized fiction and poetry; non-fiction articles on current events, history, politics, and the latest discoveries in science; book, art, music, and theater reviews; and other items of specific interest to women of the day: fashion news (and oh my goodness, some of the fashion plates are *amazing*), embroidery patterns, and sheet music. There was also a Births, Deaths, and Marriages column which often included amusing or sympathetic commentary; and in most issues the editor would respond to submissions sent in by readers with occasionally scathing comments; some of those public rejections are zingers!

Brighton in August

The London social season usually came to a close in July. Come August, everyone who had been feverishly attending every possible ball, rout, breakfast, opera performance, and dinner all spring now feverishly flocked out of London to their country home, to a rented house at some seaside venue, or—if they were extraordinarily fashionable, to Brighton, on England's south coast.

Why Brighton, which until the last quarter of the 18th century had been a sleepy, declining little fishing village named Brighthelmstone? Well, because in 1783 the young Prince of Wales (eventually the Prince Regent/King George IV) went there to stay with his uncle on the advice of his doctors to indulge in some sea-bathing, thought to be a sovereign cure for everything from epilepsy to gout, and loved it—the sea, the relaxed, informal atmosphere at the theater and assembly rooms—and decided to buy himself a small farmhouse there. Brighton quickly became THE place to go in August after the end of the season because that's where the young, fashionable prince went.

Of course, the small farmhouse was soon replaced by something—ahem!—a little larger. But evidently it wasn't large and princely enough, because in 1815 Prinny hired architect John Nash to build him something *really* grand. Nash came through, all right: he built the Prince Regent a Mughal/Chinese fantasy palace known as the Pavilion. On the outside, it looks like the Taj Mahal's younger sibling; on the inside, it's...indescribable. Google "Brighton Pavilion Interior" and be prepared to pick your jaw up off the floor.

Prinny *loved* it.

Bartholomew Fair

Originally chartered in 1133 by King Henry I to the Priory of St. Bartholomew, Bartholomew Fair was an annual event in late August (early September after the change from the Julian to the Gregorian calendar) on the outskirts of London near Smithfield. Established primarily as a cloth fair, it outgrew that original purpose and offered many other goods for sale as well as all the usual pastimes of a pleasure fair—every type of entertainment from music and plays to tightrope walkers and freak shows, sporting events, and food and drink of every description. Everyone went, from the high and mighty (traditionally, the Lord Mayor of London opened the Fair) to the lowest, and because it was on London's doorstep, the attendance was enormous. By the 1850s, however, the decorum of the Victorian age won: Bartholomew Fair was suppressed as being too conducive to public disorder and debauchery. But hey, an over seven-hundred-year run isn't too shabby.

Goats and Horses

Horses are herd animals; their natural way of life is in a group with lots of other horses to run around and interact with. But when they can't—when they're racehorses or otherwise isolated from hanging around a field with their friends, generations of horse people have found that companion animals of other species can help a horse living alone feel—well, less alone. And one of the animals that seems to do well with horses is goats—so Georgiana taking the shape of a goat to speak to Maharahnee seems to be a logical choice...except it doesn't work as intended, in this case.

Gas Lamps in Pall Mall

Early in the 18th century, amateur scientists observed that gases found in coal mines were extremely flammable and conducted laboratory experiments with them, but it wasn't until late in the century that a Scottish engineer named William Murdoch paid serious attention to how flammable gases might be used—specifically, for lighting. In 1792 he fitted his own house with gas lights, and in 1798 outfitted the factory of his employer, the Soho Foundry steam engine works in Birmingham, with gas lighting. Notice was taken, and commercial attempts to utilize this new technology followed, along with engineering improvements, until at last in 1807, a German entrepreneur named Friedrich Winzer, who patented a coal-gas lighting system in 1804, arranged for a section of Pall Mall, one of the most fashionable streets of London, to have its oil lamps replaced with gas lights.

The public was delighted with the new brighter lighting, which made being out at night a much safer prospect. So was the Prince Regent, who immediately commissioned Winzer to illuminate the façade of his London home, Carlton House, in 1808...and in

1810 Rudolph Ackermann's print shop was lit by gas. One of William Murdoch's colleagues at the Soho Foundry, Samuel Clegg, had also been inspired by Murdoch's work and started the Gas Light & Coke Company, which in 1812 received a charter from Parliament (at Prinny's urging) to provide gas lighting for the rest of London.

Soon, the new gas lights were everywhere: by 1813, Westminster Bridge had been fitted with gaslights. By 1815 there were twenty-eight miles of gas piping under the streets of London, and Prinny had had gaslights installed in Brighton to illuminate the exterior of his beloved Pavilion (and had the interior gas-lit six years later). By 1817, the first theaters were lit by gas. Elegant lamp posts were created from the melted-down cannons used in the Napoleonic Wars to adorn the streets of the fashionable West End, some of which can still be seen in Regent's Park and St. James's. The lights of London became something of a tourist attraction; no other city in Europe would have anything close for years. Crime rates dropped as criminals no longer had the shield of darkness to conceal them. I expect the Lady Patronesses of Almack's would have approved, especially Annabel.

Dramatis Personae

Or, a brief list of who was *really* who

For those among you who are not hard-core Regency fanatics, the following are highly idiosyncratic biographical sketches of the historical figures mentioned in this first story.

But first, a quickie tutorial on title usage in England

Peers (anyone of the rank of baron, viscount, earl, marquis, or duke) have a family name or surname like their less exalted fellow humans, but then also have their title, and can be referred to by both. Let's look at an example...

John Smith is the Earl of Noodle. He is commonly known as Lord Noodle; his friends might just call him Noodle, or he might be referred to as John Noodle to differentiate him from his late father, George Noodle, if the family is being gossiped about;

but Noodle is not his surname—that's Smith. He will never be referred to as Lord John Smith or Lord John Noodle; men referred to as "Lord Firstname Surname" are usually the younger sons of marquises and dukes, who are given the courtesy title of "Lord."

His wife, Mary Smith, the Countess of Noodle, is commonly known as Lady Noodle; she might be referred to as Mary Noodle to differentiate her from her mother-in-law Jane, the Dowager Countess, who is still alive and gadding about in society, and the name might stick even after the Dowager countess is no more just because everyone has gotten used to it. Mary will *not* be called Lady Mary Noodle, or Lady Mary Smith; women referred to as "Lady Firstname Surname" are the daughters of the higher nobility— earls and above—and are permitted the use of the courtesy title of "Lady." A widow of a peer keeps her rank and title unless she remarries, when she then takes her new husband's rank (and title, if any.) In social practice, many women who married men of lower rank still kept the courtesy title they were born with.

Fred Smith, Viscount Macaroni, is Lord Noodle's eldest son. Most members of the higher nobility have multiple titles, so an eldest son (and ONLY an eldest son—there are a whole set of rules around heirs apparent—direct offspring—and heirs presumptive—brothers and nephews and cousins— that we won't get into right now) is permitted to "borrow" his father's second most prestigious title as a courtesy (though if there is a third title and if Fred has a son, the lad might get to use that one if grandpa allows it.) Fred's younger brothers are just plain Honourables (only younger sons of marquises and dukes use the courtesy title of "Lord", don't forget) but his sister is Lady Susan because the daughters of earls (and marquises and dukes) have the courtesy title of "Lady."

There are other rules—dukes have their own special set. So...

Aurelius Smith is the Duke of Megapounds. Unlike his cousin John Smith, Earl of Noodle, he is *never* known as *Lord* Megapounds. He might be addressed just by his title, Megapounds, by his friends and acquaintances... or he might be addressed as "Duke" by others of his (relative) social class or as "Your Grace" by his inferiors. When he's being gossiped about, he might be referred to as Aurelius Megapounds or as "the seventh Duke" to differentiate him from his father Julius Megapounds, the sixth Duke. Aurelius's wife Ruby Smith, the Duchess of Megapounds, is likewise addressed as "Duchess" by friends and acquaintances, or as "Your Grace" by her inferiors, or as Ruby Megapounds to differentiate her from her mother-in-law the Dowager Duchess, Pearl Megapounds.

In this installment we have a character who is a baronet, so it would seem to be a good time to introduce the rules and usage of this other rank.

While a baronetcy is an inherited title, baronets are not considered members of the peerage, but of the gentry. Baronets are known as "Sir"; in *An Event at Epsom* we have Sir Oswald Broxley, who inherited that title from his father. In conversation he would be addressed or referred to as Sir Oswald, not as Sir Broxley. Were there a female unlucky enough to have married him, she would be Lady Broxley, not Lady Firstname (unless she was the daughter of an earl or marquess or duke, in which case she would be Lady Firstname Husband'sname.) Their hypothetical children would simply be misters and misses, without the "Honourable" title that children of barons and viscounts (and younger sons of earls) have.

There are also Knights. A knighthood is a one-time award to one person, usually for some service to crown and country; the title is not inherited, but dies with the person who receives it. Other than that, it goes by all the same rules as a baronetcy (including a knight's wife being known as Lady Lastname.)

Now for the who's who…

Sally Jersey

Sarah Sophia Child Villiers, Countess of Jersey (1785-1867), known as Sally Jersey to differentiate her from her mother-in-law, also Lady Jersey (and well-known as a mistress of the Prince of Wales). She was also known by the ironic nickname "Silence" as she was reputed never to stop talking, and was a Lady Patroness of Almack's and very influential in society for many years, though never as actively interested in politics as were many of the other Lady Patronesses. Fascinatingly, she inherited the senior partnership in a bank—Child & Co.—from her maternal grandfather (as well as his fortune—she was one wealthy woman!) and on attaining the age of twenty-one took her role very seriously and was active in the bank's management for her entire life. She is reputed to have had many love affairs, including one with Henry "Cupid" Templeton, Emily Cowper's squeeze.

Georgiana Bathurst

Georgiana Bathurst, Countess Bathurst (one of the exceptions to all my rules above; in this case, the title and family surname were the same), 1765-1841. Georgiana was born a member of the Lennox family, descended from King Charles II and his mistress Louise de Kérouaille, and niece to the famous Lennox sisters, one of who nearly married George III. Aside from the basic information around her ancestry, her marriage to the 3rd Earl Bathurst who held several government positions, a list of her children, and the fact that she served as a Lady Patroness, almost no information about her seems to be commonly available. . . which left me free to create a personality for her.

Emily Cowper (pronounced "cooper")

Emily Mary Cowper, Countess Cowper (another exception where the surname and title coincide), 1787-1869. Born Emily Lamb, daughter of the well-known Lady Melbourne (another mistress of the Prince of Wales), sister of William Lamb, later Viscount Melbourne, Queen Victoria's first prime minister, and sister-in-law of crazy-cakes Caro Lamb, lover of Lord Byron. She was married at a young age to Peter Clavering-Cowper, 5th Earl Cowper who was ten years her senior. She bore him a son, then embarked on a series of love affairs in London while he remained more or less contentedly in the country at their estate in Hertfordshire. Her grand passion was Henry John "Cupid" Temple, 3rd Viscount Palmerston, who was the probable father of a few of her children and whom she married in 1839 after her first husband's death. She was a political hostess *par excellence*, being the sister of one Prime Minister and the wife of another. She was one of the most popular of the Lady Patronesses, known for her kindness and social *élan*.

Clementina Sarah Drummond-Burrell

Clementina Sarah Drummond-Burrell, later Lady Willoughby de Eresby, 1786-1865. Clementina was a Scottish heiress and daughter of an earl; her husband, Peter Burrell, added her last name to his own so that they became known as Mr. and Mrs. Drummond-Burrell. Later her husband inherited a pair of baronies from both his father and (unusually) his mother; the older, more prestigious title was his mother's Willoughby de Eresby one, so that's the one they used. While Peter pursued a political career which Clementina's fortune subsidized (as well as his habits as a dandy), Clementina pursued a social one, becoming a hostess of some renown. She was reputed to be proud and haughty in nature and a stickler for correct behavior, which inspired the power I gave her, though some historians contend that it was her mother-in-law, not her, who was so snooty. Unusually for the time (and among her fellow Lady Patronesses) Clementina's marital reputation remained unstained, and she and her husband appear to have enjoyed a faithful, devoted relationship.

Maria Sefton

Maria Molyneux, Viscountess Sefton and later Countess of Sefton, 1769-1851. While much is known about her husband William's career as both a politician and a noted friend of the Prince of Wales (as well as a founder of the exclusive Four-in-Hand Club), very little is known about Maria beyond her connection with Almack's as a Lady Patroness. Might that excessive prudence and avoidance of publicity be a function of the fact that her parents, Lord and Lady Craven, had both lived rather scandalous lives and had divorced, a rarity at the time? She was reputed to be extremely good-natured, however, and an excellent if self-effacing hostess for her busy husband.

Dorothea Lieven

Dorothea von Lieven, Countess (and later Princess) Lieven, 1785-1857. Born in Riga, Latvia, Dorothea was a Russo-German noblewoman (she was educated at a convent in Russia and served as a maid-of-honor to the Tsar's mother) who was married (at age fourteen!) to General Count Christopher von Lieven. He was sent by Tsar Alexander I to serve as the Imperial Ambassador to England in 1812 (ssh, yes, I know that's two years after the setting of my stories. I invoke my creative license.) Dorothea took to London like a duck to water. She adored politics, knew everyone, and was the first foreigner asked to serve as a Lady Patroness at Almack's. She was known to be haughty and snobbish, had multiple affairs (including one with Count Metternich of Austria and again with "Cupid" Palmerston), received her own secret diplomatic assignments from the Tsar, and generally had a grand time of it for twenty years, until her husband was recalled to Russia. Not long after that she left him to live in Paris, where she established a salon and went on her merry way with a finger in every diplomatic pie until her death.

William Almack/Mr. Willis

Although he is referred to by contemporaries as a Scot, it is not known either when or where William Almack was born (though Thirsk in Yorkshire is a likely bet—so *not* a Scot, though maybe of Scottish heritage.) Earliest reports of him are as valet to the Duke of Hamilton, but he soon went into business as a proprietor of a tavern and then as the owner-manager of a gaming club in Pall Mall to which he gave his own name—and which eventually became known as Brooks's, one of the best known of London's men's clubs and still in operation today. In 1764 he built his famous Assembly Rooms in King Street and gathered his Lady Patronesses to administer them. . . though perhaps not in quite the way told in this story! On his death, he left Almack's to his niece and her husband, Mr. Willis, who continued to run it and seems to have passed it onto other descendants, as the club was renamed "Willis's Rooms" in 1871.

The Duke of York

The second son of King George III, Prince Frederick, Duke of York and Albany (1763-1827) was associated for most of his life with the army, for better and worse. He saw active service on the continent and was made Commander in Chief of the army, a post he resigned in 1809 after being dragged into a scandal involving his mistress's illegal selling of army commissions; after it was shown that she'd been paid off by the Duke's chief accuser, he was reinstalled as C-in-C in 1811. While not a particularly able or competent field commander (that nursery rhyme about the noble Duke of York marching his ten thousand men up and down hills for no very good reason is often identified as our Fred), he was responsible for a great deal of modernizing and improving of the army, which (as the Duke of Wellington often said) made possible Britain's successful Peninsular campaign against Napoleon. He was married to Princess Frederica of Prussia, an endearingly eccentric woman who avoided London and lived at their estate, Oatlands, with dozens of dogs and other more exotic animals, but they had no children.

Lord Palmerston

Mentioned above in Emily Cowper's entry, Henry John Temple, 3rd Viscount Palmerston (1784-1865) was a British statesman, serving as Prime Minister twice (from 1855-1858 and from 1859-1865), as War Secretary, and as Foreign Secretary. He was charming, intelligent, handsome, and something of a ladies' man (as can be seen from the number of Lady Patronesses he conducted *amours* with), but remained single until the love of his life, Emily Cowper, was widowed. Their subsequent happy marriage, lasting until his death, was (according to contemporary observers) one of "perpetual courtship.

About the Author

Marissa Doyle graduated from Bryn Mawr College and went on to graduate school intending to be an archaeologist, but somehow got distracted. Eventually she figured out what she was *really* supposed to be doing and started writing. She's channeled her inner history geekiness into a successful young adult historical fantasy series and continues happily to write fantasy of various types for teens and adults. She lives in her native Massachusetts with her family, including a bossy but adorable pet rabbit, and loves quilting, gardening, and collecting antiques. Please visit her at her website, www.marissadoyle.com, and at her history blog, www.nineteenteen.com.

To keep up with new releases, news, and other fun stuff, sign up for Marissa's newsletter:

https://marissadoylenewsletter.link/

About Book View Café

Book View Café is an author-owned cooperative of professional writers publishing in a variety of genres, from fantasy to romance, mystery, and science fiction as well as select non-fiction.

Book View Café authors include New York Times and USA Today bestsellers; Nebula, Hugo, and Philip K Dick Award winners; World Fantasy Award, Campbell Award, and Rita Award nominees; and nominees and winners of multiple other publishing awards.

To keep informed of new releases, specials, and other news, sign up for Book View Café's monthly newsletter at www.bookviewcafe.com.